Dead Innocent

MAUREEN O'BRIEN

timewarner
paperbacks

A *Time Warner* Paperback

First published in Great Britain in 1999
by Constable & Company Ltd

This edition published by Time Warner Paperbacks in 2004

Copyright © 1999 Maureen O'Brien

The moral right of the author has been asserted.

A CIP catalogue record for this book
is available from the British Library.

ISBN 0 7515 3473 0

Typeset in Sabon by M Rules
Printed and bound in Great Britain
by Mackays of Chatham plc, Chatham, Kent

Time Warner Paperbacks
An imprint of
Time Warner Book Group UK
Brettenham House
Lancaster Place
London WC2E 7EN

www.twbg.co.uk

For Michael, without whom ...

Acknowledgements

Thanks to Sergeant Martin Thompson of Avon and Somerset Constabulary. He put me in touch with Inspector Pinnock at Broadbury Road Police Station, who gave generously of his time and patience. If I have taken poetic licence with some of Inspector Pinnock's invaluable information, the distortions are mine, not his. Again, I'm deeply grateful to Imogen Olsen, my perfect copy editor, for sorting out my *im*perfect hold on the time factor. To Tara, my editor, for her patience and support. And to Peter James, a great theatre director, whose unforgettable production of *As You Like It* (Designer, Roger Glossop) at the Crucible Theatre Sheffield I have shamelessly drawn upon.

1

An Opening

The gun was still in her hand. Her head was turned away but you could see from the faces of the others that hers was a horrifying sight. Neither her husband nor her friends could speak. They stared down at her in appalled silence. Then the judge said with a shudder of distaste, 'People just don't do things like that.' A nervous gasp whispered through the air. The shocked silence returned. The room slowly went dark. The silence continued. Then the applause broke out. The actors came back into light and took five calls.

Jostled out into the buzz of the foyer Bright felt shaken. 'Come round afterwards,' she'd said. But how did you do that? He fought his way through the crowd to the bar. Managed to attract the attention of a bar girl who spoke into the security phone. She gave him a sweet smile: 'Kate says that's fine. Just wait there. Someone will come to take you through.'

He waited, uneasy. The atmosphere seemed hysterical to him. The level of noise in the bar now was like a football crowd only higher pitched. And how did you face a person you'd just seen do what Kate had done? On stage she was a tiger. Beautiful, fine, clever, ruthless, vulnerable. All that she was in real life only magnified. Transformed. He was off his pitch. Out of his depth. He'd never even been backstage before. What was he doing here? What was expected of him? This was not a new question in connection with Kate. It was just more acute here, now, on the opening night of a play.

'Ankate, you're alive!'

'Just about, Maisie.'

'I really thought you were dead.' All wisps and wafts of white silky stuff, in her new frock, Maisie threw her arms round Kate. 'Oh Ankate, it was fantastic, it was the best. We're bringing all our mates, aren't we, Allie?' She dragged forward a tall shy dark-skinned girl. 'This is my friend Alison.'

Dressed in black, sophisticated for fourteen and of devastating beauty, Alison had a deep voice: 'Yurr, it was rully brullian'.' The Bristol accent came as a surprise. Some more exotic sound might better have suited her appearance.

Kate was already out of the corset and the rest of the gear. She sat to take off the make-up. The dressing-room phone rang. 'Can you get that, Maize?'

'Hello? Oh, I'll ask her.' A hoarse whisper: 'It's John Bright. Is it okay if he comes up?'

'Yes!'

'Kate says yes.' Maisie hung the phone back on the wall. 'Someone's showing him the way.'

Kate felt a sudden sand-blast of apprehension, glad her face was hidden by the mask of cleansing cream.

Maisie said to Alison, 'He's Ankate's policeman.'

'Maisie!'

Maisie laughed. She whispered to Alison, 'Detective Inspector John Bright.'

The girls watched mesmerised as Kate wiped the make-up off her face. And Kate watched them in the mirror. Maisie, tall now, with pale translucent skin, narrow limbs, and an aureole of reddish fair hair, an Arthur Rackham girl. Alison, even taller, a Nefertiti head and an easy athletic grace. The puma and the butterfly. Lovely together. Alison awed being backstage. Maisie impressed too, but acting cool. Kate said, 'What do you think of my dressing room then?'

Maisie shrugged. 'It's okay, I suppose.'

2

Alison said, 'I thought it would be more – posh, like.'

'Posh is for the punters.' Kate dragged a brush through her hair. 'They get the red plush. We get the breeze blocks.'

'Shall I put these in water for you?' Maisie picked up a cellophane-wrapped Interflora bouquet.

'Sure. Thanks.'

'Oh, they're from him,' Maisie said. 'Your policeman.'

A knock at the door. Kate said, 'Let him in. And don't call him that to his face.'

Bright sidled in. He nodded at the girls, then at Kate in the mirror, but didn't speak.

She nodded back. 'You came then.'

'A-ha.' He looked round, awkward in these surroundings, as lost for words as she was. 'So this is where you hang out.'

'Not luxurious, is it?'

'Bit like Kentish Town HQ.'

Kate introduced the girls. Maisie said, 'I've never met a detective inspector before.'

Alison said, 'Neither have I.'

'He saved Ankate's life, you know.'

'Yurr?'

'We've got all the newspaper cuttings. We kept them.' Maisie adopted a ghoulish tone. '"The Body in the Bath".'

Alison shuddered in a snaky movement from heel to head. Both girls laughed. They were flirting in that shy bold way that young girls do, not quite in control but trying to look it. Bright caught Kate's eye in the mirror and gave her a smile. He did this without moving a muscle of his face. It always gave her a shock. She still didn't know how he did it.

Alison got serious. She asked him, 'Did you like the play?'

Kate cringed.

Bright said, 'I don't know if *like* is the word.'

3

Kate drooped. This was the reason you never asked: you might get the truth.

Alison agreed with Bright. 'The people in it aren't very nice, are they?'

'Tesman and Mrs Elvsted are.' Maisie was drinking Bright with her eyes.

'Yurr, but they're boring. The nasty people are quite interesting though.'

Maisie made a swooning face. 'Yeah. I loved Eilert Lovborg.'

'Oh yurr, he's gorgeous.' Alison's deep Bristol voice gave the word a rolling relish.

'Will he be in the restaurant, Ankate?'

'See? They're not interested in art. Just sex.'

'Ankate!'

'Come on. Let's go.'

Renato's was heaving. Smoke hung in veils. No point shouting over the din. Kate mouthed, 'Red wine?' Bright muscled into a space at the bar. Waiting to be served he watched her disappear into a scrum of congratulating bodies. *Kate, you were wonderful, amazing, marvellous, fantastic.* Embraces, kisses, hugs.

The girls were gazing rapt at Eilert Lovborg, an ascetic-looking man, almost imperceptibly gay. He bathed in their adoration like asses' milk. Bright handed them their Cokes. They now barely glanced his way, more exotic fish to fry.

Kate fought through the pack and grabbed her red wine, gasping thanks. He lifted his glass and clinked it on hers. 'Get a lot of rewards in your job, don't you? They don't tell me marvellous wonderful when I get a villain to cough.'

'Trouble is believing it. I never can.'

'Well, you should.'

'You mean that?'

'A-ha.'

'Oh.' She kissed him. The kiss became more than a kiss of congratulation given and received.

'Hey! Put this woman down!' Another rampant acquaintance. Kate pulled away but kept his eyes with a kind of astonishment.

They ate one of Renato's lasagnes in the bar and downed another glass or three. The pace had quietened. Most of the punters had gone, leaving only the hard core of elated actors with their closest mates. Eilert Lovborg was seriously explaining his interpretation of the role to his two fans, whose avid eyes roamed his face as he talked. Kate and Bright sat side by side, their first chance to exchange a quiet word.

'You liked it then?' she said.

'A-ha. I liked it.'

'That's all right then.'

'You care what I think?' His voice held real surprise.

Her hair, crunched into a tight little knot to look meagre for Hedda, had sprung out on its release into a wild thicket round her head. As she turned to give him a *don't act innocent* look it swung across his face. He got a piercing shock: the palpable presence of Millie Hale. For a second he was lost. Confused. Somewhere else.

Kate was worse than a cat for picking things up. She backed off, like a cat that bucks an alien scent, the merest flicker in the eyes. He gave an inward groan. He'd screwed it up again.

'Ankate? Can we go on to dad's place?'

Kate looked at the time. 'Okay, Maisie. Sure. It's not that late.' She looked at Bright. 'Fancy going on to Dave's place?' She was distant with him now. Matey, no more.

They walked to Dave's, the air a cool surprise after the fug of the bar. The girls danced ahead, whispering, laughing. They crossed the road and went down the steps to the quay.

Boats rose and fell on the breathing water. Lights were on in some. You could see the people in their tiny rooms, drinking, talking, washing up.

The boat house rose up over to their left, a tall black wooden structure, still with its loading doors and hoists. Maisie started to run, Allie after her, both with a touching extreme of grace.

Maisie pulled on a rope and a ship's bell clanged. A window opened at the top of the boat house. A head appeared. Bright saw long ringlets hanging over the sill. 'That's Maisie's dad?'

Kate laughed at the package of misgivings crammed into Bright's tone. 'He's quite nice when you get to know him.'

They followed the girls up the dark stone staircase. On the landing the stone stairs ran out. Open-tread wooden steps took over, creaking and shifting slightly as they climbed. On the second landing they could see Dave above. Maisie ran up the last three stairs. 'Dad?'

'Maisie. Hello, hon.' He threw wide his arms and crushed Maisie to him. He was dressed in white. Thick linen tunic and loose trousers, a poetic figure. Maisie, wispy, slight and pale, was lifted off her feet. The candle and the moth, Kate thought.

Shadows flickered across the trembling light in the doorway. Music pounded from inside the loft: 'A white-er – shade of – pa-ale . . .' Bright said, 'Bloke likes Procol Harum can't be all bad, I suppose.'

'Dad? This is Allie. Allie, this is my dad.'

Dave took Alison's hand and gazed seriously into her eyes. 'Dave,' he said.

Abashed, Alison said, 'Is it a party, then?'

'Well, there's food and there's people and there's music. If that makes a party it's a party, I guess. Go on in.'

The girls disappeared inside.

'Hi, Dave.'

'Kate!'

Kate avoided being crushed by the thin powerful arms. 'This is John Bright.'

'Hi, nice to meet you. What are you doing here, Kate?'

'I opened in a play tonight, Dave, at the Old Vic.'

'Ah. I see. How was that?'

'It was pretty fucking phenomenal,' Bright said. He rarely used the Anglo-Saxon, except to make a point.

Dave got the point. He grimaced at Kate, shamefaced charm. 'Sorry, Kate, I should have known.'

'Yes, you should. I'll forgive you this once.'

'I'll catch it later in the run.'

'I bet.'

The shadows, made huge by candle-light, moved in slow frenzy in the vast wood-walled space. Twenty-odd young people danced, or lay around on cushions. Dave asked Bright, 'Would you like a drink?'

'I could use a scotch, mate. No water, just ice.'

'Sorry, I don't have alcohol. There's all kinds of juice, though, and of course, water.'

Bright was shocked into silence. He gave Kate a look that made her laugh. 'Dance?' she said.

'*Dance?*' he said.

Kate had never danced with him before. She was amazed. He danced the way he drove: with an effortless rhythmic invention that made her feel high.

'No booze?' he said. 'He a Muslim or something?'

Kate smiled but did not reply.

'Guess he finds it cool to get stoned on other substances,' Bright said.

Kate stopped smiling. She looked at Bright with a touch of alarm. He gazed back, his squint impenetrable. Was he joking or not? She sensed a shift in the room, a general movement. She stood on tiptoe to see what was going on. In a space on the wide floorboards Maisie and Allie were dancing. The whole roomful of young people one by one stopped to watch Allie and Maisie dance.

Allie's movements were strong and graceful, like a powerful black cat. Maisie, ethereal and white, the wisps of her frock sprayed round her like shreds of torn wings. They circled each other swaying, their arms turning and twisting to the intricacies of some music Kate didn't know, the ethnic drumbeat slow, the melody a subdued and undulating howl.

Nobody moved. Even breathing seemed to stop. The light trembled about the two beautiful girls, who seemed unconscious of the awe they induced. Kate knew from her own girlhood they surely were aware of the admiration, though not of the subtle and fierce longings in some of the admirers. They'd discover those later. Much later, she hoped.

Bright, leaning against the rough wooden planks that divided the kitchen area from the main room, was acutely aware of these longings, not least in himself. He felt a sudden tingle of alarm. Not sure what had caused it, he unlocked his gaze from its intense absorption in the girls and turned it on the faces around him, lit reddish by candle flames.

A young man stood a few feet away, arms folded across his chest. No awe there. No admiration. Anger gripped the mouth and lasered out of the eyes. Bright watched awhile then moved closer. He spoke in his softest catlike purr: 'What's up?'

The young man's head did not turn. 'It's hideous.'

'Two lovely kids dancing?'

'The way they're all watching.'

Bright recalled his own twinge of guilt. 'The blokes, you mean?'

'The *adults*.' The boy spat the word out like a foul taste. 'Look at them. Hungry. Predatory. Those girls won't escape. It'll get them. It'll suck them in.'

'What will?'

'What will? The corruption will. And it will get them soon. They're on the brink.'

'Innocence isn't always all it's cracked up to be, you know.'

The rage blow-torched into Bright's face. 'Innocence is real. It doesn't necessarily belong to youth. Not many possess it. But those two girls do.'

'Sometimes it's not innocence, it's just ignorance, and it gets them into trouble.'

'You work for the police, I believe.'

Bright was rocked back on his heels. 'Er . . . Yeah.'

'So you would think that, wouldn't you? Excuse me.' The young man disappeared out of the candle-light into the shadowy gloom. The music stopped. The beautiful dancing came to an end. Conversation murmured once more in corners. Bright didn't see the boy again.

'You're late.' Lizzie looked immensely tall at the top of the steps.

'Our fault, Lizzie. We went on to Dave's.'

'How are you getting home, Alison?'

'We're taking her. We're just dropping Maisie off first. This is John Bright, by the way.'

Lizzie barely gave him a glance. 'Hello.' Her tone was cold.

He had a nose for petty tyranny. Never warmed to it. He gave Lizzie a brief nod, no more. ' 'Night then, Maisie,' he said. She fluttered down the steps and hugged him, then threw her arms round Kate. She whispered 'It was a great night, Ankate, I'll never forget it as long as I live.'

'Just how I feel, Maize.'

Alison lived down the street, past the little mosque, and up a sloping crescent. Outside a house with sunflowers in the garden, heads drooping in the night air, she took a key from her pocket. Bright and Kate looked surprised. 'They trust me.' Alison gave a proud lift of her chin.

'A-ha?' Bright's expression was dubious. 'That right?'

Alison grinned. 'Dad'll be waiting up actually, he just pretends not to worry. He wants me to be independent. You know.'

And indeed a tall black man opened the door before she had got her key in the lock. She reached up and put her arms round his neck. Over her head he smiled. 'Thanks for bringing her home safe.'

'He's a bit of a contrast to your sister,' Bright said, walking back down the hill.

'Take no notice of Lizzie. She can't help her manner. It's not personal.'

'You could fool me.'

Outside his awful hotel Bright said, 'I've probably sobered up enough to give you a lift?' A silence fell. He didn't look at Kate; he looked at his shoes.

'That would be nice?' Her questioning inflection precisely echoed his own. He grinned.

She brought the mugs of coffee and led the way to her living room: angled ceilings, white walls, striped rug in shades of Etruscan red. 'Mmm,' he said.

'Nice, isn't it?'

He prowled, learning the territory, listening for rustles in the undergrowth, sniffing the air. He stopped to look out of the window. 'Great view.'

'Mmm.'

'Where do you sleep?'

'Here.' She sat on the sofa. 'It becomes a bed. With a flick of the wrist.'

'A-ha.' Non-committal. They exchanged a glance. He

10

drank some coffee, walked about again, stopped to study a painting. 'That's nice.'

'Caroline. My landlady. She's a painter.'

'The people you know.'

'Only the best.' She looked at him.

He looked back, under his eyebrows. 'That so?' he said. He sat down, on the edge of the chair, thoughtful. 'You're good at friends.'

'I am?'

'I don't have any,' he said.

'No friends?' She was shocked. 'Are you sure?'

'I'm sure.'

'But why?'

'The job. The unsocial hours.'

'No more unsocial than mine.'

'The life then.'

'What, no one wants to be friends with a cop?'

'I dunno. Acquaintances, I've got. Plenty. Blokes that I've enjoyed working with. Women that I've . . . well. You know. But not what I'd call friends.'

'There's your ma.'

'Lily? A friend?' He rubbed a hand over his hair. 'Yeah.' He sounded doubtful.

'She welcomes your people in.'

'Yeah, but they all become *her* friends.'

'Like me.'

'Like you.'

'But I was your friend first.' She sounded seven years old, heard herself and laughed. She said, 'I'm your friend.'

He didn't laugh. He said, 'You want to keep it that way?'

'Well . . . Of course I do.' She couldn't say all the things she felt about him. How highly she valued him. It would sound daft.

'See . . .' He was struggling to speak to her in a way that was hard for him. 'What happens with me' – at last he'd

11

managed to get to the point – 'When things look like getting serious I – slide out,' he said.

'So do I!'

'See, with Millie . . .'

Her heart sank. Would every conversation with him always forever come back to Millie Hale?

'See . . .' He struggled on. 'We were alone, me and Millie. I didn't know any of her people. She didn't know any of mine. We were a secret. It was like we were on an island. I mean we were on a boat, for Christsake. A boat is a kind of island, right? We were in this – secret world. We were hiding where no one could get at us. We both wanted that. Me as much as her.'

'What are you trying to say?'

'I dunno.' He shook his head. 'I used to be good at – you know – casual encounters. Coppers are good at that. We're opportunists.'

'That right?'

'You bet that's right.'

'But you've changed?'

'I seem to have, yeah.'

'Since Millie? Because of Millie?'

'Seems like that, yep.'

'You telling me I'm flogging a dead horse here?' She spoke in an airy tone, light as a feather.

'Well, I hope not dead exactly.' A hint of his old humour.

'Just resting?' she said.

He laughed. Then got serious again. 'The thing is . . .' He grimaced, squinted ferociously, scratched an ear. 'I don't want to – let you down.'

She corrected him. 'You don't want to let yourself down.'

He ignored her emendation, deep in his subject. 'I've only been – emotionally involved like that just the once. It was – like I went through a barrier. It was amazing. It was the best thing that ever happened to me. But it stopped. You see? It

12

was yanked from under me. She . . .' His fury, his desperation, his passion, silenced Kate. 'See, since then, I can't . . .'
He made a hopeless gesture, drank down his coffee and
handed her the cup. 'I shouldn't have come up here.' He
stood up and scraped a hand through his hair. 'Ah shit.
Sorry, Kate. I thought it was going to work out.'

She was close to tears. 'Well, never mind.'

'You should mind.'

'I do mind.'

'You do mind?' Intense surprise.

'I mind.'

'You always sound like you don't.'

'I'm good at casual,' she said. 'I'm good at sounding it.'

'Oh.' He folded his arms, listening.

'But, you know,' she said, 'it's possible just to – pretend.'

'Pretend what?'

'Pretend it's casual.'

'Pretend to who?'

'To yourself.'

'What for?'

'To make it possible to – begin.'

'Oh. A-ha. I see.'

'I always do that. Find out as you go along.'

'I used to do that too.' He shook his head. 'Can't, these
days.'

Her tone changed. 'You look dead tired,' she said.

'Yeah, I got an early start tomorrow.'

'And I'll be dead to the world till afternoon.' She took
him to the door and kissed him lightly goodnight, letting
him off the hook. 'Thanks for coming tonight.'

'Ha.' He gave her a look: anger with himself, tenderness
for her, despair and affection mixed. He gave her a wave
from the first-floor landing. She heard his footsteps continue down the stairs. She heard the front door closed with
care. She listened a moment then closed her door with equal

13

care. She looked at her empty flat. She'd done it again. She sure was good at getting rid of people. He'd never even taken his scruffy leather jacket off.

2

Next Year

'You've not seen much of Kate lately, John.'

'Mmm?'

'I said – '

'She's away filming, ma.'

'Till the middle of June, she said. She should be back by now.'

'A-ha?' He was deep in the newspaper pretending not to hear.

'Anything interesting in the *Standard*?' Lily was in one of her *talk to me talk to me* moods.

He put the paper down. 'All right, ma. What's on your mind?'

'There was a thing on the news this morning,' she said. 'A girl's body under someone's shed.' He didn't respond. 'Round your way,' she said.

He used his occasional squint to pretend he wasn't looking in her direction. He'd been doing that since he was two. It didn't take her in. Nothing he did deceived her. 'Is it your case?' she said.

'It's my case.'

'I see.'

'You see what, ma?'

'I see why you're in such a bad mood.'

'Yeah.' He sighed.

'Do you know who did it?'

'I've got a good idea.'

'Can you get him?'

'Not yet.'

'Why not?'

'Evidence, ma. It's always evidence.'

'You'll get it, John.'

'Not necessarily.'

'You always do.'

He gave a dry laugh. 'There's always a first time.'

She'd got him talking. She cheered up. 'I think I'll have another scotch.'

'Two? You're going it a bit. What's up?'

She wriggled in her chair, wagged her head this way then that way. 'I don't know. Everyone's away. On their holidays. Even Mary next door's gone off on a coach trip and you know her, she never goes anywhere. It's the weather. It affects people. It's too hot outside. There's nothing to do in the garden even.'

He handed her her scotch. 'That's because you've got it so nice.'

'Flattery'll get you anywhere.'

He grinned. She knew he never flattered. 'Cheers.'

'And you know me,' she said. 'I can't sit doing nothing.'

She hardly ever told him she needed him. When she did, it was serious. He was on duty tomorrow and South Norwood wasn't convenient for Kentish Town police HQ, but what the hell: he'd stay the whole weekend, not go back to his dog kennel in Crouch End. 'Well, I'm not working Sunday,' he said. 'We can go somewhere.'

She turned on him her most glorious smile. It had always been worth it, pleasing her.

Saturday he came in later than late, and looked tireder than yesterday. 'Hi, ma.'

15

'There's a fish pie in the oven.' She wheeled her chair in the direction of the kitchen.

'I'll get it.' He poured himself a scotch first. He'd already had a few, she could tell.

He stretched – 'Aagh' – standing at the french windows.

She wheeled over to join him. They gazed at her feast of a garden, creamy roses cascading over the walls. 'How's the case?' she said.

'Ma, you don't want to know.'

'Yes, I do, or I wouldn't ask. What's happened? Can't you get the bloke?'

'Yeah, we got him. The neighbour.'

'You got him? So why aren't you pleased?'

'We found some stuff. Under the floorboards in his bed-room.'

'Oh no.' She didn't want to imagine.

'And now he's talking. He's been telling me about it all afternoon. Can't shut him up.' He turned away from the window. 'That's all they want in the end. They just want to tell. And the confession won't stand up on its own. The CPS will want their pound of – yeah, well.'

'You'd better eat, my lad.'

'A-ha.' He downed the scotch and went off to the kitchen.

Lily followed. She manoeuvred her wheelchair through the doorway and watched him ladle out the steaming pie. It was one of her classics. She'd been making it since he was nine years old. Normally he'd be delighted. Tonight he ate it like it was cardboard. Casually she said, 'I rang Kate.'

'She's back then?' No interest at all. And he wasn't pre-tending tonight. He was in a bad way.

Lily persevered. 'She's found a flat.'

'Oh, has she?'

'Moving in next Saturday, she says.'

He put down his fork, folded his arms and gave her his

most piercing inquisitorial squint. 'Okay, ma. What's your point?'

Lily said with bland innocence, 'Maybe she could do with a hand.'

3

Making a Move

A big 1860s house at the end of Lady Margaret Road. Nice, even viewed through pouring rain. Paved front garden with a spiky yukka plant. Iron balcony still intact over the bay window. Mass was letting out, hordes of people running from the Catholic church, piling into their cars. Suddenly the street was empty. He parked then ran up the path to the green front door and rang the bottom bell before he chickened out.

She was smaller, standing there in her doorway, more vulnerable than the Kate he carried in his mind. She didn't say anything, or smile, just waited. It was her honest eyes that daunted him. 'How are you?' he said.

'Okay,' she said. 'You?'

'Better for seeing you.' He meant it. She gave him a wide smile.

Inside, she opened a door into a spacious entrance hall, even in this weather full of light. An arch led to a huge square room, its right side a galley kitchen with a glass roof. Kate opened the french windows.

It was all gardens at the back. All round. Trees and birdsong. The garden had grown rampant, roses and clematis and lavender bushes gone wild. The rain had slowed to a peaceful drizzle, sunshine shimmering through the drops. They strolled across an old brick terrace oozing weeds and moss.

He lifted a long whip of thorny rose so she could duck under the trellis arch and down a paved path that curved between small vegetable beds.

Standing down there at the bottom of the garden, water dripping off the trees on to the shed roof, Bright looked quizzical. 'You haven't moved far, have you?'

'Oh yes I have.'

'Your old place is just over there.'

'Yes, but I can't see it. Gardens in between, and the trees.' Changing the subject, she opened the door of the shed. 'Look, isn't this great? I've never had a garden shed before.'

He shivered.

'What's up?'

He turned away from the shed and she remembered his horrible case. 'I'm sorry, I forgot.' He seemed this tough cockney mongrel nothing could touch. But was full of surprises.

'We're all sick round the station,' he said. 'Sick.'

'The bloke who killed the neighbour's daughter?'

'Not just *this* neighbour's daughter.'

'Oh.'

'No.'

'I'm sorry.'

'You wouldn't believe the stuff we found. Assembling the evidence they call it. And are we ever.'

'You caught him. There must be satisfaction in that.'

'Nah. The stuff wasn't hard to find.'

'But you did find it.'

'Just routine.'

'But you had to suspect him, didn't you? In order to search in the first place?'

Bright shrugged. He never saw what he did as anything

18

great. 'He couldn't wait to tell me. Got an audience at last. Sometimes I think that's all they want. All the gory details. Weeping and wailing how evil he is.'

'And is he? Evil.'

'He's sick. The psychiatric reports will say he's sick. And he is. He is sick. He'll go to Rampton with all the other sick evil bastards and they'll pass round the smuggled pictures and entertain each other with their juicy stories. Why are they alive? There's three little girls dead and that craphead alive and thriving. Why?'

She'd never heard him talk so much. Or talk like this. He heard himself and stopped. He sniffed a yellow azalea that spilled over the terrace. Kate sniffed the air: 'Amazing smell.'

'A-ha. Been bred out of the others, I guess.'

'Think things ought to be bred out of humans?' she said.

'I'd be out of a job.'

'So would I.'

'How come?'

'Well, if everyone were nice and good, there wouldn't be anything to write plays about.'

'What, evil's more interesting? That what you think? Not in real life it's not. It's boring. Boring. Boring.'

'But, it's the *problem* of evil we're obsessed by. The *existence* of evil. What's it for? Evil, pain, suffering, death?'

He shook his head. 'You're the only person I know talks like this.'

'Oh. Sorry.'

'So you should be.'

She grinned. He looked more cheerful too. They went back in.

He'd never seen her like this, simple delight in simple domestic arrangements. It hit him now: her little house in Leverton Street, what its contamination had meant to her, what her enforced homelessness had meant ever since. 'Does it have a bathroom?' He squinted with wicked intent.

'Just here as a matter of fact.' A biggish room. A stained-glass panel letting in jewels of light. Stark white tiles. Nice fittings. A state of the art shower enclosed in glass. 'No bath?' he said. 'That's funny.'

'Yeah,' she said darkly, 'it's a scream.' She shut the door, on this bathroom and on memories of another. She said, 'I think I really am over it. At last.'

He nodded. They both wished he could say the same about his obsession with Millie Hale. They exchanged a look on this subject but no words. God, she was easy to get on with, was Kate, he thought. 'Show me the rest then,' he said.

She opened the tall double doors to the front room. Stripped pine floor, stripped pine fireplace, tall bay window. She opened the wooden Venetian blind. Sunlight sparkled through the rain and patterned the room with stripes of light. The tiles of the fireplace deep blue. 'Bedroom,' she said.

'A-ha.'

Silence. They both contemplated that other bedroom, in her other little house round the corner. Bedding all over the place. Someone else's stains on her sheets. At least this bedroom was empty. It had the empty smell of newly sanded pine.

'Where did you store your furniture?' he said.

She paused. 'I sold it.'

'Everything?'

'Sent it to auction.'

'Don't do things by halves, do you?'

'It stayed in store for months before I decided.'

'What decided you?'

'Earning enough to buy some more.'

He gave a short laugh. Shook his head. 'You're crazy.'

20

'I went to Habitat and said I'll have that and that and that. It was amazing. I felt like a millionaire.'

'You won't feel like one now, then.'

'No, I'm broke again now.'

'A-ha.'

'I just got the necessities. Bed, sofa, table, chairs. Like those apartments you see in the house and garden magazines. All white walls and wood floors and no mess. I'll be so stylish.'

They picnicked at her nice long table under the glass roof. She put on Radio Three while he opened the wine. It was the Bach second orchestral suite. Very joyful music. She laid out a warm French loaf and cheese. He poured the wine into her greenish glasses. She loved watching him do things, deft, spare, not a movement wasted, practical, neat, fast.

'What you looking at?' he said.

'Nothing.'

'A-ha. Cheers.'

It was going to be all right. This time, at last, it was going to work out. He broke the bread, he cut the cheese. He speared the cheese on his knife the way peasant men did, the knife a part of him. She watched his hands. He said, 'Don't do that.'

'What?'

'Watching my hands.'

'Does it make you feel shy?'

'It makes me feel randy.'

The first real honest look of the day passed between them.

'Oh, heck.' She laughed, shaky.

'Eat,' he said.

The bread was like bread, the cheese was like cheese. Both were the best she'd ever tasted. Flavours sharp, coarse,

21

raw, on lips, palate and tongue. And the wine, chosen by him: you could get drunk just sniffing it. The music ended and the news came on. She turned the wine bottle to read the label. The news reader said, 'Police in Bristol are searching today for a fifteen-year-old schoolgirl who disappeared two days ago from her home in the Totterdown area of the city . . .'

They stared at each other frozen in attitudes: she turning the bottle, he sipping the wine. The news reader moved on to the next headline. They didn't move. They didn't hear it. They heard nothing. There was no sound in the world. Kate placed both fists between her breasts in the position of her heart. Her chest would not move to admit breath. Her lungs hurt. Focusing again on Bright's face she discovered him also transfixed. He let out his held breath in a sort of silent laugh. He swallowed. He said, 'Bristol's a big place.'

'Totterdown's not such a big place.'

'A few thousand schoolgirls though.'

'Of fifteen?'

'I thought Maisie was fourteen.'

'That was last summer. She was fifteen three weeks ago.'

'Lizzie would have phoned you if Maisie had gone missing.'

'Oh! Yes!'

'She'd have expected her to come here to you.'

'Yes?'

'Wouldn't she?'

'Yes?'

'You're not convinced?'

'No.'

'Phone her.' He took his mobile out of his pocket. 'Phone Lizzie.'

'No.'

'Go on.'

'No. She'd think I was daft.'

22

Kate's phone rang. For a second they both again turned to stone. Then Kate picked it up. 'Hello?' Her voice wary.

'Kate?'

'Lizzie!'

'You heard.'

'No, Lizzie, oh God, not Maisie?'

'Not Maisie, no.'

'Oh, thank Christ. Oh, Lizzie – '

'It's Alison,' Lizzie said.

A long silence. Bright stared at Kate. She stared at him but did not see him. 'Alison?' she said.

Bright got up and stood by her.

'Yes.'

'Maisie's best friend Alison?'

'Yes.'

Kate closed her eyes. 'Alison's missing,' she said.

'They were round at Dave's two nights ago.' Lizzie's voice had no expression, flat with fear. 'Alison left about an hour after Maisie. She wasn't on her own – even Dave wouldn't let a fifteen-year-old walk home on her own – she was with two friends, students of Dave's. They say they left her outside her house. But she never went into her house. She had a key. Her parents had gone to bed. They weren't worried. They trusted her. She'd promised to be in by eleven. And she would have been if – if she'd actually gone in.' Lizzie's voice broke off.

'When did they realise – ?'

'They found her bed empty in the morning.'

'What do they think, Lizzie?'

'Well, you know Alison. She's not the type to run off without leaving a note. Or to run off at all. Or even to stay the night somewhere and not let them know. They rang me to see if she was here with Maisie. Then some other school friends. Then they rang Dave. Then they rang the police.'

'And she didn't have any plans to – ?'

23

'Maisie says not. And Maisie would have known.'

'Would she? I mean – '

'Oh Kate, for heaven's sake. Don't give me that stuff about how secretive teenagers are. She and Maisie tell each other everything.'

Kate remembered how selective best-friend confidences had been, from her own adolescence, but this wasn't the time to argue with Lizzie. 'So what do they think has happened?'

'Well, they're questioning everyone. Especially Dave, as that was the last place she went. And the students she walked home with. No one's seen her. No one has a clue. She just seems to have vanished off the face of the earth.'

4

Just Missing

She stayed at Lily's that night. Bright insisted on taking her there. 'Can't leave you alone here tonight, girl.'

Their unspoken plans for the afternoon had been spiked. Kate wondered if every place she ever lived in would be contaminated by some terrible event. Was she condemned never to have a home she could feel good about? She went with him in his car. 'I'll drive you back in the morning if you want to come.'

The familiar sense of safety at Lily's place. The room, at the back, overlooking the long and lovely garden and the railway beyond, a small square box done in a restful parchment colour with a pretty border. An old hand-operated Singer sewing machine on a table under the window. Lying between the cool cotton sheets Kate looked at the ceiling. Where was Alison tonight? Somewhere she wanted to be, or somewhere she didn't? Alone? Alive?

She rang Lizzie in the morning. No news. 'The police have been round again, asking Maisie things. Maisie's distraught. She's spending a lot of time down with Allie's parents. We're all just waiting, here.'

Bright made a call to a detective inspector he knew in Bristol. 'A-ha,' he said, 'a-ha,' in varying tones of voice. Then, 'Thanks, mate, let me know? 'Preciate it. Thanks.' He turned to her and Lily. 'They don't know anything. Nothing from boyfriends. No sightings at stations, airports. No known reason for doing a runner.' He looked depressed. His recent case had prepared him for the worst. A lot of his cases prepared him for the worst. But he was a policeman, a certain pessimism about the human race endemic to his profession.

'Girls do do things like this,' Kate said with a bleak expression.

'That's true.' Lily's face was stiff with pretended hope.

Kate didn't go back to town with Bright. He was too haunted by his recent case, his thoughts too dark. She stayed in the comfort of Lily's Scottish common sense. 'All this despair.' Lily shook her head. 'That won't help find the girl. Come on. Help me dead-head my roses, or they won't be the envy of the neighbourhood any more.'

Out in the sunshine, birdsong and scents, it was hard to believe in the wickedness Bright encountered every day. Kate began to hope. Surely their fears would be magicked away in the course of the day. Alison was bound to turn up. Rueful, defeated, or just bleary from some weird druggy experience. But safe, and, within reason, well.

On the news that night, however, the police showed her picture and appealed to the public for help. 'If you have seen this girl . . .'

'Ohh.' Lily caught her breath. 'She's beautiful, Kate.'

Yes. There was no mistaking Alison. If you had seen her you wouldn't forget. No news from Lizzie and when Kate rang there was no reply.

The next morning the item was missing from the news on Radio Four. If Alison had turned up she would have been news. Still missing she was news no longer. She would only become news again if – Kate rang Lizzie. Lizzie, dashing out to work, late as always, only had time to gasp into the phone, 'No news, got to go.'

Kate got a vision of her lovely spare clean new flat and the things she needed to do there. She kissed the top of Lily's head. 'Thanks, Lily. Give John my love. I'll be in touch.'

'I hope you mean that.'

'I mean it.'

She bought her copy of the *Big Issue* at the station. The seller was a boy of maybe eighteen, shaven head, ear-ring, scruffy small dog curled up on an old coat. The boy was thin with blemished skin. She thought about the homeless on the streets, gave him a fiver and scoffed at her prodigality: she wasn't going to give him a home, was she? Share her nice new flat with him? Would she encounter Alison one day, outside a tube station or hunched in a doorway? Would she give her a quid and walk on feeling good about herself?

She read the *Big Issue* on the train. It had changed since its early days. Not so much the news from the streets percolating up, as the news of the trendy trickling down. Still, it had a different perspective here and there, made a better read than the newspapers all round her, the same headlines on all of them, the same point of view.

Her flat looked so beautiful she almost cried. She walked through the spacious rooms. She opened the french windows and smelled roses, lavender, rosemary. She discovered you couldn't feel desperate all the time. If you were this lucky you had to rejoice in your luck, had to have a bit of gratitude at least. Even the guilt of having what other people were not lucky enough to have, shouldn't spoil the joy. Surely she was allowed to feel a little bit good?

But next morning the *Big Issue* lay open at the Missing Persons page, four blurred black and white snaps with a column of description underneath, most of them young, most lost for ever, and for no reason ever known, some depressed, some mad, some in search of adventure, and some . . . Her mind stopped there. Not Alison?

She slowly got dressed, couldn't face breakfast yet, wandered out on to the terrace, pulled up some weeds from between the uneven bricks. Gazed into the pond. A frog appeared on the surface gulping and gazing with his cheerful unblinking little eyes. 'Hello, frog,' she said sadly. Sunshine sliced across the end of the garden. She joined it there, accepting the warmth on her back while she absently dead-headed the crimson rose, letting the petals fall between her fingers. Dead-heading suddenly seemed a sinister term. Lily had used it yesterday. John Bright. It was early but he might already be at work.

'John?'

'Kate?'

'Have you got a minute?'

'Taking statements in the psycho case all day. No news?'

'No new news.'

'I'll see what I can do. Meet me lunchtime.'

'I talked to the bloke in Bristol.'

Her face turned to him full of dread. She didn't speak.

'Nothing much,' he said. 'They've questioned the two students who dropped her off. Their story seems to hold up. They didn't see her go into the house. But she went up the

27

path to her front door. They were on something. Natch. When are the kids not on something these days? They're not saying so, but . . .'

'On what?'

'Oh, just been smoking a bit of dope, I expect.' He shrugged. 'So I don't expect they're that clear about how they left her. They don't seem to be hiding anything, except the fact they were on something. But you never know. They didn't think anything could happen to her outside her own front door.'

'No.'

'And maybe it didn't.'

'What?'

'They're questioning her father.'

Kate was shocked. 'Desmond Holt? But he's a really nice man, solid, reliable – '

'They always do that. They got to. They don't suspect foul play yet. No reason to.' He gulped some beer. 'They're questioning Maisie's dad too.'

Kate winced. 'Dave?'

'Yeah. No special reason, don't get in a state. They're questioning the whole crowd of those layabout kids who were at Dave's place. And they're working through the kids in her class. Alison's a clever girl, the bloke in charge says to me, as though clever girls don't get into trouble.'

'And?' she said.

'Nothing. Nothing odd in her behaviour, nothing new in her life – that anyone knows about or is saying they know about – nothing she mentioned or did. So far. It's early days yet, the guy said.'

'Early days.' Kate shivered.

'She's probably crashed out somewhere, some bloke's place probably, lucky sod. Too much Ecstasy. Or whatever. Too much booze? Too little experience to handle it.'

'She's not the type.'

28

Bright gave her one of his sideways squinting looks. 'Come on, Kate.'

'Yes, I know that's what they always say, but – '

'Look. We only dropped in on that Dave's place for a minute after your first night party last year, but there was everything going down there. Wasn't there? Come on, don't be innocent. You can drop a kid almost anything. She could be out of it for days on a bad trip. Or even on a good one. Don't assume the worst. That's all I'm saying. Bad experience, teach her a lesson, might not even be all bad.'

Kate looked at him levelly. Knew he was right in general. Knew he was wrong in this case. She shook her head.

'A-ha,' he said. 'Yeah, I agree. She's not the type. Something about her. I'll keep in touch with the bloke in charge. If there's any inside gen I'll get to know.'

'Thanks.'

Kate's face was sad. He pushed her hair away from her temple.

She felt the peculiar dry warmth of his hand and leaned the weight of her head there for a moment. Only a moment. She put her arms round him quickly, kissed his cheek. ' 'Bye then. Thanks.'

'See you soon?' He lifted an eyebrow.

She grinned sideways, then got serious. 'I'm actually off to Bristol again in two weeks' time.'

5

Family Matters

Kate heard the announcement while she was packing the car. 'The body found today in the Bedminster area of Bristol has been identified as that of missing schoolgirl Alison Holt who disappeared from home three weeks ago. Police say they are treating it as a murder enquiry.'

She shut the boot of her yellow Beetle. She came inside. She closed the front door and sat on the bottom stair. Put her head in her hands, shaking. A feeling like bottomless hunger in the gut, bottomless space under the feet. She pulled herself up by the newel post. Walked down the hall feeling her way as though in the last few minutes the world had gone dark. Opening the door to her flat, she was surprised to see daylight through the back window.

She stood at the phone table, a fist either side of the phone. Tears fell off her face. A kid, fifteen years old. One of the most beautiful girls she'd ever seen. And someone had to kill her. Kill all that promise, all that potential, all that beauty. Why? She punched the wrong number. Her brain hadn't forgotten it; her fingers did. Like they didn't want to make the call. The third try she got it right.

'Lizzie?'

'Yes.'

'I just heard.'

'Yes.'

'How's Maisie?'

'You can imagine.'

'Is she there?'

'She's at the school. That's where all the kids have gathered. They didn't know where else to go. Even the delinquent ones are there. And some of the teachers have come back off holiday specially. They just want to be together. All these kids carrying flowers. There's a mountain of flowers in the playground and all the teachers and the kids clinging together and crying. I had to come away and leave her there. I couldn't stand it.'

Kate said, 'I'm just about to set off.'

'Where to?'

'To Bristol!'

'Oh, you don't need to come.'

'Lizzie, I'm working at the Old Vic again. We start rehearsing next week.'

'Oh, yes, I forgot, with all this.'

'So I'll see you in a few hours.'

'Take care.'

'Yes, Lizzie.'

'I know how you drive. It's time you got rid of that car.'

Lizzie. Even in this extremity she couldn't resist.

In London people would be changing lanes, cutting up, taking side roads, chancing it, keeping it moving. But here . . . Everyone obediently in slow procession, at speeds between dead slow and stop. Miles of it. Visible uphill miles.

At last she reached the roundabout. Some of the cars branched to the right towards Bedminster. She was moving now at least, only ten miles an hour but getting there. She shot across the Wells Road on to St John's Lane, hills in the distance, did the sharp right into steep Oxford Street, past the small gaggle of shops with young people hanging around on corners, downhill again past the sweet little terraced houses, to the Glasnost Restaurant, Totterdown's one claim to being upmarket, up again to the brow of William Street, and she was there.

She jumped out without unloading and ran up the steps. Lizzie opened the door, she must have been watching out. She looked fine, perfectly groomed, but for the slight hysteria in the eyes and the tight lines round the mouth. You could never hug Lizzie, she had a force field round her, particularly when terrified and in need of help. No hello, no greeting; just 'I'll help you with your bags.' And there she was down the steps, dragging stuff out of the old yellow Beetle, nagging: 'Scrap metal's all it's good for. It'll blow up on you one of these days. On the motorway probably.'

'Beetles last for ever, Lizzie.'

'Out to prove that, are you?'

Lizzie was still jealous of Liam after all this time. Jealous of their dead teenage brother who'd bequeathed Kate the car.

'Anyway I can't afford a new one,' Kate said, clinching the argument.

Lizzie turned her attention to the pile of gear in the boot. 'You've brought enough for a year.'

'I'm here for eight weeks.'

'Oh yes, I keep forgetting.'

'Lizzie! I only need one bag for now. Please let's get inside?'

'Oh.' Lizzie came to a stop. 'All right.' She hoisted Kate's big holdall on to her shoulder and trudged up the steps.

The house had been newly painted outside. Sky blue and white. 'House looks nice,' Kate said.

'Just had it done. Cost the earth.'

They went in. Kate shut the door. 'Where's Maisie?'

Lizzie leaned her head against the wall in the hallway and howled. Kate put out a tentative hand but she flinched away. All you could do was stand and wait. At last she calmed down and Kate led the way to the kitchen.

Pretty kitchen, red and white, cheerful as hell. Lizzie sat down on a shiny red chair and blew her nose; Kate put the kettle on. Familiar positions; comforting in a way. Lizzie sniffing and patting her eyes and catching the drips from her nose. Kate making tea. Lizzie sipped from the jolly clown mug and put it down. 'Maisie – ' She stopped and waited for the emotion-stricture to leave her throat. ' – won't come home.'

'Come home from where?'

'Dave's.'

'She's staying at *Dave's*?'

'She says she feels safer there.'

'Safer! With Dave?'

'It's what she says.'

'Oh, Lizzie!' Kate was full of sympathy. This wasn't just Lizzie, turning everyone's problem into *Lizzie's Problem* as she usually did; this was really bad.

'I'm the one who's supported her, nurtured her, done everything for her. He abandoned her. That's all he's ever done, leave people in the lurch. And who makes her feel safe? Who's the one she wants now? I can't bear it, Kate, I can't.'

'I'll go over there,' Kate said.

'Kate!' Dave flung his arms wide and held her in a vice. They nearly overbalanced on the rickety stairs.

'Okay, Dave, okay.'

He let her go. 'Come in.'

Light of candles, smell of incense. Young people in hippie gear lounging on cushions. It looked like a movie about the sixties, but Dave had been an infant in the sixties, his acolytes not even born. New Age music gurgled out of the rough wooden walls. Everything was wood in here, rough planks crudely nailed. And a small iron stove. It was nice. It *was* romantic. Kate felt its spell, but did not forget what she'd come for. 'Where's Maisie?' She peered into the flickering candle-gloom.

33

'I'm here, Ankate.' She sounded kind of – stoned. Kate felt alarm.

She found Maisie half lying in the laps of three nouveau hippies. A New Age *pietà*. She looked dazed, woozy, half asleep. Kate came closer. 'You okay, Maisie?'

Maisie gave a groan, didn't get up to greet her, didn't leave the cradle of arms.

Dave had separated a small cooking area off from the main room with a screen of upright planks. Kate followed him in there. Here there was electric light.

His hair was still long, ringlets down past his shoulder blades, but now it was grey in parts. He was still thin, his body hard and strong. But his face was starting to look gaunt. He stretched out his arms to take hold of her again, Dave the Great Protector. She backed to the wall and leaned there, folding her arms. He shrugged and half smiled. They knew each other well. This was his charming quality, that he accepted what you were. But his detachment from other people was the other side of that. Frightening.

'How is she?' Kate kept her voice low.

'She's safe here.'

'Safe from what?'

'Safe from what she fears.'

'What is that?'

'That whoever killed Allie will come after her next.'

'Christ.'

'Or after another one of her friends.'

6

Excerpt from a Diary

i

2 a.m. A moonless night. I crouched in the car listening. My legs had grown numb. I lifted my head for a second. Nothing. No one. I sat up. The school building loomed blacker than the night. But you never know. Someone could be lurking in the dark behind those windows. I opened the car door. Quietly. And got out.

I have good circulation but crouching so long in the cramped space on the floor of the car had turned my legs to jelly. I walked weakly a few steps. How can you suffer numbness and pain at the same time? It seemed this sensation, or lack of it, would never stop but it did. It took two minutes. Two minutes I hadn't planned for. Two minutes is a long time.

In that time I hobbled to the barrier gate that divided the road from the hill and shuffled a little way along the path. I stopped to listen. Nothing. Nobody. I turned and started back, the school a big black shadow on my left. I had to believe there was no one behind the windows. If someone saw me the game was up. I had to take that chance. I had no choice. This was the optimum place, the nearest I could park the car to the spot I had chosen. Normal feeling had returned to my feet. I sprinted softly back to the car. I listened. Nobody. Nothing. I opened the hatch-back.

The tightly wrapped bundle filled the boot space. I rolled it towards me using both hands and all my strength. Then I bent at the knees stooping to receive the weight on my right shoulder. I took the head end, hoisted it over my shoulder, held the bundle round its waist, let my thighs take the strain and rose to a standing position, pulling the legs up with me as I stood. My own legs shook with the weight. But I had practised this manoeuvre many times. I knew it could be done. And the carrying. Only a short distance. It could be done.

But I had not taken account of the fear. Nerves make you weaker. I panted. My legs shook, and not just with the weight. But I managed to lower the hatch-back without banging it shut. Then I bent at the knees and went with small swift steps through the barrier gate again, along the path a few yards to my chosen spot. Not the first opening in the bushes, but the second. Of course the first would be easier but the second was perfect for my purposes, worth the extra three yards along the path. The first opening was low, too far to bend, and the slope down was immediate and steep. The second opening was higher, the initial slope more gradual, down to a plateau, lower than the path and deep in the shadows between trees.

This was the most delicate part of the operation. To duck in under the thick bushes, without tripping, falling, or dropping my weighty burden. I tottered (I laugh now at my choice of word, so close to Totterdown, just the other side of the hill) down the slope a few steps, but somehow righted myself, trying to be silent but grunting with the strain. Branches scratched my hood but all hair was well taken care of. They'd find no traces at this scene to satisfy their craving for forensic evidence. No skin visible. No hair. Only my eyes to see with. And I *could* see now in the dark. The human eye is adaptable beyond belief.

I struggled down to my small plateau. I knelt, lowering the shoulder over which the head lolled. A thump as the head hit the earth. And a subdued thud as the rest of the bundle came to rest. (As it were.) I pressed my hands round my thighs just above the knees as though this pressure would help me to breathe more freely. My arms now trembled with the strain they had been under. A heavier burden would have been too much for me. I had to admit this now. Alive she had been light as a feather. Dead she was a weightier problem.

My lungs cleared. The drums ceased pounding in my ears. I lay down. This I had not rehearsed but my exhaustion was immense. Inexhaustible. Inexhaustible exhaustion. Many a paradox I was discovering tonight. I lay down by her side. The black sky up there through the leaves and the cool breath of the night. Imagine lying with her like this, alive, side by side on the hill. I did imagine it. For a moment. Not an altogether pleasurable moment. Then I got up. On to my knees. I took the knife out of my pocket and opened out a blade.

I quickly cut through the clothes line holding the bundle together. I cut it in six places. At the neck. The chest. The waist. The top of the thighs. The knees. The ankles. I opened up the plastic sheet. I rolled her away from me off the sheet and bundled up five of the lengths of clothes line in the plastic, squeezing the air out as I wrapped. With the sixth length I tied the whole lot together. It made an untidy parcel but heavy enough to throw. I scrambled down the slope from my plateau, between bushes and trees, to the railings that border the railway. I threw the bundle hard over the railings on to the rails.

I'm a strong thrower. Good at ball games at school. The night was too black to see how far it spun. I didn't care. The plastic and rope could be bought in any supermarket – I'd checked – and had never been touched by human flesh. Hand in glove.

Everything is a question of time. It would take them time to find the parcel. When they did the plastic and rope would be ragged, snagged on bushes, blown by wind, soaked by rain, shat on by birds, run over by trains. Traces of me and mine weathered away. Withered away. Whither away?

Now I could return to her. I composed myself. I crawled back slowly up the slope through the thicket to my plateau, where she lay and where I could stand upright. I looked down at her. She was on her front, face pressed into the grass and weeds. I knelt by her and rolled her on to her back. A blade of grass and a torn leaf adhered to her right cheek. I removed them gently. Stroked them away.

Her eyes were shut. I had shut them myself. I feared at the time that they might open again. But they had not. And they did not now. It was unlikely they would at this stage, but the fear persisted. Rigor mortis had not yet set in but I did not have much time. I had got down a book from the medical section of the library at work. I found that though rigor mortis occurs quite quickly, it can go off again in as little as twenty-four hours, especially in the summer months. No one had ever told me this. I had wanted to keep her by me longer but knew now I must not. Rigor had always seemed to me a necessary concomitant of death. Just as no one tells you the facts of life, so no one tells you the facts of death. Her eyelids stayed closed down over her eyes.

The fine gold chain round her neck had got twisted. I worked it round so that the cross hung dead centre (dead centre, that's good) resting in the soft declivity of her throat between the delicate branches of her collar bone. I had left on her bra and pants for modesty. The white shapes hovered, it seemed, over the darkness which was her brown flesh. I took her right hand and bent her arm so that her hand rested on her left breast. Then I did the same with her left hand, placing it on her right breast. I straightened her legs, running my hands from knee to ankle, bringing her feet together. Her feet were bare. Shoes weigh a lot, would have made her heavier to carry. Also, her feet were beautiful.

Long, narrow, smooth, strong. Amazon's feet. With long straight toes.

I was kneeling on the damp grass. The night was barely cooler than the day. I wanted to stay there by her side, stretch out again, even sleep a while. But I must not linger. I touched her hands briefly but could feel nothing. I longed to peel off the gloves and feel her flesh with my hands. I stood. I turned my back on her. I squeezed my eyes shut and said a quick prayer. For her. For me. A prayer. That's a joke. The things we do.

I stooped to make my way out of the bushes. Cool leaves stroked my face. I heard the noise of a train, distant, approaching, the heavy clatter of goods wagons, getting closer, its noise splitting my skull. I put my gloved hands over my ears until the noise faded. Noise is bad for me. Something happens in my head. I held on until the noise had completely gone then took my fists away. And heard a closer noise. A smaller, more sinister noise. I stayed still, not breathing at all, for minutes, while the pressure mounted in my skull, in my chest, in my throat.

The footsteps came from the same direction I had come ten minutes before. This person had passed my car. Had been watching my activities in the dark? You can hear footsteps clearly there on the tarmac path, at night. Only one set of footsteps, in this case, but a voice went along with them. A voice, whispering, intensely sibilant. Did this mean there were two people, one in shoes, the other in trainers? (Trainers are silent, I wear them myself for that reason.) Or one person, talking to itself, hurrying along in the night earnestly settling a score?

This whispering was real, as the footsteps were. It was not in my head. Schizophrenics hear voices in their heads. It has recently been discovered that where most of us can distinguish between our own thoughts and the voices of others, schizophrenics cannot. Their own thoughts come to them as outside voices. This does not happen to me. But of course I talk to myself. I believe others do. Most others perhaps?

I could not creep out to see how many shadowy figures were passing by outside the bushes. For a moment there seemed to be many, a multitude, gliding silent and swift, fiercely whispering. I just had to wait.

I crouched, waiting, a long time, determined not to give in to the temptation to move, to creep up the slope and peep. So I shall never know how many people passed. I shall always see a shadowy three-legged racer. A person with his shadow strapped to his side. Whispering.

All the time I was listening I forgot her behind me there. Which is strange because she after all was the reason I was listening so hard, hiding there, and waiting. But now that I was about to leave her I received the most terrible stab of pain. A physical jolt of longing, to turn and go back to her and lay my face on her body. I had to go, however. I knew the time had come.

I turned just once to look upon her, unsullied, uncorrupt, perfect, fixed. I held my breath. Then I ducked out of the bushes. I did it fast. Anyone could have heard me. But my shadowy passer-by had long gone. And at two thirty in the morning surely not that many people would be crossing Windmill Hill. Night after night I'd been out there and hardly seen a soul.

I jogged in my silent trainers down the path back through the barrier gate. These days it's less suspicious to run than to walk. Joggers are out at all hours now. Keeping fit. Keeping trim. Keeping in shape. Anoraks on the move. And it was better, running. More in time with my heartbeat, jerky, uneven, but fast.

There are still five cars parked along there. I jog past mine. I can barely believe my will-power. In this supreme testing moment of my life, I have the supreme strength not to get into my car and drive off. A kind of rejoicing floods me. Freedom, pride, excitement. A joyous exhilaration buzzes my head. I nearly lift my arms with clenched fists to punch the night air.

But I go on running in a steady earnest way like the serious types you see every day, timing themselves. What are they keeping fit *for*? To carry on running? I nearly laugh out loud but I don't because I'm now down by the awful tunnel and it's only this lucky euphoria that impels me in there.

Shiny slime in the dark running down the brown brick soot-encrusted walls. The hollow drip, arhythmic, magnified, like my heartbeat. The pale horseshoe at the far end of the tunnel doesn't get any bigger, like I'm running on the spot. My feet squelch in a sudden silver puddle and when I look up the pale horseshoe of hope is bigger than me and within seconds I'm out. Through hope and out the other side?

I cross the road. Nobody. Jog down past the city farm. Nobody. Even the rare-breed sheep asleep. Past the printing works. Lights and the faint sound of machinery but nobody. Nobody. I come to the Philip Street Chapel. *We have peace with God*, the poster tells me, *through Our Lord Jesus Christ*. Yeah.

A step or two from Bedminster Parade I hear a car engine. I can tell the car is going slowly but I can't see it from here. Its lights waver towards me. I'm across the street from *Motaman. Car Parts And Accessories*. I'd like to flatten myself into a doorway but there is no doorway deep enough. So I scuttle silently back round the chapel corner into Bartley Street. I can keep watch from here on the Parade, if I keep still and out of the light.

A police car comes into my sights, crawling along the Parade in my direction. So slow. Like they're looking for someone. Like they're looking for me. I guess they do this every night, trawling for thieves. Maybe I should pretend. Pretend what? That I'm merely a thief? For a moment I

41

actually consider this. But quickly regain my senses and stay where I am.

They crawl past. Slow motion. They didn't see me. Unless they're pretending, waiting out of sight for me to emerge into the Parade? I'm gripped now by the urgent need to empty my bladder. And my bowels. I can't stay here any longer, I have to get home. Quick. Now.

I strolled. I did. I strolled, in spite of the fear, in spite of my urgent bodily needs, out into the Parade, past the shiny hub caps and complex tools in the car-parts window, and sauntered round the corner without even peeping round first. Nobody. The squad car gone. Nothing else moving. Litter in the street lights. In spite of the red-brick library and the grey stone police-cum-fire station long disused, this is a mean place. A place for what my mother would call 'the common people'. Not for the uncommon people. Like her. Like me, now, I realise. Like me. An uncommon person like me. I wonder what proportion of the population has done what I've done. Killed. A fellow person. Killed. Not in war or accident. But like me. How many? I must find out. Statistically interesting. I'll look it up. Add my name to the list. I do let out a laugh now. You don't get on a list till you're found out. The only list worth belonging to is the one that can't be made. I ran again.

I ran all the way home. I ran to jingles to take my mind off my more and more urgent guts. This little piggy went to market, this little piggy stayed at home. This little piggy had roast beef, this little piggy had none. Had none. This little piggy had none. It was a hell of a run – now here's a clue for anyone who might find this and read it – I have not yet found my perfect reader – uphill all the way. And I didn't meet a soul.

Later.

More comfortable now. A complete evacuation. I even

vomited. That's curious. Interesting. Purgative. Macbeth uses that imagery, to the doctor, to whom of course it would have relevance: purgatives, rhubarb, senna, talking about tearing out a rooted sorrow from the mind, as evil from a land. Sins are purged. I was purging mine perhaps. Rambling thoughts. I didn't sleep.

Very early in the morning I went downstairs to the kitchen. I heard the change-over from World Service to Radio Four. Then hours of news while I drank tea, shivering slightly on a stool. I couldn't eat. I took up mother's breakfast. And when I came down again they were making the announcement. It was strange hearing it in bald words like that: 'The body of a girl . . .' A jogger found her. I could barely suppress a laugh. Just what I had hoped. He must have been out at the crack of dawn. Poor chap.

I hung about for as long as I could. Mustn't be too early. Then I went down to Temple Meads station. I waited for the London train to come in. I watched the people coming through the barrier. The barrier was unmanned. Some passengers dropped their tickets on the ground. One or two placed them in the litter bins. The litter bins were full so it was easy to retrieve a few tickets. The first one I picked out was a return half. Lucky first time. And it gave yesterday's date as the journey time. I could barely believe this smooth silent slotting-in to my plan. Though I know it's nonsense, I felt I was controlling events. My will had willed this.

I pocketed the ticket and slipped out of the station, mingling with the people who *had* been on the train. I had a bag with me, of course, in case police should be watching. Or any observant person. Actually I believe there hardly is such a thing as an observant person. They walk round deaf and blind to the world around them. Their world is a little hard ball of self-interest located in their skull, their stomach, their genitals, their purse. I loathe them, one and all. Well, never mind that.

43

I wondered if I should draw attention to myself in some way in case of complications later. It might be as well to have been noticed here, now. But I decided against it. Those little tricks can easily misfire. The person who saw me would swear it was a different day or a different time or even a different place. So I strolled over the crossing and up towards the roundabout. Then, turning right, over the muddy river down towards Bedminster, I avoided Windmill Hill. Must not draw too much attention to myself. The police would still be up there, milling about, keeping an eye out for suspicious characters. Like me.

I came down the top end of the Parade, before the pedestrianised section, and turned the corner. My heart, interestingly, took on an insistent rhythm, pounding as though located actually in my ears. And when I crossed the road approaching the tunnel my legs actually began to shake. I noted all these reactions. The reason the legs shake in such circumstances is that all the muscles in the back, the neck, and the legs themselves, go rigid, contracted, tense. The legs do not shake out of weakness but out of a kind of concentrated strength. Too much strength.

I breathed out slow, slow, long breaths as I have taught myself to do, out and out and out, expelling the last atom of air, thus relaxing stomach, neck, back muscles. Out, out. That was better. My legs shook less. Even in the dank tunnel their function continued to improve. I came out of the tunnel into the lane alongside the school.

The police had stretched blue and white tape all round the parked cars. There were five cars. Mine farthest away at the front. A young policeman stood close to the back car. I approached him. 'Excuse me, officer,' I said.

He looked at me. He felt a spurt of excitement and terror at the sight of me. I might be the murderer! Speaking to him! Imagine! He did not allow any expression of these feelings to appear on his face. 'Yes?' he said.

'I suppose all this is because of that young girl?' I said.

'That's right, sir.'

I assumed an expression of concern. 'Yes, I see. Only I don't quite know what to do. You see, one of these cars is mine.'

Again he managed to stop the thrill showing in his face. Good control. I admire that. 'Yes, sir? Which one would that be?'

'The Renault. The grey one. You see?' Nothing ostentatious for me. Oh no.

'The one parked closest to the barrier, sir?'

'Yes, it is.'

'Can I ask you why it is parked just there?'

'Oh yes. I always park there in the morning if I can and then run over the hill.'

'Why, sir?'

'Well, it's a good place to run. And there are those exercise bars. I use them. Cheaper than a gym. And in the open air too.'

He looked blank this time. Floored. Couldn't think what to ask me next.

I helped him out. 'I visit people over there.'

'Visit?'

'I work for social services.'

'You're a social worker?'

'Of sorts. I assess people with special needs and report back. Yes.'

'So why was you parked there overnight?'

Here we go. 'Well, yesterday I had to go to London. We have a small flat there which we rent out. It's between tenants now and my mother asked me to go and make sure it was okay. So I parked early yesterday, did my run et cetera, then caught my train to London. I've only just got back.'

It was a good story. He didn't know what to think now. 'I see.' He looked round as if for help. None came. He said, 'Wait here a moment, would you, sir?'

'Yes, of course.' I must remember not to talk too much. Not to say too much. Explaining about the flat was quite unnecessary. Round and round the garden like a teddy bear. One step, two step . . . He's coming back, accompanied by an older man in a suit. A type I hate. Big. Square body, tight belly, beery face. But eyes that weigh you. Cold.

'Hello, sir,' he says. So genial. Baked Alaska.

'Er, hello?'

'James Ryan, CID. I'm in charge here.'

'Oh. Yes.'

'The Renault at the front. That's yours, I hear.'

'Yes.'

'We're going to have to impound it, sir.'

'Yes?'

'Forensic will want to search it thoroughly.'

'Oh. Well, yes, of course.'

'That all right?'

'Yes!'

'You don't mind?'

'No, of course not.'

'It's not just yours, sir. It's all the cars parked here overnight.'

'I understand.'

'Routine, sir. Has to be done.'

'Yes, yes, it's fine.' In spite of all this co-operation with the Law I allow myself to look a little bit scared. Because anyone would be, wouldn't they? The most innocuous person. The innocent.

'Will you give your details to the constable, sir? We'll let you know when we've finished with the car. Sorry for the inconvenience. And we'll need to ask you a few questions later on. I hear you use the hill quite a bit.'

'Yes, I do.'

'Yes, so you might have noticed something. See if you can think of something. Anything. Help us out. Anything at all

46

unusual. Or usual come to that. Yesterday morning. Thank you, sir. Go ahead, constable.' And he strolled off back to the hill. Hard, nasty. Really quite menacing. A worthy opponent, actually.

I gave the young policeman my name, address, phone number et cetera. I said, 'Can I go across the hill now, or is it out of bounds?'

'You have to go the long way round, sir, I'm afraid. Up this way and over through the garden bit.'

'Oh fine, I'll go that way.'

'Just one thing, sir.'

'Yes?'

'Can I have a look in your bag, please?'

'Oh yes. It's just my overnight stuff. And my running gear, of course.'

I opened my bag. Watched his hands touching my things. Feeling around. Looking for clues. I didn't like this at all. I felt invaded, contaminated. Strange. Just things, aren't they? Not me. My self. My flesh. Just things.

'Okay, sir. Thank you. Just routine.'

I wonder if they say that on Death Row as they strap them into the chair: Just routine, sir. Okay?

I zipped the bag up again. 'That's all right,' I said casually. ''Bye. 'Bye!' And off I went up behind the school, where I could have looked down at the police goings-on but didn't. I went through the 'garden bit' to the other side of the hill.

7

Justice at Work

The slow buzzing pace of the court limped on. What kind of nonsense was this where every word the witness said had to be repeated for the recording then read back again at the end of the testimony to make sure it was correct? This was trial by tedium. Bright was fed up. He'd done everything to catch this gook. Not easy. His wife and all his mates off the estate keeping stumm or telling the same story: he's a really nice bloke, loves kids, wouldn't harm a fly.

The prosecution lawyer was Jack Grimley, stocky cock-of-the-walk body in a sharp suit. Natty dresser, big gold signet ring on the little finger. Yellow hair, florid face. But he did the business. He'd done his homework, cross-examined all the cagey relations and the mumbling witnesses.

The defence was crap. Two depressed-looking blokes, brothers, inherited the firm from their dad, looked like they'd been dug up, dandruff on their miserable grey suits, searching vainly through their papers, losing their place, can't find the crucial document, haven't even called the psychiatric expert.

You do the leg work, you want your result, but Christ – the Gook should at least have a chance. Bright could have done a better defence job himself. The prosecution had to prove intent to kill. That was all. A decent defence could have turned it around. Not responsible for his actions, criminally insane.

He felt the rage and misery of the dead girls' families breathing down his neck from the little gallery behind him. And the loathing of the Gook's family farther along. All together in one box, the only place to watch the proceedings. Nice families. All here because one sick bastard couldn't keep his hands off little girls.

The magistrate called recess for lunch. The Gook was led downstairs eyeing his mother with despair. The families filed out of the box, Gook's family glaring at Bright with hate, eyes darting venom as they passed him one by one. You had to get used to that. He was hated by a few families of guys in jug. It was all about families in the end. That was the job.

He told his DC to get him a pint and a sandwich in the pub, found a small room down the corridor and got on his mobile. Got through to Bristol HQ and asked for DI Ryan.

'Ryan here.'

'Oh, yeah. Look, we met at that evidence conference last year. John Bright, Kentish Town CID.'

'Oh yes?'

'I've got a bit of an interest in this case of yours.'

'And what case would that be, then?'

'Come on, mate. The black kid found in the bushes.'

'Oh, that case?'

'Just wondering how you're treating it.'

'We're treating it as murder.'

'Er, yeah, a-ha, I read that in the papers. Are you looking at the serial angle?' Silence. 'Just a thought.'

'It's a possibility.'

'Yeah, I—'

'One of many.'

'A-ha?'

'The case is wide open at the moment.'

'No assault, I gather, no signs of—'

'I remember you now. You're that *little* geezer. Gave a speech, didn't you? At that conference. Scruffy leather jacket. The rest of us in suits, the hoi polloi.'

'Er—'

'Yes, I remember you.'

Bright got the message. 'Okay. Sorry. It's just I'm connected to the case personally. The er – the niece of a – friend of mine was the victim's best friend, and I just wondered . . . Yeah. Never mind, mate. I'll wait for the six o'clock news like everyone else. Forget I called.'

'It wasn't a bad speech as I recall.'

'Oh?'

'How the work's being screwed up by PACE. All the f – All the paperwork.'

'Right.'

'You want to come here, I'll talk to you. On the phone, forget it.'

'I'm in court this next day or two. A committal hearing. Looks like the charge'll be murder.'

'Feather in your cap.'

'Hmph.' Bright had never heard himself say hmph before. Thought he must be getting old.

The rich Irish voice at the other end said, 'See you in a few days then, maybe.'

'Thanks, mate. 'Preciate it.'

'Sure.'

8

Loss and Gain

Later in the night Maisie extricated herself from the arms of her sleeping protectors and threw herself on Kate. Kate put her arms round the lacewing-light body. 'Did the doc give you something to calm you down?'

'Yeah. Valium, I think. It's knocked me out. I don't like it.'

'Won't do you any harm, just at the moment.'

'Don't want any more.'

'I'll tell them.'

'Oh Ankate, it's so terrible.'

'I know.'

'Nobody can know.'

'Well, no.'

'It's like I lost my dad. All over again. I lost my dad . . .' Her voice went up in a glissando scale.

Kate rocked her like a baby. Tears rolled out of Maisie's eyes. Kate gave her a handful of tissues. She knew this: how one loss stands for all losses, brings back old losses, worse losses, adds its pain to the great hollow knowledge of loss. Maisie's burst of crying began to subside.

'My best friend and my dad.' Her voice was small again, diminished.

'Is that why you wanted to stay with your dad?'

Maisie nodded, then said, 'I dunno really. Yes. It must be that.'

'I'll tell Lizzie.'

'I know what mum thinks. I told her it wasn't because I didn't – you know – want to be with her. I asked her to come with me. We could all be here together.'

'I can imagine how she'd react to that.'

Maisie gave a wan smile. 'Yeah. So now I've injured mum as well.'

'Maisie, you haven't injured anyone.'

Maisie wiped more tears away but didn't pursue this subject. She yawned suddenly.

'Where do you sleep round here? Apart from draped around the floor.'

Maisie pointed up. 'That's a sleeping platform up there. But there's people on it.'

51

'What about your dad's room?'

'That's his private space. He never shares that.'

'Not even tonight?'

Maisie's hopeless eyes looked almost black in the candle-light.

'Stay here.' Kate loosened the girl's arms and stood up groaning – her legs had gone to sleep. She hobbled to the door in the wooden wall at the opposite end to the kitchen.

A big space, nearly as big as the main room, two Velux windows in the pitched roof, the moon dead centre in one of them. In the moonlight she made out a big futon on the floor, on it Dave, on his back, straight out, arms crossed on his chest. Alone. When she opened the door he was up and on his knees in an instant. 'Who's that?'

'Dave?'

'Kate – ' He was ready to give her the spiel how this was his private space and he never shared it.

'Dave, you're going to have to share your private space tonight. You have a daughter here in need of a little contact comfort.'

He looked angry a moment, then – was it scared? – Then – maybe knowing how it would look to refuse – he said nothing at all.

'Okay?' Kate stood her ground.

'Sure.' As much welcome in his voice as he could muster.

'Maisie?' Kate brought her in.

He'd got himself together by now and was holding out those protecting arms. Maisie walked into them. Kate wouldn't have liked it but Maisie did. Kate hobbled back to her uncomfortable chair.

9

Excerpt from a Diary

ii

The stomach clenched like a fist. Bubbles of fear rising now and then to the throat. Sudden production of salt saliva. Sudden loss of voice as something interferes with the flow of breath through the vocal cords. Is this how an actor feels waiting for the curtain to go up? The process is not totally unpleasant. I am enjoying it, in the way that an actor must who knows in spite of his nerves that he is a great actor and that he is going to get them hanging on his every word.

They won't find a thing in the car. The plastic sheet I parcelled up and threw over the railings down on to the railway line. It will be anywhere by now, churned up by trains, soaked in standing water, blown away by winds, too contaminated by extraneous gunge to reveal original traces. And of course she had never been in my car. Except dead. And plastic-wrapped.

They'll go over it with minute precision in their space suits and plastic gloves. They are plastic-wrapped too. An ironic detail I hadn't anticipated. They'll collect dust particles, wading through all the old gunk that collects in a car like mine. It's a tip. I pride myself on my unsmart car. The detritus that squeezes down between the seats and in the ridges of those awful rubber mats on the floor. And the boot. Ah, the boot. Spills of potting compost, bought at any supermarket garden centre, and a puddle of toilet cleaner – ditto – not very well wiped up. I love to think of them going to work on all that with their tweezers and little plastic bags. The worker ants. The scavenger wasps, eating up the messes others leave behind.

The phone rings at five o'clock. It's not the great Irish wolfhound Inspector Ryan, just one of his minions. 'Just to let you know we're finished with your car. You can collect it at any time between ten and four tomorrow. Sorry for the inconvenience.'

'That's okay. I've managed without it.'

'We'll be in touch regarding a few more questions if that's okay.'

'Yes, sure.' I'd like to keep him chatting, suddenly. About the hill. About police work. I want to know what they found in my car. But there's no question I can formulate at this moment that won't implicate me.

'By the way, sir, you'll be glad to know your car was clean.'

I laugh. 'Clean? I'm afraid it was shamefully dirty.'

'Well, you know what I mean, sir.'

'Yes. Sorry. Of course I do. Thanks.' My car was 'clean'. I knew that. Of course I did. But there's always that little niggle of doubt. A hair, a fragment of skin, an eyelash. You never know. And maybe they were pretending, to catch me off my guard. How about that for an idea?

10

Missing and Matching

'How'd it go?'

'One up to us.'

'It's to be a murder charge, you mean?'

'That's it, ma.'

'Is it the right thing?'

'Well, he's in the system now. He'll get life. They'll do worse things to him in jail than he'd get in the loony bin. If he'd had a better defence it coulda been Rampton. Take your pick. At least the neighbours' daughters'll be safe. Till the next sick bastard. Sorry, ma.'

'You look tired, John.'

'Long few days.'

'Are you suited to this work?'

'It's what I know how to do. The due process of law. Want a drink?' He was already mixing her scotch. Half an inch in the big glass she liked, two lumps of ice, a flick of the wrist with the water, just to wet it. Poured one neat for himself, swallowed it in one, poured another over ice and swirled it a bit. 'There you are, ma. Cheers.'

'Cheers. Congratulations, anyway.'

'A-ha.'

They clinked glasses. She sipped and sighed. 'Ah that's good.' She wheeled into the living room and they drank looking out at the garden. Tired August time but she always had it nice. He would cut the grass next weekend.

'Kate rang,' she said.

'What?'

'Before you got back.'

'What she say?'

'She got your message at her sister's. Things are not so good there, she says, everyone upset and scared, but okay apart from that, and will you call her.'

All the time she's talking he's swirling the drink in his glass and watching it closely. Now he took a big mouthful – 'Okay' – and put the glass down. He went out into the hall and up the stairs, a bit of the bounce back in him, two at a time.

*

Kate came down the stairs. 'Who was that on the phone?'

'Your policeman.' Lizzie was crushing the shopping into the fridge.

'I suppose you mean John Bright?'

'I told him you were in the shower. He said he'd phone back.'

'My policeman!' Kate started washing the lettuce for dinner.

Lizzie said, 'Are you sure she's all right round there?'

'Well, *I* wouldn't be, and you wouldn't be. But yes. She's surrounded by all these people. Ever such nice gentle souls. Oozing Lurv. You know. I'd punch their faces in if they laid a hand on me. But they sit there holding her close for hours on end making encouraging noises. And Dave occasionally opens those wide enfolding arms.'

'The human harbour.'

They both laughed, a rare event with Lizzie. Forgiveness. Good terms precariously restored. Kate moved close to her, placed the lettuce leaves in a tea towel. 'She *is* okay, Lizzie. And I think she'll get tired of it quite soon.' Kate did not believe this, but Lizzie needed cheering up. It was no use trying to explain about the complex twining of two losses, father and friend. Lizzie might get the drift but she'd pretend not to, and get mad, and the whole thing would end in tears over the salad. Kate reverted to John Bright: 'He's coming down, by the way.'

'Your policeman?'

'I'm warning you, Lizzie.'

'When?'

'Tomorrow.'

'Where's he staying?' This was not a simple question. Like a lot of Lizzie's questions it carried hidden weight: Do you sleep together? Do you expect him to stay here? Will you be staying with him elsewhere?

'Well, maybe he could have Maisie's room while—'

Lizzie looked mutinous.

'Just while he gets fixed up somewhere else? A couple of days? A day?'

Lizzie's knife sliced into a tomato. 'Is it serious, Kate?'

'Oh for heaven's sake, Lizzie.'

Lizzie piled the scarlet slices into a bowl. 'Because I don't think he's right for you.'

'Right for me? In what sense precisely? As a lover? As a companion on life's weary way? As a financial adviser? A gardener? *Right* for me? We're *friends*!'

Lizzie looked a little abashed. A little. Not much. 'Well, he doesn't seem . . .'

'What? Seem what? In the right class? Out of the right drawer? Remember where we came from, Lizzie.'

'He doesn't seem – good enough for you, that's all.' Lizzie was mumbling, unlike her.

'Well, thanks for the advice. You're a fine one to be advising others in their choice of blokes, I must say.'

Lizzie turned away. Kate could tell by the set of her shoulders that she'd gone too far. Not fair, alluding to the fiasco of her relationship with Dave. 'Sorry, Lizzie, but you don't half provoke a person. He is coming here to help.'

'Kate.' Lizzie turned solidly to face her. 'I don't like him.'

Kate groaned. 'Lizzie, nobody likes him. That's the whole point.'

'But you do, for some reason.'

'I got to know him. And there is the small factor that he saved my life.'

Doubt crossed Lizzie's face, the merest passing cloud, but Kate took advantage. 'You have to admit, Lizzie, with a lot of blokes it's the other way round. You like them a lot before you get to know them, and a lot less after.'

Lizzie scowled but didn't give up. She slapped down her strongest card: 'He looks like a crook, Kate.'

'Oh for heaven's sake!' Kate's sudden anger startled both

of them. 'Forget it. I'll book him into a hotel. That gruesome place near the station should suit him fine, it's exactly like Wormwood Scrubs.'

'Kate!'

But she'd gone, slamming the door, stomping up the stairs just like all their childhood rows. Nothing changed since Lizzie was twelve and she was seven. Two little figures popping in and out of a clock, controlled by a mechanism they couldn't dismantle, couldn't change.

Standing at the window looking down at the street, Kate calmed down. Just the knowledge that he was coming made her safer. Made them all safer.

11

Excerpt from a Diary

iii

Well, I got my car back. It looks unnaturally neat. It's the way I'd like it to look all the time, frenziedly clean, the crumbs sucked out of the interstices. But that would not suit my purpose: I'm seen as the easy-going type, relaxed, laid back. I'm so cool! No anal characteristics, no obsessional neuroses. You read all the books, you create for yourself the character you want. It's just the same as what an actor does. Only an actor does it serially, one character after another, grown then discarded like snake skins. I spend my life perfecting just this one character. A supreme creation that takes everyone in. I'm a comedian but I'm the only member of the audience in on the joke, the only one laughing. I can see I could tire of that one day. I can see the temptation to hint, then even to tell . . . I wonder. I wonder now . . .

Later.

I've been QUESTIONED! At the STATION! Inspector Ryan popped in to look at me. Is that an indication of my status? I'm important? A prime suspect. THE prime suspect even?

I told my story again in a windowless room. They asked if I had proof of my journey to London. 'Well . . .' I scratched my fetchingly tousled head. 'I might still have my ticket. There was nobody collecting them at the barrier when I got back.'

'Have you got it on you, sir?'

I felt in my pockets. 'I'm afraid not. But it might be somewhere at home. You know the way you empty your pockets. Where would I have . . .? Anyway, I'll have a look when I get back.'

'P'raps one of my officers could accompany you home while you look for it, sir?'

I looked startled.

'Not unless it suits you, of course,' says Ryan in his most silkily threatening Irish tone.

'No, no, sure,' said I, like I'm seeing my place in my mind's eye, a little bit uneasy. They don't know if I'm worried because: a. there is no ticket; b. there is a ticket but my place is a bit of a mess for guests to see; c. anyone worries about the police coming to their place; d. I'm nervous because I'm guilty; e. I'm guilty of something but not necessarily this – some minor misdemeanour – porno mags, S&M videos, paedophilia on the Internet. Could be anything.

I can see them guessing, getting intrigued. I really enjoy this. It's scary. That flutter in the throat. They DON'T suspect I'm enjoying it, I'm sure. I let them speculate a bit. Then: 'It's just my mother,' I say. 'She's a bit of an invalid. She'll be a bit worried. You know, the police coming to the house.'

Their metaphorical brows clear. 'Don't worry about that, sir. We'll send a woman officer. We won't alarm her.'

'Well . . . Okay then.'

'Right, sir. Shall we go?'

'Now?'

'Why not?'

'Oh. Yes. Okay.' I'm still looking perturbed as we leave. They've primed me now. They've given me the idea. This is improvisation. It's titillating. Lives with his mother. Bit of a momma's boy, bit feeble, tied to her apron strings, under her thumb, possibly gay; probably gay. They've got to follow me up, obviously.

So they come with me. Well, after me. Me in my nice 'clean' car, nondescript, ten a penny. To mother's house. Oh! Nice house! I can hear them thinking. I know what they expected: a first floor over a shop in Montpelier; a basement – sorry, garden-flat – in Kingsdown Parade; not this, impressive classic Georgian, up here in Clifton.

They look oddly at me when I await them on the pavement. For the first time they see me as an anachronism. They nod at me, then look up at the house. Nice shiny paint, navy front door, shiny brass knocker, geraniums in pots. They follow me up the steps and wait patiently while I unlock the front door.

The hall is cool. It smells of flowers and furniture polish.

Mother says all houses should smell of those two things. She's right. She calls out, 'Is that you, darling?' as we come in.

'Yes, it's me.'

'Are there people with you?'

'Yes. A couple of people from work. Come to pick up some case notes.'

'Oh.' I hear her taking this in. 'Hello there!' she calls.

The policeman coughs and says 'Hello' in a subdued way. He actually blushes. But the policewoman is tough, in a pretty, blonde, English blue-eyed kind of way. 'Hello there!' she calls back, confident.

I hear mother grow silent. I can't call out don't worry, it's only a colleague, or any other elaboration of my deception; I'd risk sounding quite mad. It will have to wait. Mother calls out peevishly, 'I really need my tea, darling!' And I say, 'I won't be long, truly.'

I show them into the living room. I'm always struck myself by its beauty. There's a bunch of anemones in a blue and white Chinese bowl on the mahogany table in the back window. Light through the garden leaves and reflections in the polished surface. I invite them through to the kitchen: 'Do you mind if I just put the kettle on for my mother's tea? I am a bit late.'

'No, go ahead.'

Their eyes are going everywhere, it's weird. You feel quite vulnerable as these eyes sweep round all the pots and jars, weighing up what could be lurking under the disguise of innocent household substances, self-raising flour or sugar or dried ceps. They weigh it up against the likelihoods. I want to say something clever, daring them to look in the jars, but I don't. I'm much too clever to be clever with them.

'What's wrong with your mother?' That's the policewoman. She's much brighter than her colleague. Knows what to ask.

'Well, giving birth many years ago, something went wrong. It was the epidural. Too much of something, or something. She doesn't talk about the details. Well, not to me. That's all I've been able to glean. Paralysed legs.'

'Giving birth to you?' she asks.

I'm busy with the tea. 'No,' I say. My back is to them. 'To my sister,' I say.

'And where is she now? Your sister.' She makes her questions sound like anyone's, showing interest, making conversation. She's good. But so am I. I'm not taken in by this. 'She lives in Ireland now. West Cork. She runs a B&B. All by herself. It's a lovely place.'

'It's usually the girl who stays and looks after the mother.'

I shrug. 'Oh well. Yes. She escaped and I got sort of – landed. But actually I don't mind.' I meet the police-woman's eyes for the first time and give a slight smile. She nearly smiles back, a real smile, not a professional one. She doesn't let herself go all the way. But she has felt my charm. Not too much; just a pinprick. In her flesh. I can always tell. She looks away.

'Now,' – I've filled the kettle and emptied the old tea-leaves out of the pot, placed the Doulton cup and saucer and the milk jug on the tray. I switch the kettle on – 'I'll just have a look for that ticket.'

I pick up my overnight bag which I've dumped on the kitchen chair next to my briefcase. I go right through both bags, I don't know how I have the nerve. I dump every single thing out on to the kitchen table. 'No. Not here.' I stand, hands on hips, thinking hard. 'Where could I have put it?' They watch me. 'I'm sure I've still got it. I'm sure I didn't throw it away.' I look embarrassed. 'Honestly!' Suddenly I hit my forehead with the flat of my hand. 'I know!' I race from the room and pound up the stairs. So boyish, so genuine. I shout from up there, 'Got it!'

Mother calls, 'What?'

'Nothing.'

'Not my tea?'

'I'll get it now.'

'What about your friends?'

'Going soon.'

'They don't have to rush away.'

I dance down brandishing the ticket. 'In my other jacket!' I shake my head. 'Of course. How could I have forgotten?' and hand it over.

The constable or whatever he is scrutinises it. The woman says, holding my eyes, 'She seems nice.'

'My mother? She's okay.'

Constable Mastermind has finished his minute perusal of the piece of red and yellow card. 'Well, sir, that seems to be in order.'

'Yes?' I smile, so relieved.

She's still looking at me. She stretches out a hand for the ticket. Gives it a comprehensive glance, nods and hands it back to me. 'Keep it in a safe place,' she says. 'Don't throw it away, okay?'

'Oh. Right. Yes. Thanks.' It's great, this acting lark. I've noticed the closer you stick to your own real feelings the easier it is and the better the effect. I did feel a certain relief, a certain gratitude. The only factor I concealed was my delight, my triumph. I hid behind a becoming modesty. This policewoman was my audience. In the palm of my hand. She was ready to be caught though she did not know it. She's lucky she's not my type. Ten years too old for a start, and too fat. Well, plump, to be charitable. Sturdy policewoman's legs.

She smiled again when I said thanks. I did sound a bit absurd. I meant to. 'Can I say hello to your mother?' she said.

Oh, she wasn't such a pushover after all, playing the same game as I, I discovered.

'Oh.' I got all nervous again. 'Well, the thing is, you're a policewoman and—'

'Woman police officer.'

'Oh yes, sorry.'

'And?'

'Well, actually she's – my mother might be—'

'Give her a shock, you think?'

'Well, yes. I don't think she knows about the awful – I didn't let her read the papers. It could prey on her mind.'

'No, I see.'

They look at each other – What do you think? He on the level? Well, let's leave it for now, get further instructions – and she says, 'Oh well.' She gives me this really inviting smile. 'I can always come back another time. Maybe in plain clothes.'

I laugh, a little uneasily. 'Oh, er, yes, of course.'

'All right, sir. Thanks very much.' He's got the door open on to the sunny street.

She gives me a last conspiratorial smile and follows him out. 'Thanks,' she says. 'I might drop by some time.'

I watch her plump little bottom tremble as her feet hit the steps. Then I go in.

The kettle has boiled. I measure out two teaspoonfuls of Lapsang, reboil the water, pour it into the Chinese teapot and put both my arms round my own body, hugging myself while I wait for the tea to infuse.

12

Private Life, Private Death

He was never happy outside London. He got this nervous feeling on the M4, the rolling hills flashing by, pretty but worrying. What did people do out here in the sticks? Bristol wasn't bad, it was a city, it had personality. But the country? Fearsome. All this wide green space.

It wasn't the countryside making him nervous, though. It was Kate. Was he right to invite himself? Did she really want him there? Could he be of use or was he just muscling in? And was he walking into another stand-off without the guts to see the thing through? And what did he want anyway? They'd have to talk. And he feared that the most. Talking about this stuff – how did you do it? He'd talked to Millie, no problem, didn't know why that was, no explaining it, no barrier, like talking to yourself.

They'd just walked into it, he and Millie, this conversation, like old mates, old sparring partners, suddenly met in another country, on another plane, something, he couldn't explain it. Trouble was, it had him by the balls. Other women – he liked them, fancied them to hell, like Kate. But when it came to it – he just couldn't – go through with it. And it was Millie's fault. How much longer could she stick around to ruin his life? He tried to get angry at her and couldn't. Just got the usual sick sense of loss in his gut. How could he explain this to Kate, in any way that she could tolerate? And what did he want her to say: *Oh, I understand, darling, and of course I'll wait?*

An articulated truck thirty feet long pulled out in front without signalling, just as he started to overtake it. A flash in the mirror showed a car coming up in the outside lane. If he braked, the car on his tail in the middle lane would be up his arse and he'd be under the truck. He had to risk pulling out. He flashed his lights and honked long and hard as he went. The truck swerved back to the inside lane. The car coming up on the outside braked squealing and Bright swept on accelerating like a jumbo jet on the runway, praying as fast as he moved.

It was over. He was okay. All was okay. No one was dead. He felt suddenly cheerful. What the hell. Things change. Living things change. Just like Millie: nearly got him killed for just thinking about another woman. He slowed down to eighty in the middle lane as he overtook a mock-Tudor Morris, then cruised into the inside lane and tootled along at eighty-five. A glorious day and the sun not round to his windshield yet. He got his mind back to the case. After all, the reason for his trip.

Alison. She's dead. No change possible there. He wished he hadn't met her. He wished she wasn't connected to Maisie who was connected to Kate. It was tough clearing the decks in your head to think hard and straight about the thing.

Alison. Beautiful, bright, fifteen years old. And black. That might be a factor. Leaves Maisie's dad's place – Dave, is he called? – with two other young people round ten thirty at night. Dave and all his guests are agreed on that. This does not make it true.

These two young people leave her at her door.

Correction: They say they leave her at her door.

She never gets into her house.

Correction: The parents say she never gets into her house.

No one sees her again.

Correction: So far no one has been found who saw her again.

Someone sure as hell saw her again because she turns up dead three weeks later and someone was responsible for that. And for the laying out. He's heard of some things but to lay a body out on a hillside to be found, like an effigy on a cathedral tomb, hands crossed on her breast, legs straight out, face to the sky. Kind of reverent. And untouched. No one laid a finger on her.

So where was she those three weeks? Who with? Who did that to her? Did what to her? Was she killed or did she die? Why was she left there? By whom? One or more than one? Did she disappear by choice? Or by abduction? And did she know her abductor? Why would she go with this person? Unless this person was known to her. She was too bright to be tricked. That's what people would say. Only, no matter how bright they are, well-brought-up kids of

Alison's age have an innocence the rest of us can barely recall. And the brightest can be the easiest to fool.

Maisie, Kate's niece, a little cracker, thin as a twig, hair like candy floss, eyes like a puppy dog. Full of fireworks, going off in all directions, and clever. Maisie wrecked. What do you do at fifteen when this happens to your best mate? Then the mother, Lizzie. He knew his charm was not of the ingratiating kind, but most women kind of responded, given time. Not the formidable Lizzie. He winced at the memory. 'Hello, Lizzie, I've heard a lot about you. Nice to meet you at last.'

She was polite. Brutally polite. Graciously insulting: 'How do you do? Come in. I won't offer you tea because you'll want to get an early start, I expect. When are you going back to London?'

Maisie whispered to him, 'Take no notice of mum, she's just like that. It's not personal.'

'Oh yes it is.' Kate grinned. 'She hates you, mate.'

He winced.

'I thought you liked to be disliked. I thought that was your stock in trade.'

'Yeah, but in this instance I was actually trying to be nice!'

'Well, there you are, you see. You shouldn't act out of character. Just be horrible like you usually are, and Lizzie will be eating out of your hand.' Mind you, Kate was mad at him that day because – The sign for the A32 to Bristol appeared in the middle of this vaguely disturbing reverie and he sat up and signalled. He got an uneasy feeling as he slid on to the slip road. He was moving off his patch into unmapped territory.

13

Visitation Rights

The bell clanged. It was a big brass bell like a school bell, three floors down. You rang it by pulling on a rope. Maisie leaned out of the window. She was about to throw down the key, the normal way to let people in when the boathouse door was shut. But she saw it was a policeman down there. With a policewoman. The policewoman called up, 'Could you let us in, love?'

Maisie said, 'It's the police.' In the room there was a hiatus, then a slow silent bustling, people moving around, purposefully purposeless. 'Shall I go down, dad?'

'Yes, Maisie, fine.' His face had that concentrated hawkish look, staring like she wasn't there. She thought for a moment he was a bit scared. But he had no reason to be scared. Did he? Except of course all people with radical attitudes, with the courage to live life by their own rules, their own beliefs, and not to go along with convention, maybe they were all a bit scared of the police. And maybe they were right to be scared.

She felt stronger, protective, as she made her way down the dark stone staircase of the lower floors. She unlocked the door with the big key.

The police held out their cards just like on the telly. She didn't dare look closely to see if they were who they said they were. She wondered if anyone ever did.

'Who are you, love?' the policewoman said in quite a friendly way.

'I'm Maisie Creech.'

'We're looking for David Fowler.'

'That's my dad.'

'Your dad?'

'That's right.'

'What you say your name was again?'

Maisie knew what they were implying: *funny, father and daughter, different names, weird set-up here.* Just the usual conventional attitudes. She was used to it. 'I have my mum's name. Yes, he's in.'

'We'd like to have a word with him. Thanks.'

She was shocked. They were already in and on the way upstairs without her permission like they already knew where to go. She wanted to protest but had no idea what to say. Feeling humiliated she shut the big door and locked it again, then ran lightly up behind them.

'Is it about—' She stopped a moment then said, 'Allie?'

'She was your best friend, that right?' The policewoman was quite young, could almost have been a sixth year at Maisie's school. Sounded sympathetic.

Maisie nodded. She dared not speak in case of starting to howl again. The policewoman didn't go on. Seemed to realise.

The policeman said, 'How long's your dad lived here then?' He wasn't sympathetic at all.

'Oh, years.' Maisie had got her voice under control. 'About ten years, I think.' He'd been there ages before it became the thing to live in lofts, he was ahead of his time in so many ways.

'A lot of his students hang out here, that right?'

'Yes.' She tried to find words dignified enough to express the amazing rapport Dave had with the young people he taught, and even with those he didn't. 'They think very highly of him,' she said.

The police people exchanged a glance but didn't say anything.

'Why aren't you at home with your mum?' The woman did not sound unfriendly saying this.

'Well, I just wanted to be with my father for a while, that's all.'

The woman gave her a little smile. She was nice. 'Stay with him quite a lot, do you?'

'Well . . .' Maisie was torn between the picture she wanted to paint, and the truth. 'Well, no actually. We get on very well but I have so much homework and everything, there usually just isn't time.'

'But you stay with him sometimes?'

'Just once or twice really. When my mum's had to go away somewhere.'

'You stay here on your own with your dad?'

Maisie felt uneasy about this question without quite knowing why, like they were implying something horrible: 'Not really. There's always a lot of people here. Dad's really popular. Lots of people don't get on with their parents, things like that, and dad says it's important that someone is there for them.'

'And he is there for them, right?'

'Yes, he is, always.'

The policeman looked at the policewoman. He had a funny expression but he didn't say anything. The rickety wooden stairs took over from the cold stone ones below. The next floor was Dave's place. The woman said, 'Did Allie come here?'

Maisie felt uneasy, wary, she didn't know why, felt she might have betrayed someone or something, felt it had all moved too fast for her, she'd lost track. 'Yes, she came here with me sometimes.'

'To stay?'

'No, not to stay, no.'

'She ever come here on her own? Without you?'

'She never said she did.'

'Would she have told you?'

Maisie's face showed shock. 'She was my best friend.'

70

Tears filled up her eyes. The policewoman looked abashed.

They were at the top of the stairs. The man banged on the door then pushed it open without waiting. Everyone was lounging about as before but now they looked somehow posed, stagey, deliberately arranged in casual attitudes.

Maisie went straight to Dave. Into his arms. Enfolding her, he faced the Law. 'What have you been saying to her?'

'Just chatting, sir, on the way up.'

'Look at her!'

The policewoman said, 'I think it was just the mention of Alison, wasn't it, Maisie?'

Maisie didn't reply. She knew this to be not quite the truth but it was too complex to explain and anyway she was too upset to speak.

Dave said, 'What about Alison?'

'Just wondering if she ever stayed here, sir.'

Maisie felt Dave's body stiffen and go quite still. Pressed against his chest, she couldn't see his face but his voice came out quite smooth. 'Did she, Maisie? I can't remember.'

'They asked me if she stayed here on her own.'

'Just if she came here on her own, sir.'

'Yes, I believe she did, once or twice.'

Maisie looked up at his face. It had the look she found perplexing. A very truthful helpful look, but under it she sensed – not a lie exactly – but a different truth, a version withheld. She wanted to say, 'Allie never told me,' but she felt Dave willing her not to. So she looked at him and said nothing.

'Why would she come on her own, sir?'

'Well, as you see . . .' Dave looked round the room. There were at least five people scattered about on cushions in here and someone standing in the kitchen doorway. 'Young people do tend to hang out here.'

'Why is that, sir?'

'I wish you'd stop calling me sir. Sounds very odd. Well, I think you should ask them. Why do you hang out here, Josie?'

A large soft girl with big brown eyes fingered the fat plait over her shoulder and said, 'Oh, Lord, well, I dunno, just because it's nice here, it's a good feeling, and Dave kind of helps, you know? If you've got a problem or anything, Dave's the person you think of to discuss it with. There's love and peace here, you know?' Her cheeks glowed red and, embarrassed, she faded away, sticking the end of her plait in her mouth as if to stop herself saying more.

The boy in the kitchen door said, 'Cool, Josie, yeah. It's a place to chill out, man, you know? It's a haven.'

A voice from the floor said, 'Yo.'

Dave gave the police a faint smile. He shrugged. 'I also hold seminars here.'

'Seminars?'

'I lecture in English Literature.'

'At the university, we know.'

'Sometimes this is an atmosphere more conducive to learning. Well, to intelligent discussion anyway.'

The policeman made no comment. 'So, can I ask all of you when you last saw Alison Holt?'

General shifting. People sat up, looked at each other.

'You first, sir.'

Dave loosened his grip on Maisie, held her lightly with one arm. 'Missing Persons took a statement at the time she was reported missing.'

'Yes, sir.'

Dave said, 'Well, it was three weeks ago. Her parents rang the next day to find out if she was still here.'

'And she wasn't here?'

'No. She'd been here the night before – the Friday. She'd left about ten. This must all be on record.'

'Yes, sir.' The policeman waited.

72

'She left with two or three other people. You'll have their names on record. Who lived in the same direction.'

'And had she been staying here?'

'No, just visiting. With Maisie.'

Maisie, in tears again, nodded.

'You didn't leave with her, love?' The policewoman was always the one who addressed Maisie, as though the man were not allowed to.

'No. I left first, round nine thirty, with Lennie, a friend of ours. He walked me back home. My mum likes me to be in by ten. Allie gets a special dispensation Friday nights.'

'Alison left about ten, I think,' Dave said.

Josie took the plait out of her mouth, said, 'I was with her,' and put it back in.

The boy in the doorway said, 'So was I.'

'Who are you, sir?'

'Stephen Hudson. Steve.'

'Anyone else with you?'

'Yeah. Martin, wasn't it, Jose?'

'Martin, yeah. I was with them up as far as – as – Windmill Hill, then they went up the steps to Totterdown, you know, Pylle Hill Crescent and Richmond Street and all that, and I went off to my place. Yeah.'

'We went along St Luke's Crescent then up Alison's street. We all chatted outside Alison's place,' Steve said. 'Then she went in, we thought, and Martin and I went off to the Indian chippy, you know, top of Alison's street near the shops. There was a queue so we decided to go down into town. We bumped into a mate of mine down by Temple Meads. Andy. And he got us into this club in King Street. I lost track of the others right away in there. You took statements at the time, you know.'

'Yes, sir. Thank you.'

Dave said, 'Anything I or any of us can do to help, I'm sure . . .' He looked around and all the people nodded. The boy flat on the floor raised a hand in agreement. '. . . we will. Anything.'

'Well, we would like a word with you in private, sir, now you mention it. Down at the station, if you don't mind.'

'Down at the station?'

Even the supine boy sat up straight. Josie said, 'Dave?' in a panic-stricken voice. Stephen said, 'Are you arresting him?'

Dave said, 'Well? Are you?'

The policeman said, 'No. But Inspector Ryan would like to ask a few questions. You're not being accused of anything but you might have things to tell us.'

'I think I've told you everything I can remember.' Dave was about to go on but didn't. Maisie knew he stopped speaking out of fear, that dry throat that won't let your voice escape. And she could feel his heart. Dave? Scared? Then she thought, So would I be scared if they wanted to take me to the police station. It is frightening.

'Could you come with us now, sir?'

'Well . . .' Dave looked round, thinking of things to keep him there. All the young people watched him like dogs losing their master.

Stephen said, 'Listen, man—'

But Dave said, 'It's okay, Steve. I don't mind.' He tossed Stephen the keys. 'Keep an eye on the place, will you, till I get back?'

'Yeah, man.'

'Dad? Shall I come with you?'

'Christ. Listen, I'm going to have to make some arrangements about my daughter here.'

'That's okay, sir, we'll drop her off at her mother's.'

'Will Lizzie be in yet, Maisie?'

'Dad?' She wanted to stay there till he came back at least.

'Better go, Maize.' Dave picked up the phone and punched Lizzie's number.

'Our colleagues are waiting down the street. You can follow them in your own car, sir.'

'I don't own a car,' Dave snapped. 'It's against my principles.' He spoke into the phone: 'Oh, Kate, it's you.'

The young people milled about collecting their belongings while Dave explained the situation to Kate.

The policeman said, 'We'd like you all to stay here, please.'

They looked at each other, wary.

'Why?' A girl with long blonde hair appeared, looking down from the sleeping platform. Maisie had not seen her before.

'Just a few questions, love.'

'No obligation,' the policewoman said. 'But you don't mind, do you?'

The girl looked as though she had not long been awake. The policewoman grinned. 'Doesn't look like you've got anywhere that urgent to go.'

'Oh.' The girl swept her hair back with a pale hand. 'No. I guess . . . not.'

'So?'

'Okay then.'

Dave put the phone down. 'Kate's coming over for you, Maize.'

Maisie nodded, miserable with the dread of her mother's reaction when she arrived home, tail between her legs. 'Okay, dad.'

Dave looked round the room: 'And listen, help these guys. We've all got to help as much as we can. We all knew Alison, a little at least. We might be able to throw some light.' He had pulled himself together. The young people straightened up, bathed in the light of his restored confidence.

'Okay, Dave.' The blonde girl gave Dave a special kind of look as she came down the ladder.

'What's your name, love?'

The girl swept her hair back again and said shyly, still looking at Dave in that special way, 'Sally. Sally Leventon.'

Maisie felt a particular misery surge up inside her. She'd had this feeling before when girls looked at her father like that. Maybe it wouldn't be such a bad thing to be back at her mother's just now.

'How's mum?'

'Well, Maisie, you're going to have to—'

'—to be careful. I know.'

'She'll be glad to have you back.'

'Yeah but she won't show it, will she?'

'She can't.'

'Why not? Dad does.'

Kate bit her tongue. She did not say Lizzie cares more than he does, she said, 'She cares too much.'

'I know.' Maisie groaned. 'She just makes everything so heavy.'

'Yup.' Kate came to an unexpected halt. The Ford Capri in front waited to make sure the traffic lights were well and truly green to take off his handbrake and put his car in gear. 'Oh, these Bristol drivers.' She had a swift mind-flash – John Bright's capable hands on the steering wheel, his instinctive handling, more like flying than driving – which led her to add, 'By the way, John Bright's coming down.'

'Your policeman!'

'Maisie!'

'It's what mum calls him.'

'Exactly.'

'Is he coming down to solve the case?'

'Hell, no. I mean, he might be able to glean a bit of inside information from the bloke in charge, but that's about it. This is not his patch.'

'So why is he coming then?'

'Well . . .'

'Is it because he's your bloke?'

Kate glanced into Maisie's pure young eyes. 'Christ, Maisie, the things you say.'

'Well, I thought—'

'No, he's not my bloke.'

'Not yet anyway,' Maisie said.

'Maisie!'

'Well, you haven't given up, have you?'

Kate, speechless for a moment, rallied. 'No. Actually. I haven't.'

'I liked him.' Maisie offered her sturdy support.

'Oh well then, in that case, I'd better not give up.'

Silence for a block while trains of thought took separate tracks. Then Maisie said, 'That's the first time I've stopped thinking about Allie since . . .'

Kate looked at the tired pale face.

Maisie said, 'I don't want to stop thinking about her. Not for a minute. If I forget her a minute, a little bit of her goes and I'll never get it back.'

'Oh Maisie.'

'I can't stand it, Ankate. I don't know how to stand it.'

Kate took a hand off the wheel and held Maisie's hand.

'And what did they take dad for?' Maisie wailed.

14

Helping the Police with their Enquiries

Ryan's bulk made him feel flimsy, made of muslin, ghost-like, but he was holding his ground. He sat with his arms folded firmly across his chest and held the gaze of whoever spoke to him.

'Listen, son.' Ryan was only five years older than Dave, if that. 'Listen, son, there's no need to be defensive. We're not accusing you of anything.'

'I should think not.'

'Like my officer said, we just want you to tell us everything you know.'

'You took me away in a squad car in front of my daughter and my students—'

'I know, son, and I'm sorry about that.'

'Oh, are you?'

'I am, and the sooner we get this over with the sooner you can get back to your daughter and your – students.'

'Not all your students, are they, sir?' The hard-faced policeman assisting Ryan.

'Not all, no. Not officially.'

'Quite a number of nubile young females, I'm told, sir.'

Dave managed to say nothing.

'Wouldn't you say so, sir?'

Dave addressed Ryan: 'This officer seems to be making insinuations which in the tragic circumstances I find offensive. And if this is to be the level of your questioning I want a lawyer. I want to call my solicitor now and I refuse to say another word until you allow me to do that.' He found himself standing up, had no idea how this had come about, but knew he made a daunting figure when roused.

However, these two hard-noses remained undaunted. 'Sit down, please, sir,' Ryan said, bored.

Dave could have said, I won't sit down, and got himself involved in a farcical stand-off, or stand-up, but he knew too well as a teacher not to get into a battle you can't win. He stood irresolute.

'I told you,' Ryan said, 'you're not accused of anything. My officer DC Hughes apologises for getting out of line. Don't you?'

Hughes eyed Dave with contempt. 'Yes, sir. Sure.'

'Obviously heartfelt, DC Hughes.' Dave spoke with the sarcasm he used on the clever clogs student trying to put him down in front of the rest – you got the odd one now and then. He was pleased to see it work on Hughes if only to rile him up. Dave kept his eyes on the guy's face as he lowered himself back into the chair, then he took the initiative. 'Look,' he said. 'I met Allie – Alison – a few times. Three, to the best of my knowledge. Maisie brought her once or twice. And once, I think, she came by herself. And yes, I have young girlfriends, but I am not a child-molester. The girls I have affairs with are well of age and never up to now in my experience, virgins. I'm not saying I haven't been tempted. I doubt if you could meet a male who could state honestly that he hadn't been tempted . . .' He looked hopefully into the two faces across the table. They remained impassive. 'And Alison was, I have to admit, a little bit smitten. I gave her an avuncular talk and, basically, sent her off to get on with her homework.'

The two cops looked at each other. Ryan said, 'What does avuncular mean, DC Hughes?' Hughes said, 'I don't know, guv, we'll have to look it up.' It had gone wrong. This sort of stuff didn't wash with them. In their eyes everyone was guilty unless proved innocent. The more truthful you managed to sound, the better a liar that proved you to be. They let a long silence elapse.

Then the DC said, 'I imagine if we searched your place we might find the odd illegal substance stashed here and there, sir. Don't you think so?'

'That right, Mr Fowler?' Ryan said.

Dave felt like a deep sea diver about to get the bends. He could get no grip. He didn't know what to do. Condemned by speech, condemned by silence, condemned simply by their suspicion, he felt paralysed. He actually wanted to weep. Only pride and bloody-mindedness stopped him. He crossed his fingers against his heart and hoped to die. 'I very much doubt it,' he said. He hoped every scrap of dope had been gathered up when Maisie went down to let the bastards in. But you never know. And if they decided to raid the place . . . Or search the young friends they'd detained there . . . 'And I hardly see the relevance anyhow.'

'There's things a young girl might do stoned out of her gills that she wouldn't do sober, sir.'

'Is that so?' Dave wished he had not said that. Cheeky, feeble. Their expressions showed they knew they had provoked him. He crossed his arms harder, tighter, across his crossed fingers, across his heart.

Ryan looked through the file on the table in front of him. He looked up. He said, 'I see from your statement when Alison first went missing you didn't mention this crush she had on you.'

15

No Place Like Home

Bright stood at the window, bouncing slightly on the balls of his feet, jangling the change in his pockets. Lizzie watched him. He'd given up attempts at conversation. He wished she would at least leave the room. She knew this and sat on. Even though she had things to do. She embarrassed him on purpose. At last she said, 'Why would they be questioning Dave again?'

'It's a murder enquiry now. They got to start again. Don't suppose they suspect him in particular. They got to start somewhere.'

'Why with him?'

'Alison went there a few times, you said.'

'Well, so what?' Lizzie had no idea why she was suddenly defending Dave. Except that she disliked Bright more.

'I didn't arrest him.' Bright turned his oh so amused squinting glance on her, those small brown eyes, sharp as broken glass.

Her face went pink. 'No. Of course not. But they questioned him at the time and . . .'

He relented. 'It'll be the same with every bloke she had contact with, from the postman to her eight-year-old cousin. They got to turn all the stones.' She wasn't convinced, he could see. He hoped he was speaking the truth. For Maisie's sake, and therefore for Kate's. And speaking of Kate—

The yellow Beetle yakkered to a halt on the steep street outside. She saw him at once and pretended not to. He felt oddly pleased by this. Maisie dawdled up the steps, head

81

down, Kate nudging her to be nice to Lizzie. Lizzie had shot out to the front door.

Bright expected to hear the nagging start as soon as she opened it. But no. Silence. Maisie at last came into the room.

'Hi, Maisie.'

She moved her mouth – you couldn't call it a smile – and gave him a sort of wave.

'Sorry to hear . . .' He nodded the rest of the sentence and she nodded back.

Kate had gone into the kitchen with Lizzie. Maisie came to stand by the window with him. They looked at the house opposite with its depressing replacement windows and bottle glass front door. After a minute or two she said, 'They took my dad.'

'A-ha, I heard.'

'What will they do to him?'

'They got to question people at the station these days. Get it all down on tape. It's just rules.'

'Will they lock him up?'

'I don't think so.'

'Why not?'

'Well, I don't think they suspect him of doing anything bad. They just think maybe he knows something. Something maybe he forgot last time.'

'Knows something?'

'Or someone.'

'You mean one of his student people?' Maisie turned this white strained face on him that would break your heart. You lose your best friend like this, and then they start accusing your father of untold crimes.

'I'll find out,' he said.

'From the police?'

'A-ha.'

'Will they tell you?'

'They might.'

'Because you're a policeman too?'

'A-ha.' He didn't say because he was a policeman with a certain amount of clout in this field. He said, 'I'm not making any promises, okay?'

She sighed and sat down. 'Even mum doesn't want him arrested,' she said.

'Hello.' Kate stood in the doorway. Hair all over the place, eyes with that challenging look when she wasn't sure of her ground but was giving it a go. 'Came here first then?'

'A-ha.' What did she mean, first? He didn't ask.

'Well, I'd better take you to where you'll be staying.'

'Oh.' This was a surprise. He didn't show it. 'Right.' He picked up his bag. Felt a bit daft assuming he'd be staying here. She raised her eyebrows in conspiratorial amusement. This made him feel marginally less daft. 'Now?' he said.

'Probably a good idea. What do you think, Maisie?'

'What? Oh. Yes.'

Kate laid a hand on her niece's head. 'Go and get a cup of tea in the kitchen. You're starved.'

Maisie got up and moved slowly to the door. She turned and looked at Bright. 'I'm glad you're here anyway,' she said.

Bright, touched, didn't know where to look. His eyes met Kate's and the old thing happened again. Islanded in a dangerous place, no way forward, no way back, no way in, no way out.

She ended it: 'Come on then, let's go.'

The hotel foyer was like a huge airport departure lounge. Insidious noise loosely describable as music filled the air-conditioned infinitely carpeted pinkish space. Employees like cabin staff discreetly handed out forms to be filled, electronic room keys that also turned on the lights, offers to carry baggage too small to be worthy of the name.

'Think I can manage, thanks.' Bright lifted his small overnight bag, hated all this deferential bullshit. Kate grinned.

'And Mrs Bright?' The smooth young man gave her a toothful smile. Kate blushed, felt idiotic. Bright made a muffled groan and Kate laughed. 'I'll help him carry his baggage,' she said. 'I haven't got any.'

The room too was pinkly carpeted and lit. 'I'm sorry about this,' she said. 'Lizzie just—'

'A-ha. Don't explain. I got the picture.' He threw his bag on the bed. 'Well? What now?'

She decided to keep this impersonal. 'I wish I knew.'

'I guess I phone Ryan.'

'Really?' Her face filled with hopes he felt certain to disappoint.

'Not that I expect to find out much.'

'You won't be able to protect Dave?'

'No.'

'No.' She put her hand over her eyes. 'It's Maisie. I just can't bear—'

'No.'

'And nor can Lizzie. It's worse for her.'

'A-ha.'

She sat on the bed while he took his toothbrush out of his pocket and placed it in the glass in the pink-tiled ensuite bathroom. 'Want to meet later on?' he said.

'Oh.' He was telling her he had to be alone to phone Ryan. She felt stupid. Stood up. Ran through her Bristol haunts and ended up with the one she always chose. 'See you at – eightish – in Renato's. Next to the Old Vic. In King Street.'

'I remember.'

'Italian place. Well, obviously.'

'I remember.'

'Oh yes.' She was flushed, flustered. 'We could eat there too.'

84

'I remember, okay?' She aroused a tenderness he found hard to withstand. ' 'Course I remember.'

'When you came to the play.'

'When I saw you're this great actress.'

'Oh, piss off.'

'Which I already knew.'

'Okay, I'm going. You certainly know how to get rid of a girl.'

'I have my methods.'

'I've noticed.' She was at the door. So was he but she didn't hang about. 'See you at eight.' She was gone.

16

Excerpt from a Diary

iv

I bought the paper today. Pictures of the grieving children at the school. They LOOK like children in the pictures. With their teachers. By the piles of flowers in the playground. But they're not children really. They're women and young men. They are to a certain extent innocent – or should I rather say ignorant? – of the ways of the world. But they are not children. She was a woman. Perfect in every detail. Before the world could touch her. Contaminate her perfection. It was about to begin, the contamination. It was beginning. I saw her smoking spliff with those types who visit Mr Wonderful. In his loft. The lofty types. Next it would be something a little more sophisticated, a little more exciting, a little more dangerous. I'm sure like all of them she took Es like sweeties.

In a few weeks, or even days, her virginity would have gone and she'd be just like all the rest. Spoiled. The spoils of a vile kleptomaniac who would have to have that, just that, for himself. To add to his collection. His stash.

I'm crying again, looking at these pictures. The problem is, I can't explain to them. They think she's lost. I can't explain to them that she's saved. One perfect unspoiled thing saved. I'm sorry to have to hurt them all like this. If only there were some way to tell them WHY.

The picture of her parents is not very good. They're rather blurred. Gazing straight out, sitting at a table. Oh yes, it's when they were on TV making their appeal. That's why it looks odd. Those lines across the picture. They have got what they deserve. They allowed her into these dangerous ways. Freedom they call it. It has got to stop. Oh, for the general run it will do. But there are certain rare creatures of such perfection of form, of grace, of soul, of mind, that the world must not be allowed to corrupt them. If these people do not realise what they have been entrusted with, have not learned to protect it, they must be taught. It is hard. But they must learn. They have other children. Perhaps they'll be more careful of them now. I'm not a cruel person, not at all, I am tortured with tenderness. But in my silent secret way I will teach the world this lesson. They will see. Eventually.

And they'll see I'm not cruel. I didn't harm her. I preserved her perfection. They'll see that. These people, journalists, police, are used to adding two and two together, it's their job. They'll pick it up, won't they? Surely they will.

I went to a house today. There were two small boys under school age. No trousers, snot running down their faces. They played on a littered floor, sticky with spilt drinks and food. The baby lay in its pram with food all over its face and a nappy soaked and soiled. No father to be seen, of course, and the mother lying back, eyes rolling in her head, the gear lying on the floor by the couch within reach of the children. Everybody happy.

Why not kill them, you'll ask. They're already killed, that's why. They're gone. 'Special needs?' You bet. I'll fill in the forms for them. Get them to write their names. If they can. As I was leaving she said, 'Got a fag, love?' She said, 'I got to have a fag, see, just to keep floatin'.' I gave her a cigarette. I don't smoke myself. I loathe it, detest it, but sometimes it's the only way to break the ice. It's currency. They all smoke, these people. All of them. They have skin like wrinkled grey paper. From the age of nine. Earlier, some of them. I've never figured out how they survive at all. Those of us with the money and the nous to eat the right food, stuffing ourselves with the right vitamins and minerals and the ginseng and the royal jelly and the evening primrose oil and the echinacea, from morning till night, can barely survive. While these creatures of the underclass spawn, as profligate with their genes as sycamore and thistle, breeding on waste ground.

17

Muscling In

The Broadbury Road police HQ, a terrible seventies building, stood on a windy corner surrounded by roadworks in a housing estate of red-brick pseudo cottages that would have been nice with their original windows and doors. Bright crossed the tarmac car-park into the public entrance and stated his business through a microphone and bulletproof glass. He was getting the impression this was a rough area.

Ryan came out of the pass door with Dave. Bright turned his back as best he could in the cramped entrance. He didn't want to embarrass Dave. He also didn't want Ryan to see they knew each other. Not yet.

Dave said to Ryan, 'An Irish detective inspector. It seems odd somehow, incongruous. Not in Ireland of course, but here. Don't you think?' He meant it man to man but it didn't come out like that; it came out big lad cheeking teacher. Bright felt glad he'd turned his back.

Ryan saw Dave off the premises without a word, came back scowling and saw Bright. 'Oh, it's you,' he snarled.

' 'Fraid so.'

'Yeah, sorry. That guy gets on my tits: "Incongruous, don't you think"! Doesn't take anyone in, that stuff. Him with the long hair down his back. Not that I'm prejudiced, mind. Ringlets down to your arse doesn't make you a criminal. But it sure as hell gets up my nose.'

'How's it going?'

Ryan got coffee from the machine on the landing outside his office. 'Uniform branch just blew it.'

'Jumping the gun?'

'They march in there when he's surrounded by his so-called students. We were hoping to catch him with something incriminating just to have something to hold him on. They'd have everything flushed down the toilet before those guys were up the stairs.'

'You figure him then?'

Ryan growled. 'Maybe he didn't kill the girl. Maybe. Maybe he didn't abduct her. Maybe. But he's not telling everything, not by a long chalk. He's done something, or he knows something, that he's not telling us. Something has happened that connects him. Something. I've a nose for guilt and Mr Guru Man stinks of it. Clever he may be, and charismatic for these poor kids maybe, but the fear coming off him is a stench to a nostril like mine.'

Bright took his coffee, impressed. 'I'd better state my interest.'

'You already did.'

'I've met the guy socially. I know his daughter.'

'You're screwing her auntie the actress, that's the word round here.'

Bright covered the lower half of his face with his hand, his eyes contorted into one of his fiercer squints. He had to decide fast which way to jump with this guy. On impulse he said, 'Not screwing as it happens. No such luck. We're – friends, that's all. Since—'

'Since the body in the bath case.'

'A-ha.'

'That right, now?' said Ryan. 'She's a great-looking girl. Not many guys round here would say no to a piece of that.'

'Nor would I, believe me, mate. It just hasn't happened. Looks as though it never will.'

Why his frank admission of lack of success with Kate should endear him to Ryan he hadn't a clue. But it did. He'd spoken on instinct. He knew Ryan would assume the refusal was on her part. Well, anyone would. A copper screwing a key person in a case like this was a bad risk. Being turned down by a foxy lady, however, was not a thing a bloke liked admitting. So the admission was likely to be true. Ryan thought so anyway. He sat back in his chair, relaxed. He seemed to grow in size. He regarded Bright, nodding his big head several times. 'So what do you want to know that the papers can't tell you?'

'I dunno. The stuff that gives you the feel. The scene, the pictures, the lab reports—'

'Alcohol and barbiturates and no struggle, looks like the old polythene bag.'

'But you're sure it's murder?'

'The way she was laid out. Weird.'

'A ritual killing?'

Ryan shook his head. 'No. Only one set of footprints. Trainers. No distinguishing marks.'

'How are the evidence reports looking?'

Ryan groaned. 'Any idea the sheer number of witnesses? Kids know so many people. The whole feckin' school have got something to tell you, some vital sighting on the day or the day before or the day before that, something she said in the changing room before gym or the school hall during assembly, it drives you mental.'

'Got it on the PNC?'

Ryan nodded. 'And we're setting up HOLMES.'

'Where's your incident room?'

'Bishopsworth. You're not getting in there.'

Bright grinned. 'Nothing to go on? Apart from Dave?'

Ryan sighed and shook his head. 'Nothing you can get hold of. We've got six uniforms knocking on doors.'

'Heard you were talking to her father.'

'Nothing there. Well . . .'

'A-ha?'

'He's hiding something but I don't think it's anything to do with this.'

'Why?'

'No sign of anything wrong in the house. No abuse. Nothing.'

'Talk to the guy who found her?'

'The jogger? Poor sod. Yeah, shitting himself. Imagine, you go into the bushes for a quiet piss and what do you find? Black Beauty lying dead at your feet.'

'Any history?'

'No. Never seen a corpse in his life before. Nothing there either. Clean as a whistle.'

'So that's it then. No one else been questioned?'

'A few people who had their cars parked close by. You

know the Bedminster approach to the hill? Right by the kid's school, where my fellas had been asking questions for days. Five cars had been parked there overnight. All gone over with a fine-tooth comb. All clean. But one of the uniform branch, pretty little mare by the name of Goldilocks. Helen Goldie, that is. Hang on . . .' He riffled through the files on his desk. 'Here we are: she fancied one of these car-owners for it. Guy who lives up in Clifton. Don't know why him. His car was pure as the driven snow. No evidence whatever. But Goldilocks Had A Feeling.'

'Worth following up?'

'Not on the basis of female intuition. Sorry.'

'No other connection to Alison? Or anyone who might know Alison?'

Ryan looked at Bright. Something had changed in the guy's posture. Or something. His little brown eyes. Sometimes they squinted, sometimes they didn't, weird. Something in him had perked up. His eyes had sharpened like needles. A hard metallic light that hadn't been there before. Ryan said slowly, 'You suffering from female intuition as well?'

'I dunno. Why was his car parked there if he lives in Clifton?'

'He works in the Bedminster/Totterdown area, some kind of social services thing. Home assessment visits, something.'

'Could he have done a home assessment visit to Alison's family?'

'They're not that kind of black. Father works in the DSS. Managerial. The mother's a teacher. They're the respectable type.'

'Why would he leave his car just there?'

'Health-conscious. He jogs over the hill on his way to work and on his way back.'

'To work? Jogging makes you sweat. He the type to arrive at work sweaty?'

'Well, his car was a mess. And he's another long-hair. Not like our friend Dave Fowler the guru but aiming for that league. Holes in his sweater, that sort of stuff. And the kind of people he's visiting? Believe me, they wouldn't notice if he smelled like a doss house. But I don't know. I don't know.' Ryan's big fist came up to his mouth. He pondered over the file then handed it suddenly to Bright. 'Have a look at it, I'm busy. Don't tell a soul. And don't remove it from this office.'

18

Partings and Meetings

Maisie insisted on going to the school, so Kate went with her. A river of flowers flowed from the site on the hill where the body had been found, down the path, spilled in a bank along the wall of the school to the gate, through the gate, ending at a kind of altar in the playground where some people knelt and prayed.

Kate thought, This is the new mourning. People of the national disaster generation have invented it for themselves. It's television. It creates national news, and that creates demonstrations. Outward signs of inward grief. Maisie left her, to join two girls who put out their arms. They stood entwined, the Three Graces.

Kate looked at the pictures of Alison, the poems and messages attached to the flowers. A young woman stood next to her. She said, 'Excuse me, but you're Kate Creech, aren't you?'

'Yes. How – ?'

'I go to the Old Vic. I saw your Hedda.'

'Oh.' Kate didn't want this conversation over the grieving flowers.

The young woman saw her discomfort. 'Sorry. Not the place. I just wanted to say – Well, it was remarkable, that's all.'

'Oh. Right. Thanks.' She never knew how to deal with this kind of thing. Gave the girl an awkward smile.

The girl didn't smile back. 'Did you know Alison?' she said.

'Yes. She was a friend of my niece.'

'Oh.' The young woman looked over at Maisie. 'Maisie,' she said.

'You know Maisie?'

She smiled and nodded.

'Are you a teacher here?'

She shook her head.

'A neighbour?'

'I know her father,' she said.

'Dave?' She didn't look Dave's type. She was tall, athletic-looking, with a strong face, long eyes set wide apart, an amused mouth, mid-length mid-brown hair. Dave liked them more ethereal – long blonde hair and long soft frocks, diaphanous and sweet. And younger. This girl wore a flow-ered cotton dress down to her calves and sensible sandals. She looked capable, practical.

Maisie left her friends and came back wiping her eyes. The young woman said, 'Hello, Maisie.'

Maisie looked blank.

'We met at your dad's place. I'm Margaret.'

'Oh. Yeah. Hi.'

Margaret gazed at Maisie, eyes full of sympathy and sorrow.

Maisie turned to Kate. 'Let's go, Ankate.'

'Okay.'

'No use being here.' She wandered towards the gate.

Kate turned to say goodbye to the young woman, but she had gone. She caught up with Maisie at the gate. 'Who was that?'

'Who? That woman?' Maisie shrugged. 'There's always so many women at dad's place. I can't remember them all.'

'You made a greater impression on her than she did on you, then.'

'Oh well, I'm dad's daughter. They have to keep in with me, don't they?' She gave Kate a wan smile.

They stood at a loss for a while outside the school walls. Where now? What now?

Kate said, 'Fancy seeing my digs?'

Kingsdown Parade was a high point of the city. Not as high up, geographically or socially, as Clifton, but with lovely Georgian houses, and a certain village feel. Kate had stayed up here last summer, an attic flat five floors up, windows looking through breaks in the roof parapet, nothing grand, just a kitchen you could eat in and living room you could sleep in. Nice. She liked it. And she liked the family downstairs. Luke lectured at the university, media studies. Caroline painted, still lifes of flowers, mainly for classy greetings cards.

Kate opened a door in the garden wall and led the way up a brick path overgrown with silvery things, lavender, rosemary, curry plants, all releasing heady aromas as they brushed past. The best of the summer flowers were over but honeysuckle was making a last ditch stand and some late roses swelled on the trellis. Maisie trailed after her and stood passive on the step while Kate rang the bell.

'Kate! How are you? It's great to have you back!' Caroline and the youngest, Thomas, leapt on Kate. The cat, Harry, more circumspect, kept his watchful distance but didn't run away. Caroline made space on the table, pushing aside her painting things and a bowl of tall spiky flowers of an extraordinary blue. 'The last of my delphiniums,' she said. 'I'm recording them for posterity.'

'They deserve it. They're gorgeous.'

'They are.'

Thomas leaned against Maisie's knees, gazing up into her face. 'This is my train,' he said. He waved the bright painted wooden object under her nose. Tears ran down Maisie's face. 'You're cryin',' he said.

Maisie nodded and cried more.

I cry,' he stated proudly. 'A lot.'

'That's certainly true.' Caroline poured tea. 'It's Earl Grey. Is that all right?'

'We were down at the school,' Kate said.

Caroline passed round big mugs of tea. Thomas stared at Maisie. Caroline and Kate stared at each other. The cat Harry stared at Kate. Even Maisie's crying made no noise. Thomas placed his train in Maisie's lap then clambered up after it. He settled himself back against her. She put her arms round him and rested her cheek on his head. It was the first time Kate had seen her look truly comforted.

'Joe Paxton's got the flat. He leaves tomorrow morning,' Caroline said. 'I'll change the sheets and stuff tomorrow and you can move in the next day. Is that okay?'

'That'll be fine,' Kate said. She turned her head and met the eyes of Harry, a chunky tabby. He knew her of old but was taking his time, just checking. He made a sudden leap from the window sill and landed in her lap. He turned round a few times, trying out positions, fixed on one curled sideways, his back pressed against her stomach. She too felt oddly comforted.

19

A Way In

Bright spent a few hours going through the file. There was nothing you could put your finger on. The parents were beyond suspicion. The neighbours, heartbroken, bewildered, equally easy to eliminate. Ryan was right. Dave, and the atmosphere surrounding Dave, were the nearest anyone could get to something odd. And the fact that Alison had been there last was damning.

The report on the visit to the guy in Clifton with the invalid mother was the last in the file. Bright read it twice then got up and left the office.

The CID room went quiet when he walked in. People got busy. Bright understood: it made them feel wankers, thinking the boss had called him in. They didn't like it and weren't bothering to hide their feelings. He stopped at the first table. A guy staring into a computer screen pretended he didn't see him then got real startled when Bright spoke. 'Oh! Sorry! What did you say?' He didn't do it well. His performance lacked subtlety to say the least.

'I'm looking for WPC Goldie. Helen Goldie.'

A few laughs, and a guy down the room whistled. 'Aren't we all, mate?'

Bright's squint intensified but no amusement showed. Glances were exchanged.

'Canteen, I should think.' The computer guy went back to his screen.

She was easy to recognise. A bit on the plump side for him

but pretty, all right. And the blonde looked almost natural. 'WPC Goldie?'

' 'S right.'

He introduced himself. She looked impressed. 'You're the one who got that garden shed bloke.'

'A-ha.'

'Did Ryan invite you down to help with this?'

'No. I invited myself.'

'We could do with some help. Not getting far.'

'I wanted to ask you about this guy in Clifton.'

'Why?'

'Your report. You thought he should be followed up.'

Her fine blonde skin coloured, pearly pink. 'My guv'nor said—'

'A-ha. I know.'

'And the DC who went with me. He thought the guy was okay.'

'But?'

'Well, I don't know . . .'

'Yes you do. You say I don't know in that vague way and they'll all go on ignoring you. Come on, give it some elbow, love.'

'Oh.' She coloured again, this time as though he'd goosed her. She looked at his face. He had a slight squint, now she looked close. It gave him a foxy look, kind of amused, only the rest of his face stayed stock still, like a mask, like he was listening behind it, like what she said might be important.

'Take your time,' he said.

She shut her eyes and clasped her hands as though she were praying, and maybe she was. She opened them, hands and eyes. 'Okay,' she said. 'Right. He was – it sounds daft but he was, like, crowing.' She looked at him, ready to be mocked, but his face didn't move. Only the squint had gone. Was that possible? And needle points of light had come into the small brown eyes.

'A-ha?' he said.

'Well, it was like he was *glad* we were there, like he wanted to be questioned, like he thought he was okay, we couldn't touch him for some reason. This posh house and everything.'

'Having a posh house doesn't necessarily make you a killer.'

'Oh.' She looked upset. 'No . . .'

'Though it can help, of course.'

She looked at him closely then laughed. 'No, I don't mean that, only it was like he knew we'd think he was all right because he was posh and lived in Clifton and had this posh invalid mother.'

'I've got an invalid mother.'

'Have you?'

'A-ha. But she's not posh. So I'm all right.'

She knew now he was teasing her. She relaxed. 'He wouldn't let me see his mother. Kept saying how the police would startle her and all that.'

'How'd you rate him in the pulling stakes?'

'What?'

'Don't you call it that out here in the sticks? Did you fancy him?'

'Oh! Oh right!' No superior officer had ever talked to her like this before. 'Oh, well, no, I didn't fancy him, but you could see someone could. He certainly seemed to fancy himself.'

'Pretty boy?'

'Yeah, very, like, boyish, you know? Lovely hair, a little bit long but not too much, and kind of scruffy but, you know? streetwise. Long sweater with holes, and jeans with holes, and these nice boots. This lovely neck.' She stopped for a moment.

'You sure you didn't fancy him?'

She gave him a come-off-it look and a small smile.

'Lovely neck, nice smooth brownish skin, and square shoulders, and no spare flesh.'

'Well, he jogs.'

'Yes. Over Windmill Hill.' She spoke with serious significance.

'Exactly,' Bright said. 'Just like about three hundred other people.'

'Yes, but they don't live up there where he lives.'

'Eh?'

'He lives in Clifton. The Downs are three minutes away. There's miles of Downs to jog over. Up there, looking down on the suspension bridge and the river and all that fresh air and – space. I mean if I lived up there I wouldn't go over to Windmill Hill to jog. Would you?'

'There you are,' he said. 'You've done it.'

'What?'

'You have a feeling, you have to go at it. Prod away at it till you come up with the bit of it that isn't just a feeling. Anything will do if it convinces the right people. See what I mean?'

'Oh. Yeah!'

'That's a significant anomaly you've found there.' He squinted at her and waited.

She gave her small smile again. 'I know what anomaly means, thanks.'

He laughed, revealing these surprising white teeth and at the same time a curious beauty. Talking of fancying, she fancied him all right. She was shocked at this discovery and looked down at the table to hide her eyes.

He saw all this. He felt bad for a moment. She wasn't his type and anyway he ruled colleagues out, no matter how fetching. And this one was nearly young enough to be his daughter. 'Okay,' he said. 'You have discovered the one serious anomaly in his behaviour. That's the significant fact that should go in your report.'

'Yes. Sure. I see that. But I've only just realised that.'

'Because you talked it through.'

'Yes, but I couldn't talk it through with anyone here. They wouldn't listen.'

No, he thought, too busy twinkling into those blue eyes and lusting after that lovely mouth. 'So talk it over with yourself.'

'Okay.'

'And once you've got your big anomaly to convince the guys, then you get back to the serious stuff.'

'Serious stuff?'

'Your funny feeling about the guy.'

'Oh!' *You're wonderful*, her eyes said. *I'm yours for ever.* He rubbed his face all over. 'Come on then,' he said.

'Right. Okay. Well, he was flirting with me.'

There's a surprise, Bright thought. 'And were you flirting back?' he said.

'Oh yes.'

'I thought you told me—'

'I was putting it on.' She spoke with easy scorn for the gullibility of the male.

'Oh, were you now?'

'Yes, because he wanted me to think he had me in the palm of his hand. Know what I mean? I don't know if he fell for it or not. But – ' she got excited here – 'he liked it, whether I was pretending or not! See what I mean? He liked the kind of – sport – of it. You know? The – contest? Well, that's what I thought anyway.' Bright sat back and really smiled at her. She smiled back into his eyes and he fully appreciated that whether a bloke was sure or not he would certainly enjoy the contest. 'Could you get back in there?' he said.

'Well, I told him I might come back. Out of uniform.' She blushed again, pale pink like a little seashell.

'And what was his reaction?'

'He said he'd like that.'

'A-ha?'

100

20

The Living and the Dead

They came out of the door in the garden wall. It felt like the expulsion from the Garden of Eden. They stood skinless, vulnerable in the blinding afternoon sun.

'What now, Ankate?'

'I don't know, Maisie. Any ideas?'

'It was nice in there.'

'Yes.'

'I wish I had some brothers and sisters.'

'It doesn't always work out so well.'

'No, but at least they're there. When you need them.'

Kate thought of her beloved brother Liam dead at seventeen. 'Well . . .' she said.

'Oh Ankate, I'm sorry. I always forget.'

'It's okay, Maisie. You've got things on your mind.'

'You've been through the same thing.'

'A long time ago.'

'But you've never got over it.'

'No.'

'Does that mean I'll never get over Alison?'

'Probably.'

'I'm glad. I don't want to get over it.'

'It gets gentler. Most of the time. But every now and then, you can be standing in the queue in Sainsbury's, or just going into your dressing room at lunchtime, or taking your washing out of the machine, and it comes back as though it's only just happened, and you find yourself in tears. But then it goes away for long periods. Only you do think of the person every single day. In that sense they're still alive. And they're still alive as they were. Liam was seventeen. I was only a year older. So he's never older than seventeen. I'll be old enough to be his mother soon.'

'Will you have any babies?'

'God, Maisie.'

'But do you think about it?'

'I seem to think about it continuously these days.'

'I do.'

'Do you?'

'Alison and I used to talk about it a lot. She wanted six children.'

'And you?'

'I just want a baby. I want one so much, Ankate.'

'Don't start getting ideas. I shouldn't have brought you to this house. I shouldn't have introduced you to Thomas. What would Lizzie do to me if you got pregnant? I'd get the blame. She'd even forget there had probably been some male involved.'

Maisie laughed with a note of hysteria. So did Kate.

'He's a lovely baby though, isn't he, Ankate?'

'You can come and visit there when I move in.'

'Would they let me baby-sit?'

'Let you? They'd anoint your feet with oil.'

'Wheee!' Maisie raised her arms in the air and danced a few steps. Then she turned a horrified face to Kate. 'Allie's dead and I'm . . .'

'And you're alive,' Kate said.

21

Excerpt from a Diary

v

Well, she said she would come to see me again, and she came. Wasn't that nice? Out of uniform too. Dressed all in summer style, gauzy flowered frock and the blonde hair loose and nice gentle eyeshadow, not too much but just enough to bring out the blue.

The doorbell rang this afternoon. I had just taken mother her tea. She complained of pain and wanted me to rub her back. But the doorbell rang. I looked out of the landing window and there was my little police lady. I got a surge of excitement that shot from my groin to the top of my head like an electric shock. Left my scalp tingling.

'Who is that?' mother called out in that fearful way she has always faced the ring on the doorbell.

'It's all right. One of my colleagues from the other day. She won't be here long. Then I'll rub your back.'

She smiled so shyly when I opened the door. She blushed, even. I thought of actors again. Eleonora Duse was said to blush, literally, when the part required it. But can we really achieve control over our involuntary physical reactions? And could someone like this, an ordinary little English scrubber in the police force of all things, possibly be able to harness her emotions as skilfully as an actor, to blush to order? I think not. I think she is really a little smitten. Oho, this is fun.

I smiled shyly myself. And played it very surprised to see her. 'I hardly recognise you,' I told her, 'looking so – well – ethereal.'

She laughed. 'I don't think ethereal is the word exactly,' she said. 'Not unless I lose a few pounds.'

There was an awkward moment then. She didn't know if I was going to invite her in. And, I have to admit, neither did I. I allowed this moment to lengthen a little.

'Well . . .' She smiled.

'Well . . .' I smiled. I flirted into her eyes and she flirted back. Then she looked down as though embarrassed. It was then I decided to invite her in. But I played with her a little longer. 'Is this allowed?' I said. 'A police officer consorting with a suspect?'

Her head came up. 'A suspect? But you're not—' She broke off.

'Is that so?' I said.

'Well, no more than anyone else in this enquiry.' She put a hand over her mouth. 'I shouldn't have told you that.'

I knew of course now that she was attempting to trap me. Why do people who think they are clever always do something blatantly stupid? I hope of course that this does not apply to me! I am aware at any moment that it could. No, dearie, you *shouldn't* have told me that. So why did you? She can't have seen in my eyes what I thought of this ruse. I looked dawning relief disguised by nonchalance. I was very good, I knew it. Again I wished I had an audience to appreciate the conviction and subtlety of my performance. But she startled me.

'I'm sorry.' She spoke in a different tone. Without the flirtation but still with a certain shyness. 'I shouldn't have said that. And it's not true anyway. You are still on the list, because of obvious reasons. No more so than a few other people they're questioning. But I wanted to see you anyway. If my governor got to know, I'd be in trouble.'

No. Not convincing. I know the sort of person that goes into the police. They like rules. They obey orders. They suspect everyone and do nothing without a purpose. On the other hand, nothing said by me in such a situation would be on the record. Even if I admitted everything and she had it all on tape, they'd do her for entrapment. Look at the Wimbledon Common murder. They've got to do it by the book these days. I suddenly laughed.

'Look,' I said. 'Come in anyway. What on earth does it matter? Come and have a cup of tea.'

Following me through the dim and fragrant hall she said, 'You always seem to be making tea.'

'My mother is an addict, and so am I.'

'Oh. It's coffee with me.'

I could see the conversation was going to be scintillating at this rate. Why is it always the dullards who wield the power? This little miss, not fit to lick my boots (or any other part of me, I hope), has the right to barge into my life, question me, spy on me. Make me a little nervous if the truth were told. She might have considerable native cunning but she is no intellect, that's for sure.

In the kitchen I had my back to her and I suddenly turned. 'You're all the same, aren't you?' I said.

She looked startled so I explained: 'Your eyes.'

She didn't know whether I meant the eyes of pretty young girls or the eyes of policemen. 'Eyes?'

'Always darting about, aren't they? Making sure they don't miss anything. It's all right, you can look in all my jars if you like.' I picked up a charcuterie knife we brought back from France years ago. It's the sharpest thing I've ever seen. I cut myself on it once. An event that gives me the jitters even to think about. I held it quite easily in a way that might or might not be threatening. 'And this,' I said. 'This is a very sharp instrument. It's meant for cutting up meat. But you have to see it as a potential weapon. You have to suspect everyone you see of being up to something criminal. Don't you find that a strain sometimes?'

She watched me quite calmly. That took some nerve. I

did admire her. 'Yes,' she simply said. 'But it beats working in an office. Or in a supermarket.'

'Surely it would not have come to that?'

'Well, things are tough these days. Jobs aren't easy to come by. You must be aware of that. Your line of work.'

She had turned the conversation round, with consummate ease and considerable courage. I felt almost in love with her.

'Ah, my job. Yes indeed.'

'We're in the same field in a way,' she said.

'Are we?' I did not relish this idea and almost allowed the coldness I felt to appear in my tone.

'Well, we deal with mostly society's rejects, don't we? We both pick up the pieces.'

'Well, you pick them up to put them in prison. I pick them up to keep them out.'

'A lot of the time we're just called in to put the victims in the body bags.'

I gave a shudder. 'Like Alison Holt,' I said. I put down the knife.

'Did you know her family?'

'No.' They had omitted to ask me this down at the station. Her effrontery took my breath away. They should make her police superintendent.

'Oh. I thought you might have been called in to them some time, in your job.'

'No.' I had recovered. 'From what I've read they seem to be a rather respectable family. Quite comfortably off.'

'Yes, but they mightn't have always been like that.'

'No, I suppose not.' I was finding it hard to keep up my bantering superior pose with this determined creature.

'I wondered if you'd met her dad.'

'What?' Lucky for me the kettle boiled then. Gave me an excuse to turn my back on her. Gave my hands something to do.

'Well, you both work for the DSS, don't you?'

They had not asked me that either, down at the station. Was she thinking up these piercing questions all by herself? Or had she been told to ask them? 'Yes,' I said. 'But in different departments. It's a pretty big organisation, you know.'

'Yes, but you worked in the same building for a while, didn't you?'

I carefully placed the tea cosy over the pot. 'Did we?'

'Nine months ago, actually.'

'Is that so?'

'Yes. I checked.'

I wondered if I might arrange a little accident with the boiling kettle. That would put paid to the peaches and cream complexion and the smug determination. 'You checked? Why?'

'I didn't want to – you know – get to know a person socially who might have – well, you know . . .'

'Who might have what? Killed someone? Abducted and killed someone?' I blazed anger at her. Again I discovered that when you are acting it is good to stick close to your real feelings. Use them. 'And did you check whether I had met Alison's father?'

'He said you hadn't met. But with so many employees he mightn't remember.'

'He's quite right. I certainly don't remember him.'

'And one black man is hard to distinguish from another anyway, don't you find?'

'How dare you say a thing like that?'

'Well, I find that.'

'That's because you are a—' I was furious. How dare she imply that I feel racial prejudice. That the killing of Alison was some kind of racial attack. Was this the line they were pursuing? I controlled myself. 'Are you a racist?' I said. 'I know the police tend to be.' I didn't give her time to reply.

'Because I would like to state here and now that I am not. On the contrary. Most of my work up to now has been in the St Paul's area of Bristol. I prefer black people as a matter of fact. Most of them have more beauty and more life and more humour and more wit and certainly more grace in their little fingers, as we say, than—'

'Okay, okay!' She was actually smiling. She held up her little plump hands. 'I'm sorry!'

'The police think Alison was killed by a racist?'

'We think it might have been that. Perhaps even a racist group.'

'But surely a racist group would have inflicted damage, harm, defilement. She was undefiled, wasn't she?' Oh dear, I suddenly couldn't remember if this was a fact generally known. I had actually allowed her to goad me into saying too much.

I was standing facing her. Silence fell between us. She looked at me and I looked at her and I knew and she knew that I might as well have said in so many words that I myself was the killer.

She had a serious expression. I don't know how I looked. There have not been many occasions in my life of which I could say the same. I suspect I looked somewhat wild. I felt that my hair stood out round my head like a nest of writhing snakes. I also have no idea how long we stood like that staring. I realised quite slowly that she was afraid now and I wondered why. Then of course it was obvious why: now that she knew almost for certain she was standing in a kitchen with a man who murdered girls and not from racist motives, a man with a super-sharp knife, and no one in the house but a crippled woman upstairs – oho – she was in acute danger.

But – I quickly saw – she was only in danger if I knew that she knew. People always distrust their own first impressions. If I were to behave with utter innocence, I could turn this whole thing around. At least for long enough to do the things I should have to do now.

So I let go of the work surface behind me and blinked. 'Heavens,' I said, laughing. 'That made me angry. I'm so sorry. I frightened you, I think? It's just that I hate racism in all its forms. I see so much of it. I mean the results of it. Systemised racism, the relegation of those with dark skin to the lower class, the joblessness, the discrimination by teachers, employers, psychiatrists, police of course, officials of all sorts. It really horrifies me. I see the end results of it. The drug addiction, the neglected children. All the children who die from neglect and drug abuse.' Suddenly this was my own anger speaking as it had only ever spoken before to myself. No Acting Required. Dangerous. I stopped and laughed again but actually strangely felt close to tears. Closer than I had felt since the night I laid Alison out on the hill.

'Sorry again,' I said quietly. 'Look, I'll take this tea up to my mother. And then we'll go up on the Downs. How would you like that?'

'Well . . .' She was a little breathless, hesitant.

'Listen.' I moved just a little closer to her. She didn't flinch, brave little thing. 'I know you think there's some weird reason why I wouldn't introduce you to my mother. But it's really simple. She's terrified of people. Yes! I know she calls out nice messages when she thinks I have friends here. But what she is really saying to me is GET RID OF THEM FAST, GET THEM OUT OF THE HOUSE. She's always been the same. My sister and I always knew that. We were never allowed to have people in.'

'You had no friends, then?'

'It made friendship difficult though not impossible. But my sister and I were very close.'

'You must miss her now.'

'Oh, I visit her every now and then.'

'What does your mother do if you are away?'

'I leave her food for several days. She has a little fridge in her room. And a Teasmade. She can manage certain things for herself.'

I watched the disguised policewoman. She wanted to ask about my mother's bodily functions, but her English upbringing made her hesitate.

'Yes,' I said. 'I know what you are thinking. She can lever herself out of the bed on to her commode chair. And vice versa. Not comfortable or easy. But she can manage. If she could not, I wouldn't be able to work, would I?' I was telling her the utter truth. She felt it.

'Oh . . .' She almost sighed the word. 'I was wondering about that, yes.'

'You can creep up and peep in her room if you like. Just hope she doesn't spot you. I wouldn't like you to think I was keeping any secrets from you.' I gave her my sexiest, feeliest smile.

She didn't smile back. She was having second thoughts. She was also a bit scared to go upstairs.

'Go on,' I said. 'I dare you.'

'Did you use to do this as kids? Dare your friends to creep up there.'

I smiled. Wouldn't she like to know?

She said, 'I need to use the loo actually anyway.'

I went up the stairs with her. On the landing I spoke to mother. 'Here's your tea, darling.' I pushed mother's door a little and Miss Policewoman peeped in as she tiptoed past. I put mother's tea on her bedside table, sped out of the room, heard the noises of decorous toilet use behind the closed bathroom door, and descended to the ground floor. I opened the door under the stairs, closed it behind me and descended one floor more to the basement. Well, it's more of a cellar really. Just the place to keep a young girl prisoner for three or four weeks, wouldn't you say? I opened the door under the stone steps and left the house by the back way.

110

22

Cover Blown

She peeped in again coming out of the loo. The woman in the bed held a cup to her face. But she bore a resemblance all right. Helen didn't know what she'd expected. A ventriloquist's doll, a full-sized blow-up toy, an embalmed corpse, a tape recorder with recorded messages? To see a real woman shocked her. This level of imagination was not essential for a job in the police force. Mostly it told against her. Not till John Bright—

Helen said, 'Hello?'

The woman in the bed looked frightened. A person on the landing, not her son? Frozen in tea-drinking mode, staring at the doorway, she didn't speak.

Helen pushed the door a little. 'Sorry to disturb you. I just came to see your son about some work. I'm Helen.' She went no closer. The woman sat petrified, the cup shaking on the saucer. 'Sorry, sorry.' Helen backed off. 'It's okay, I'm going now. I'm going, really.'

She closed the door behind her and tripped lightly down the stairs. The stairs were lit from a long window on the landing but the window was draped with lace curtains and the back of the house faced north, so the light was dim. In the hall she called, 'Hello?'

She felt the silence and knew the kitchen would be empty. She knew he'd done a runner. She knew she'd blown it. She wanted to impress John Bright so much it had thrown her way off beam. She ran to the front door and opened it. The blaze of sunshine hit her like a punch in the face.

Bright saw her and sat up. He was out of the car, over the road, and up the path faster than she could blink.

She said, 'Did he come out this way?'

'Think I'd still be sitting there if he had?' Bright whizzed past her, into the house. He darted into the drawing room and out again, into the kitchen and out again. Stood a second in the hallway. Opened the cupboard under the stairs and disappeared. His voice came back thin and muffled: 'Is there a light switch up there?'

She fumbled over the surface of the wall. Hit a switch. The hall lit up, and the lobby down by the kitchen. Hit another and the dark stairs below appeared, in the light of a forty watt bulb that swung on a wire fifty years old. Bright's feet sounded on stone.

'We didn't know there was a basement.' She sounded feeble, she knew.

'There isn't at the front. It's all these hills.' Bright pushed a door, pushed harder, and it jumped open. They went out into a stone-flagged yard. The stones were black, not the clean honey beige of the house front. High walls, a small stone outhouse, neglected plant pots, two dustbins. The outhouse was locked, its small window opaque with grime. Bright dragged at the door in the far wall and it scraped open on to an alley. Weedy cobbles and high garden walls. The alley was dark in the shade of the tall houses. One end was shut off by a double garage where men were working. Helen ran that way without discussion. Bright ran down the other way towards the street.

Two ten-year-old lads stood astride their bikes on the pavement where he emerged. 'See anyone come out of here, lads?'

'When?'

'Maybe five minutes ago?'

'Are you the cops?'

'A-ha. CID.'

'Wow! Is it a murder?'

'Yes,' he said.

'You're kidding us!'

'A young man, nice-looking, scruffy long sweater, jeans, mid-length brown hair.'

The lads longed to have seen him. But they hadn't. Regretfully they shook their heads, Bright all the time searching the main street with his eyes.

He joined Helen at the garage where the men with spanners and oily rags shook their heads in the same regretful way.

'Do you know the people who live at number seven?'

'No. Only the woman who lives here at the end house. She gets fed up with the noise, comes and bawls us out. Otherwise they come out to get their cars. No one talks to us. We're the lowest of the low round here.'

'Keep your eyes open. It's the murdered girl.'

A tall young black man turned round, sharp. 'Alison?'

'You knew her?'

'No, man. But she a sister, you know?'

'This bloke at number seven done it?'

'We don't know. We'd like to talk to him. Or to anyone who knows him.'

'Believe me, man, we find him, you'll have him. After we finish with him.'

Bright tried every garden door, peered into yards. Tried basement doors, found them locked. They went back round the front. At the house on the left they got no reply. At the one on the right a tall Indian woman in her thirties opened the door. A small boy with round brown eyes clung to her skirt. 'Oh,' she said. 'I know who you mean. He never speaks to us. Nor does his sister.'

'Sister?' Bright stared at Helen.

'He told me she lives in Ireland.'

'Oh, she might do,' the Indian woman said. 'I wouldn't know. I see her now and then.'

'How do you know it's his sister?'

'She told me she was. She's a bit more friendly than him. Just visiting, she said she was. While her brother was away. To look after the mother. The mother's an invalid. I've never seen her.'

'She's bedridden.'

'I offered to look in on her. I thought the young bloke was going to hit me. He was offended, you know? Said he could manage fine by himself. So I never offered again.'

'She doesn't like strangers.'

In the car Bright said, 'Alert social services. The mother is going to need help.'

'You think he's really done a runner?'

'You were too good, Helen. You got your man.'

'I let him go. I lost him.'

'My fault,' Bright said.

'No. I questioned him too hard. I went too far. I could have done a convincing job, you know, that I fancied him et cetera. But I got carried away. I had to go upstairs to see his mother. I couldn't just leave it alone. Impatience, you see.'

'It was my idea, this stupid piece of entrapment. I'm supposed to be your superior, not just in rank but in experience and wisdom, and I've blown this. This is not just your ordinary villain, this is a murderer of young girls. On the run. Ryan is going to have me busted. And it's no more than I deserve.'

She looked terrified.

'Don't worry, I take full responsibility. You did good.'

But when he dropped her at her car even her flimsy dress drooped. He was tempted to take her for a drink, cheer her up. Cheer himself up.

He drove on, to present himself to Ryan. He couldn't wait.

23

Sally Makes a Sacrifice

Sally was waiting in the big doorway when Dave returned. He was pale. His face was grim. Harsh lines and hollows from eyes to chin. His body shook a little. A tremor that was not precisely visible.

'Oh . . .' First afraid – he hadn't expected anyone to be there – then dulled. 'Sally.'

'Aren't you pleased I waited?'

'Er, yes, I . . .' First appalled then polite. 'Yes, of course.'

'Would you rather be alone?'

His eyes looked beyond her. 'No. No.'

She had to take the key from him and put it in the door. His hand shook. Before they entered the cavernous stairwell he looked behind him. A car passed and he watched it down to the end of the street and round the corner before he would go in. She went ahead of him up the stairs. He looked behind him all the time.

Inside the big room she lit candles. He sat on an old basket chair. He put his long hands over his eyes. She moved about the loft in bare feet. Her small noises comforted him. She brought him a mug of steaming tea. 'Thanks, love,' he said. He sat with both hands round the mug. She smiled, grateful for his thanks and glowing that he'd called her love. She sat cross-legged on the floor at his feet. She leaned against his legs.

After he had drunk all the tea he said, 'They've been following me. They've been watching me. All these weeks. They've been watching this place. They know everyone who's been here, when, with whom, and for how long.

115

They know everything I've done, everywhere I've been. They think I killed Alison.' His voice rose and he began to sob. He got up and walked about wiping tears and snot with his hands, his shirt hem, his sleeves.

Sally was frightened. She said, 'What can I do, Dave?'

He said, 'Lizzie. I need Lizzie. I need her so much.' He was in the kitchen doorway holding on to the door-frame with either hand.

Sally knew Lizzie was his former – not wife exactly – the mother of his child, the exquisite daughter Maisie that all the girls wanted to look like. Sally had never thought to be jealous of Lizzie – heavens, she must be the same age as Dave and everyone knew men had no use for women their own age. But now a sharp pain pierced her. 'Lizzie?' she said.

He was crying so bad, these big heaving noises, he didn't seem to hear her. But her devotion knew no bounds. No matter her pain: if he wanted Lizzie, he should have her. She knew Maisie's name was Creech. She pulled the phone book from under the table. There it was: E. Creech and an address in Totterdown. She dialled the number.

Lizzie toiled up the hill from Temple Meads. Painting clowns' faces on mugs all day was not the best therapy for her present state. And panting up the hill afterwards wore her out, but it beat sitting in a bus in ossified traffic. Sarah from next door had stayed on the bus and would still be sitting there, still down by the roundabout, roasting behind glass.

Around lunchtime Lizzie had called home with the certain knowledge that something had happened to Maisie. She felt Maisie's danger in every limb, every pore. Her finger-ends tingled with it. And when she rang there was no reply. She told herself Kate was there and Kate would not leave Maisie alone. Just like the pair of them to go waltzing off without leaving word. *Oh, Lizzie will be all right.* All afternoon her fear fed her anger and her anger her fear. Both fuelled her climb up the hill, pounding in her ears.

When she opened the door the phone was ringing. It was the police to tell her Maisie was missing, she knew this. 'Yes? Who is this?'

'I'm – I'm sorry. I'm – I'm – Sally. I'm a – friend of Dave's.' The breathy little voice nearly gave out in shock at the rage in Lizzie's voice.

'Dave?' Of all the people she did not want to hear from now—

'He – he needs your – he needs – he asked me to call you.'

'What's happened? Is it Maisie? Has he heard something about Maisie?'

'Maisie? No.'

'Yes, Maisie, his daughter Maisie. If he's got news of Maisie I want to know. If he doesn't, I don't.'

'Oh. No. Sorry. I'm sorry to bother you.'

'I should think so.' Lizzie smashed down the phone. And now didn't know where to call, whom to ask. She looked into the living room. Cushions and newspapers everywhere, specks all over the carpet. *Typical. Go out toiling for the daily bread and what do they do? Lounge around chatting. Maisie telling Kate all the secret things she would never tell me.* She pounded up the stairs. Maybe they were both asleep. Or Maisie prone with headphones clamped to her ears.

Maisie was not in her room. Every garment she owned had been thrown in the air, whirled in a vortex and dropped. It looked normal. It looked normal for when Maisie had just gone out. It was oddly reassuring, the typhoon effect.

Some of her fear dissipated but the anger filled the space. She dragged the vacuum cleaner out of the landing cupboard and bumped it downstairs. So when they did come in she didn't hear them.

'Mum!' Maisie hit her between the shoulder blades. 'We're back!' and then backed away at the sight of her face. 'What's the matter?'

Lizzie couldn't speak. She shut off the cleaner, yanked the plug out of the socket, manhandled the thing upstairs and threw it into the cupboard. Kate and Maisie flattened themselves against the wall as she came downstairs and thrust past them to the kitchen.

They stared at each other as cupboard doors slammed and plates clattered, Lizzie's footsteps clomping back and forth on the floor. She didn't need to say what they'd done wrong. They knew. They had no excuse. Kate had more courage than Maisie. She went and stood in the kitchen door. 'I'm sorry, Lizzie. I didn't think.'

More banging. Lizzie's implacable back. A hot volcanic torrent of water spurting into the sink over the neglected breakfast washing-up. No use now to say, *I'll do that, I'll do everything, I will not only make the supper, I will be the supper*. It was too late. 'I was just thinking of Maisie. How to keep her occupied and try to—'

'Excuse me.' Muttered through clenched teeth as Lizzie pushed past her in the doorway, a bag of garbage clutched in her fist. Sudden street noise and the clash of dustbin lids. Then the bang of the front door as she clomped back in. Kate felt exhausted with guilt.

'Lizzie, listen, don't make supper. Why don't we all go out? I'll take us out to eat.'

'Oh yes, that's always your answer, isn't it? Let's go out. Let's escape from whatever we're supposed to be doing. Let's leave it all and go out. Only it's always waiting, Kate. It's always waiting there for you for when you come back. It's frozen vegetarian chilli and you'll have to lump it.'

'Don't do that, Lizzie.'

'Don't do what?'

118

'Don't pretend you think I want to go out because I don't like your food. You know it's not true and it's not fair.'

'Oh, isn't it?'

They were both yelling.

'Fight about what you're fighting about.'

'And what's that? That nobody cares enough to let me know where they are even though if they did give it a moment's thought they'd know I was worried sick? And right to be?'

'Yes, that's right! Nobody gives a fuck about you. Especially me and Maisie. There. You believe that? You see? You don't really believe that. You just use it as a big stick to beat people with.'

'Out of sight out of mind—'

'This child is grieving. And all you can do is berate her for not putting you at the forefront of her mind every minute of her day and night. You're supposed to take care of her; not she of you! You're the mother, for Christsake; not Maisie!'

Lizzie's face was a picture. Kate followed her eyes. Maisie stood in the doorway appalled. In the silence, she said, 'Phone, Ankate.'

'Lizzie, we all follow your example and spend most of our time thinking about how much we fail you.' Kate said this quietly. She was taking advantage and she knew it. But her blood was up and for once she refused to resist temptation. 'Nobody can please you whatever they do.' She made a *my God what have I done* face at Maisie, passing her in the doorway.

Maisie whispered, 'It's John Bright.'

When she came back to the kitchen Lizzie was sitting at the table. Maisie half-leaned against her, the closest you could get to an embrace in Lizzie's behaviour code. The room was quiet. Just the friendly buzz of the fridge.

Kate said, 'He's waiting at Renato's. I totally forgot we had an arrangement.'

Nobody replied.

'We were in such a state about getting back in time for you, Lizzie, you see. Everything else went out of our heads.' She tried a sheepish grin.

Maisie flinched and shut one eye. Lizzie leaned her tired face on one hand and gave Kate a long silent stare. She sighed heavily.

'I thought we could all go,' Kate risked. 'We could just have a spaghetti in the bar.'

Maisie looked anxiously at Lizzie, but didn't push her luck.

'You wouldn't have to cook,' Kate went bravely on. 'I'll pay. I'm rich at the moment.'

Lizzie was looking at her fingernails with close attention.

'I know you don't like John Bright, Lizzie. But I think Maisie might like the change of scene.'

'Well?' Lizzie turned to Maisie.

'Renato's is nice, mum.'

'I look a mess.'

'You don't.'

'I'll have to change.'

'Okay.'

'I'll be ten minutes.'

'We'll wait.'

'Put that chilli back in the fridge, Maisie.' Lizzie marched out of the room. 'We'll just have to eat it tomorrow now.'

24

Drowning Sorrows

Renato's was quiet. It was Monday night. And it was early.
Bright was emptying a large scotch when they walked in. It
was clear to Kate this was not his first. He ordered their
wine and another large scotch for himself. They took a
table near the bar.

Kate introduced her family to Signor and Signora
Renato. They remarked on Maisie's loveliness and noticed
her resemblance to Lizzie. While they talked, Kate asked
John Bright, 'What's the matter?'

'I think I know who killed Alison.'

Kate went white.

'Don't worry. It's not Dave.'

She bent her head, let out a breath.

'I found him and I let him go. He's done a runner.'

'How could you find him in so short a time?'

'I'm a fucking genius, how d'you think?' He swallowed
the scotch like it was full of goldfish.

As he so seldom swore, she decided to ask no more questions. 'I think you'd better eat,' she said.

'Whatever.'

She went to the counter and ordered him lasagne. Maisie
joined her. 'Lasagne for mum. Napolitana pizza for me.'
Maisie looked around her at the black and white ten by
eights of actors on the walls. 'I love this place, Ankate. It's
really theatrical, isn't it?'

Kate thought of all the bars in all the cities, the refuges of
actors away from home, in need of a place to celebrate or
commiserate. This was one of the best. 'It truly is, Maize.'

Maisie leaned close and whispered, 'What's up with John Bright?'

'I'll tell you later.'

Bright sat staring into his drink at one end of the table. Lizzie chatted with Signora Renato at the other. Kate and Maisie looked on. The evening did not look like being a social success.

But later a couple of actors turned up. They had just arrived in Bristol to start rehearsing *As You Like It* and come to Renato's first, the one place where they were sure to find comrades. Kate introduced Lizzie. Alan Tate, a man of no mean charm, decided to chat Lizzie up. Lizzie, who seldom went out, and seldom drank, on her second glass of Chianti began to glow.

Maisie, on her second glass of Coke, freed from looking after Lizzie, entered into a deep conversation with John Bright to try and cheer him up. They had embarked on the subject of fathers. During a lull, John Bright was heard to say, 'I had no dad because he died. Your dad isn't dead.'

Lizzie suddenly looked stricken and covered her face. She gathered her handbag and left the table.

'Lizzie?' Kate came into the Ladies, concerned.

'Kate, I am such a bitch.'

Kate decided to keep it light. 'Well, I won't argue with you there.'

But Lizzie drove on. 'Dave rang me. Well, he didn't ring me; he got some bloody girl to ring me, that's partly why I got so mad. I told her to piss off, basically, I refused to speak to him. But I just realised: he must have been in an awful state to get her to ring me. They must have just let him go. The police.'

'We could drop by on the way back.'

Lizzie looked horrified. She had never set foot in Dave's Bachelor Pad, as she called it.

'Come on, Lizzie. Why not? There's got to be a first time.'

'Why?'

'He's not a suspect any more, by the way. John Bright has managed to – well – get the enquiry moving in another direction.'

'No?' A Mexican wave of serial emotions ran over Lizzie's face. 'You mean they've caught someone?'

Kate took a breath. She must not knock John Bright off the pedestal Lizzie had just put him on. 'It's not as simple as that, apparently.'

'Why?'

Lizzie drunk asked impossibly simple questions.

'Well, I think it's a question of gathering evidence or – something.'

'I see. But they know who it is. So Dave's off the hook?'

'Looks like it, yes.'

'Oh, Kate.'

'You didn't think it was Dave, did you, Lizzie?'

Lizzie lifted her hair off her brow and gazed into the mirror. 'Frankly, I thought him capable of anything.'

'Oh,' Kate said in wonder.

'But when John Bright said to Maisie her dad wasn't dead, I thought, what have I done? I've made it so hard for her all these years. What you said tonight—' Tears came running out of Lizzie's eyes. Kate was appalled. 'It was all true, I deserve it. Why do I have to be such a bitch?'

Kate watched her big sister sob. She had never in her life before seen Lizzie humbled and contrite. She said, 'It's just unhappiness, Lizzie. You've always had too much responsibility.'

'Oh God, I look a sight.'

'No. You don't.'

'What will Alan Tate think?'

'He'll think he's had more of an effect than usual.'

Lizzie actually laughed. 'Okay then.' She wiped carefully under her eyes where the mascara had run, and blew her nose, smoothed down her white linen blouse and skirt, and turned to face Kate. 'Let's go and visit Dave.'

25

Excerpt from a Diary

vi

It was extraordinary going out on to the cobbled alley. The sense of escape. Fleeing. Flying. Fleet of foot. The men at the garage didn't see me. It wouldn't have mattered if they had. They've seen me a hundred times and not seen me, why should they care? Out in the street some boys on their bikes jousted and laughed, too absorbed to notice an adult of no interest to them. One of them was the beautiful boy Laurie from next door. I have watched that child from afar, his graceful manners, Swiss milk chocolate brown skin, innocent shining eyes. If his parents knew that my eye was upon him! I, the Preserver of Innocence. They would remove him from my path. Now they will never know because I can never return. I knew this day would come at last. When I would leave this life behind. I embrace my flight.

I sped past, wings on my heels. My bag was not heavy, did not slow me down, but I had to find a place to change my clothes. My absence would be discovered in no time. I must not answer their description. The nearest possible place was Clifton Village. I went round the edge of Victoria Square under the trees. The diagonal path across the middle was too exposed. Briskly under the stone arch, past the pharmacy, the florist. I thought of going into the high-class second-hand clothes shop, a changing room the obvious place, to go in as one thing and come out as another. But the shop was empty apart from the assistant. Again, too exposed. I needed a place crowded with people intent on their own affairs.

I crossed into the village. The bakery café was too empty and too genteel. The Clifton ladies in there would notice an anachronism such as I. Almost next door was the more raffish hippie-type market. Many different stalls, lighting not too bright. I went in. Up the central aisle past the clothes, into the handmade sofas, past the posters and cards. This was a favorite haunt of my youth. I knew it by heart. But I couldn't for the life of me recall a loo. So I zipped to the left through the junk shop and out into quiet little Wellington Street.

Up to my right the Rainbow, the restful café with the secondhand books. Yes! The door was open. I squeezed between the gaggle of customers in the queue and trod lightly down the aisle between the tables. No one gave me a glance. My worst danger would be that someone should already be using the loo. I pushed the door with my fingers actually crossed. Empty. And cool. I bolted the nice pine door, changed in less than a minute, thought about leaving my bag and old clothes there, decided that would be too conspicuous.

Two people looked up as I came back through into the café, but with no interest, intent on cake and conversation. No idea even that I had come from the loo. I could have been leaving after a pleasant lunch. No queue now at the counter, and all the staff had their backs to me, preparing food for their customers.

I walked out into a wall of light and heat. Opposite, the big garage where they sell old clothes and junk was just opening up. What better place for some old clothes than an old clothes shop? The depressing person who presides there was deep in the gloom of the interior. I left the bag with my clothes in it behind a forties tea trolley piled with cracked plates and tarnished cooking implements. So suitable.

I could afford to relax a little now. A little but not too much. I had to think what to do next. Many courses of action were open to me. I had to fix on my next immediate step. The sense of untrammelled flight was going from me now. I could feel the descent to earth. I even suffered a pang about mother. But mother has had the use of me all these years. Oh has she ever! It could not last for always. She must have known that. Now it is someone else's task. Someone else will turn up. People like her always find somebody. They have to.

I had cut off a whole side of me. A whole side of my life. No one, now, in the world, knew who or where I was. There was nowhere I had to be. At this point in my thinking, I also suffered a pang about my job. I had hated almost every moment of that job. I hated the squalor. I hated the people I dealt with. I loathed the hapless emptiness and mess of their miserable lives. I feel disgust for the social order that robs such people of culture and education, of the desire for culture and education. And I loathe myself for being part of that social order, perpetuating it with the hand-outs that enable such vermin to stay just about alive, running like rats, feeding on the leftovers that the rest of us cannot manage to consume. And yet I would miss it.

I found myself already passing the front of the university. Though this was vacation time there were always students. Summer courses. Out on the grass soaking up sunshine and knowledge. I recalled my days there and felt rage choking me. Mr Wonderful. And Mr Wonderful's favourites. The coterie. The subtle ways they have of making it clear they do not want you around. The little fortresses they make to keep themselves feeling good. They the Insiders. Fortresses with human walls, walls of human flesh. More impregnable than stone. Unscalable. The heat of humiliation spread over me like a strawberry mark spreads over the skin. This heat was hotter than the sun. Altogether too hot.

Distracted by this detritus in my head I took the left fork below the university building. I had meant naturally to go down Park Street past the design centre and George's many bookshops, unnoticeable in the crowds. Instead here I was in the wide dull street inaptly named Park Row. I crossed to the shady side. Cooler at least. In all senses. I had shaken off the torment. The intolerable torment of my thoughts. I only state them here because I believe that somebody should one day understand me. Should understand what has made me, formed me. This attempt at clarification will now fill my days. My diary shall become the centrepiece of my life. It will take the place of my job, and of my mother.

As I reached this precise point in my thought, there appeared across the road, illuminated by the blazing sun, as though my thoughts had conjured them up, two people . . . I stood still. I watched them as they got into the little yellow Volkswagen. I watched while the car nosed out into the traffic and disappeared down the hill. And I laughed inside my head. I laughed. The perfection, the smooth rounded beauty of the perfect moment. How was it possible to explain this sublime synchronicity?

The whole thing came together in my mind. Connections, you see. E. M. Forster is not the only one to have made the great discovery. Everything is connection. Connections are mysterious and sometimes almost miraculous. And when a connection clarifies itself to you, at that moment you feel in your body a jolt, of power, an electrical current that seems to have thrust from far out in the universe to hit you like a comet, like you are the focus of all the fates. It is impossible to describe the physical and mental shock, the terror and the ecstasy of these moments, these leaps of understanding. These sudden apprehensions of connection are not generated by me but revealed to me. That's what you have to understand.

Now I have her. She will be told day by day what I have done, what I do, what I mean to do. She will not know who I am. Or where I am. But she will be my Recipient. My Repository. She will almost in a sense be the cause. The Onlie Begetter. I will become part of her life. She of mine. Our destinies will be intertwined. In a sense this means they have always been intertwined. All time comes together here. I have taken the threads of fate and tied them together. Here. Now. This sense of power intoxicates me. The beauty of the idea intoxicates me. All eternity of these little lives, I have ordered into significance. It has been worth living for this.

26

Families Function

'Listen, Lizzie. John looks a bit the worse for wear. I think I'd better take him back to his hotel. I can join you at Dave's afterwards?'

'Don't do this, Kate.'

'What? Do what?'

'You always do this. You get people jumping to your tune and then you leave them in the lurch.'

This accusation left Kate speechless, it seemed so wide of the mark. Maisie stifled a laugh. Maisie too by now had consumed a fair amount of good Italian red wine. Though not of the best Italian grappa, Signor Renato's welcome-back gesture after their meal.

'I cannot go to Dave's on my own,' Lizzie insisted.

'I'll be there, mum.'

Lizzie barely acknowledged Maisie's crumb of comfort. 'After all these years. How can I just walk in there: Hello, Dave, how's things?'

'Sounds like quite a good opening line.'

'Listen.' Bright spoke low and slow. 'You go. I'll be okay. Just point me in the direction of that barracks they call a hotel. I don't need a chaperone.'

Maisie rolled her eyes. 'You are really drunk,' she said.

'What?' Bright reeled back. 'Who is this child? She is wise beyond her ears.'

Maisie and Kate started to laugh. 'What's so funny?' Lizzie hated to be left out of their laughter.

'Wise beyond her ears.'

Bright smiled. 'And eyes *between* her ears.'

Maisie stopped laughing. She took his arm, stood on tiptoe and kissed him.

'What'd I do to deserve that?'

'Come and see my dad with us. He makes good coffee. Then mum won't have to go on her own. On her own with me.'

Kate said quickly, 'It's the best solution, Lizzie.'

Bright and Maisie, arm in arm, swayed along ten yards ahead.

'It's a big space, Dave's loft. I'll disappear John when we get there. Put him to sleep in some dark corner. You'll never notice him.' Lizzie and Kate were already drawn along in the wake of the two in front.

Lizzie sighed. 'Nothing ever goes my way.'

Maisie guided Bright through the traffic. They crossed to the quayside and waited. Lizzie made Kate wait for the lights to change. The cobbles shone like polished metal in the lamplight. The water held a rippling moon. Even this time of night the heat had not left the air. Warm eddies lapped their faces, their arms. The boats hardly moved on the water. A few people strolled like them enjoying the warm night. At the end of the quay on their left the boat house loomed up black. There were no lights even in Dave's windows on the top floor. Or were there? That wavering glow could be candles, could be reflection of sky, moon, lamplight.

Lizzie held Kate back by the arm. 'I can't do this, Kate.'

'Yes you can. Remember what you said at Renato's.'

'That was an impulse. It's gone off me.'

'Well, it was a good impulse. Stick with it.'

'Anyway, look, it's in darkness, he's gone to bed, he's asleep, we don't want to wake him up.'

Dong dong dong. Maisie pulled on the bell. A window was pushed up, on the top floor. Dave's hair came over the sill, like Rapunzel in the fairy tale. 'Dad? It's us.'

Dave stayed quite still a moment then disappeared.

'Oh God,' Lizzie said. 'He's coming down.'

He reappeared in the window. 'Catch!'

Maisie caught the key like an expert and unlocked the small door cut out of the big boat door. They ducked through the opening in single file. Into a dark lofty space, where the stone stairs rose into deeper darkness.

'It's okay.' Maisie led the way. 'Dad'll bring a candle in a minute.'

Sure enough above them a shaky flame created shadows that jerked and swayed up the stairs.

Dave saw that one of them was Lizzie. He stood quite still with shock.

She eyed him, defiant. 'Hello, Dave.'

He nodded, speechless, and gestured for everyone to go in, shook hands with John Bright, no idea who he was, but did not take his eyes off Lizzie.

There were candles lit in the room but the space swallowed their feeble light. Maisie went round lighting more. The only person there was the young woman who had spoken to Kate in the school yard that morning. 'Hi.' She sat, unusually for Dave's visitors, in a chair, and was still in her practical cotton print frock. She was friendly and relaxed. 'We met this morning,' she said to Kate.

'Yes. Margaret, isn't it?'

'You remember!'

'Well, yes.'

'They let Dave out this afternoon.'

'Are you the only person here?'

'I think the others are a bit scared to come back. After the police raid.'

Kate looked at John Bright. 'Raid?'

'Hoping to find dope – or whatever – something to pin on him.'

'But they didn't?'

Bright shook his head. 'Went off at half cock.'

Kate saw Margaret's puzzled face. 'Oh, sorry. Margaret – this is John Bright. He's a – '

'I'm a copper, love.'

'And a friend of mine.'

'You're here as a friend then,' Margaret said.

'That's it.'

'From London?'

'Yup. Off my patch.'

'Is it very different here?'

'It is for me, love.'

Maisie had been busy in the kitchen. She brought him a coffee. 'It's really strong,' she warned.

'Thanks. I'll be careful.'

Dave and Lizzie had remained on the landing. Now they came in. Lizzie looked uncomfortable but gratified. As though she had leapt a chasm and was surprised to find herself safe on the other side. She looked up at the big sleeping platform, the rafters and lofty roof, the amazing moon through a Velux window; and around at the cushions and lovely drapes, the old basket chairs, the fifties juke box. She looked into Dave's sleeping room: dark wood and white linen, peaceful and calm. She looked into the kitchen: primitive wooden surfaces and minimal mod cons, but attractive, warm. Her head moved from side to side in surprise. Kate wondered what she had imagined. A brothel draped in purple velvet?

'Oh Lizzie, this is Margaret. Margaret, this is my sister Lizzie.'

'Oh.' Margaret stood to shake Lizzie's hand. 'You're Maisie's mother. I've heard a lot about you.'

'How?' Lizzie's brusqueness stopped just this side of rude.

'Well, from Dave.'

'Oh? You must have expected the wicked witch of the west.'

Margaret smiled. She had a beautiful smile. Her face in repose had a slightly lifeless quality. Her smile irradiated it. 'Not at all. I expected a sort of goddess.'

'Oh, I see. Made of stone.'

'Well, marble at least.'

'Ha.' Lizzie looked baffled, pleased, offended, all at once.

Kate and Maisie laughed. Margaret smiled.

Dave said, 'I'm so glad you came.' He addressed all of them but clearly he meant the words for Lizzie.

Maisie curled herself around Dave. Lizzie looked away, whether because the sight gave her pleasure or pain or both, Kate couldn't tell.

'Was it terrible at the police, dad?'

'Yes, it was terrible, Maisie.'

'They gotta do it, mate.'

'What?' Dave gave Bright his most arrogant look, head high, tossing the ringlets back.

'Dad, you met him before. He's John Bright.' Dave looked blank. 'Kate's policeman.'

Kate rolled her eyes at Bright. 'They insist on calling you that.'

'A-ha.' Bright's inscrutable mask, but she suspected a

complex reaction behind it. As complex as her own. She was glad of the weak flickering candle-light.

Margaret smiled from him to Kate. 'How did you meet?'

'He saved my life. I was a—'

'She was a suspect in a murder case.' Bright and Kate spoke together.

'A dead body was found in Ankate's bath.'

'They thought Kate had done it.' Lizzie made this sound like a typical act of carelessness on Kate's part.

'John didn't think so.'

'So she has to be grateful now for the rest of her life.' Bright squinted at Kate.

'For my life.' Kate did not smile at all.

Dave said, awed, 'Of course. You've been through this, Kate. I forgot.'

'If you don't want to be around mysterious deaths, you probably shouldn't be around me.' Kate spoke lightly.

'Certainly shouldn't be around me,' Bright said.

'Or any of us, now.' Maisie's little face crumpled. Dave hugged her tighter. Lizzie's expression couldn't be read. Kate suspected a deep joy which Lizzie would refuse to admit.

'It is hard not to be superstitious about these things.' Margaret's voice had a peaceful resonance.

'What things?' Bright liked brass tacks.

'Well, coincidences, patterns.'

'Being around one murder is hardly a pattern.'

'Two now,' Kate murmured.

Margaret said, 'Two is the beginning of a pattern.'

Bright stood up and walked round the room. He didn't like this conversation. He stopped near Margaret. 'What do you do?'

'How do you mean?'

'For a job, love.'

His tone was insulting. She chose to ignore that. 'Well, I've done various things. I got my English degree. Dave was one of my teachers. But then I worked mostly with animals. Things for charities. A donkey sanctuary, for instance, in North Devon. Now I've stopped work for a while. I'm . . .' She hesitated then plunged. 'Well, I'm trying to write.'

Dave spoke dutifully. 'That's good, Margaret.'

Lizzie did not hide her disdain. 'Write what?'

Margaret squirmed a bit. It was the first time Kate had seen her less than composed. She caught Kate's eye. 'I hesitate to say drama, but . . .'

'Plays?' Kate tried to sound encouraging.

'Well, I don't think I could write for the theatre. I think that's too difficult. But I've got a number of television ideas and almost-finished scripts and I'm hoping if I give myself enough time to concentrate, I might actually complete something. I know it's a hard world to break into, but – well – you have to try in this life or – '

'I agree.' Kate summoned more enthusiasm into her voice than she felt. 'You have to give it a go.'

Lizzie disapproved: 'What are you going to live on?'

'I've saved a bit. Not much; I'll probably have to get a part-time job soon. But I can last for three months, I think. I'm very frugal.'

'Oh.' Lizzie's expression relented a little.

'I'm hoping to get some advice and criticism from Dave. That's why I came round.'

'Glad of your company,' Dave said.

Kate said, 'This is the first time I've ever seen this place not draped with people. How do you stand that wall-to-wall social life, Dave? I'd go mad.'

'I need it. I'm not self-sufficient like you and Lizzie.'

Lizzie refused to return his look.

'Gotta go.' John Bright made a slightly unsteady route to the door.

'I'll come with you.' Kate stood up.

Margaret also stood. 'Mind if I come along? I live in Totterdown too.'

'Oh.' Kate and Bright looked at each other. He gave her what she had come to recognise as a smile. 'Can you find your way back to the hotel, John?'

'If I can't I'll ask a policeman,' he said.

Down by the water the night had grown cooler. Kate shivered. ''Night then, John. I've hardly seen you.'

'I need sleep. Ryan will be flaying me alive tomorrow.'

'And I've got the read-through in the morning.'

'I'll see you for lunch if Ryan hasn't had me deported.'

'Where?'

'The theatre bar?'

He put his arms round her. She smelt his biscuity smell, felt his warmth, the firm pressure of his hands on her back. His hands made her feel safe. Even the sight of them. She held the back of his neck a moment and thought they ought to get a little drunk more often. 'Take care, John.'

He released his hold. 'I'd see you ladies home but I do not think I'm likely to be a lot of use to you just at this time.' He raised a hand and walked off down the quay, keeping a careful straight line. Kate always hated seeing him go.

Crossing the little foot-bridge Margaret said, 'Mr Bright seems rather unusual.'

'Yes, he is. Seems like your average little cockney wide boy, but actually – well, he has unexpected qualities.'

'I suspect he's good at his job.'

'Oh, he's that all right.'

'So why is he in trouble?'

Kate, embarrassed, suddenly did not know how much she should say. 'Oh, I don't know. He offered to help out because he's recently been involved in a case like this. A chap in London who had killed his neighbour's daughter and buried her under his garden shed.'

'Oh, that case!' Margaret looked impressed. 'But he said he's going to be hauled over the coals?'

'Well, he thought he'd found Alison's killer. But apparently it didn't work out.'

'I'm sorry. I've embarrassed you.'

'No—'

'Yes. Obviously you shouldn't be talking about it. He'd have told you in confidence. I'm so sorry.'

'No.' Kate warmed to the girl's simple straightforward style. 'Only, I don't know how much I'm supposed to know. Things were a bit confused tonight.'

They walked in silence for a while. Just as they were about to enter under the railway bridge Margaret shivered. Kate looked surprised. The girl was so strong-looking, and taller than Kate. 'I don't like tunnels,' she said.

'Well, they're scary in the dark.'

'I think it's the echo.'

Kate listened. 'Yes. You can't be sure there's not someone behind you.'

At last they came out into the open. The houses of Totterdown rose in tiers to their left, the black shape of Windmill Hill sloped gracefully up to their right.

Margaret let out a breath. 'I'm always glad to be out the other side.'

Kate laughed. 'I wouldn't come this way alone. Especially now.'

'No. Especially now. How's Maisie coping?'

'Well, it's hard. I don't know how well she's doing. In a sense nobody copes well.'

'No, because you're coping with an absence. Not with a thing but with nothing.'

'Yes, that's it!' Kate almost found herself speaking of her brother, a thing she seldom did with friend or stranger. She stopped. 'At least with this there's something to focus the anger on.'

Margaret seemed puzzled. 'What do you mean?'

'Well, somebody did it. Somebody killed Alison. Deliberately. Somebody knew where she was for three weeks and didn't let anybody know and then they killed her.'

'They are sure of that? That she was deliberately killed?'

'They're treating it as murder, yes!'

'You feel mainly anger. Yes.'

'Grief is mostly anger in my experience.' Kate sounded grim. 'Only in most cases there's nowhere to place the anger. No one to blame.'

'I've never lost anyone close to me. So I wouldn't know. My father had already disappeared from my mother's life before my brother and I were born.'

'Orphans.'

'As good as. He seduced my mother when she was fifteen. He was the father of her best friend at school. Awful scandal. Kept quiet, of course. They were rather a prominent family. My mother was their guilty secret. He put money in a trust for her. So we've never been short – of a bob or two as they say. But after he abandoned us she lost touch with all the people she knew. They were hypocrites.'

They fell silent climbing the steep steps up to Richmond Street. They needed their breath. At the top Kate marvelled at this strange little area, Totterdown. The way the pretty little terraced houses climbed over the hill and round the hill. These on her left backed on to the railway cutting, a ravine rivalling the Avon Gorge in depth. She and Margaret looked back down at Windmill Hill, way below them now.

'That's where she was found,' Margaret said. Even from up here they could see the shimmering mounds of flowers that had been placed at the scene, like a ghostly lake in the moonlight.

'Yes.' Kate sighed. 'Poor child.'

'They shall not grow old . . .' She had a beautiful voice, this Margaret.

'That's no comfort to me, I'm afraid. They shall not grow up either, or grow anything, or grow at all. And anyway, no one had the right to decide for her.'

Margaret nodded. 'Sorry. There's nothing one can say actually, is there?'

'Well, I'd better get over to William Street.'

'Is that where you live?'

'Where my sister lives. I've got digs up near Kingsdown Parade. I'll be moving there soon.'

'They'll miss you.'

Kate winced. 'I know. But I'm here to work. That's what I'm being paid for. And I need my own place. I need to concentrate. I'm a bit of an all-or-nothing-er.'

Margaret spoke shyly. 'You can tell by your work. That you're very – dedicated.'

'Oh hell.' Kate laughed, embarrassed.

'Your Hedda really was remarkable. I wasn't exaggerating this morning. The way you played her hatred of the pregnancy? It's usually played as though she's repelled by the physical humiliation, the loathsome marriage. You played it that she *wanted* to give birth – not to a human being – she feels nothing but despair for the human race – she respects only Art. She yearns to be part of the genesis of a work of art. So when she burned the manuscript and said, I'm burning our child, one felt the real sacrilege of what she was doing. You somehow got to the depth of the tragedy. I'd never cared about her so much before.'

'Heavens.' Kate felt uncomfortable. As she always did in the presence of a True Fan. She didn't know what to say. Suddenly stifled by the clingy intense atmosphere she became distant, awkward, formal. 'Well, thanks.' She had to get away.

'I'd really like to talk about it one day.'

'Yes, that would be nice. Bit late tonight. Well, lovely to meet you. See you again, I hope.' Lying.

'Oh. Yes. Sorry.'

'No, thanks for being so nice – '

'Anyway, I live just down here. So . . .' The girl hovered, not knowing what gesture to make. Did they shake hands or what? Kate thrust out her hand and the girl took it. A good firm handshake. Kate felt remorse. 'Look, I'm sorry. You must think I'm really rude. It's just I never know what to say.'

'Oh, I understand.'

'And just now. You know. This Alison business. It's hard to think about anything else.'

'Yes. One never knows whether to speak. But if I never met you except this once and I hadn't said – '

'Yes. I really would like to discuss *Hedda* some time. It's full of fascinating problems. Just bad timing.'

Margaret looked at her in silence. 'Bad timing. Yes. Well, thank you, anyway.'

'For what?'

'For not dismissing me as just another Fan.'

'I did, initially.'

'I know.'

'Thanks for not minding.'

They grinned in the moonlight and parted, Margaret down Pylle Hill Crescent, Kate up the steep Richmond Street. Kate felt lightened by the encounter, indeed oddly blessed.

27

Bright Takes the Rap

'I let her go in there, knowing she was a rookie kid. I could at least have organised someone on watch at the back.'

'You didn't have anyone. I couldn't spare anyone. This is not under your jurisdiction, if you remember.'

'Anyone would have done. Didn't have to be a copper. Anyone can make a citizen's arrest.'

'I knew you were not on to the right bloke anyway.' Ryan towered over him.

'You're wrong.' Hoarse with hangover – scotch then wine was par for the course – the three grappas were the big mistake. 'You're wrong, Ryan.'

Ryan was unmoved. 'This Mark Leighton was in London when the body was being left on the hill. He didn't get back till the next morning.'

'Have you checked?'

'Of course I've checked! He had his train ticket. He produced it. We've seen it.'

'He had *a* train ticket. Doesn't mean he was on a train.'

'Where did he get it then?'

'A ticket's easy enough to come by. He could have picked one up at Temple Meads on the way up to get his car. He told you there was no one collecting tickets at the barrier. Someone coming off the London train coulda dropped one. He just has to pick it up.'

'Far-fetched, John.'

'Anyone see him in London? Or on the train? Or getting off it?' Every word he spoke hammered a nail in his skull.

'We didn't check because there was no reason to suspect him. Only the vivid imagination of little Goldilocks.'

'So why's he done a runner?'

'It's what I'd do in the circumstances. A police officer turning up to flirt with me all dressed up in her frilly frock.'

'No you wouldn't. You'd ring up the officer in charge and complain of police entrapment.'

'You know the public don't react like that.'

'He left an invalid mother behind, Ryan. Do the public react like that?'

140

Ryan sat, a brooding presence. He seemed to overflow his desk. He put a big hand up to scratch his big nose. 'Yes, that's odd, sure enough.'

Bright laughed. It hurt the bones in his face. 'It's more than odd, Ryan.'

'He's not exactly your macho man. These fellas can be scared off easy. And maybe there's something he didn't want us to know. Something nothing to do with this, but that he wouldn't like to come out. That happens in cases like this, you know that. All sorts of stones get turned over and some nasty creepy-crawlies are found underneath. I'm not saying anything necessarily criminal but something he mightn't like his mother to know.'

Big brawny Ryan would assume that such a slim pretty lad was queer. 'Should check out the gay clubs if that's the way you're thinking.'

'All I've got is his name. No photo. No fingerprints.'

'You'll get a good photofit from Goldie's description.'

Ryan scowled.

'Have you run a check on him for previous?'

'Same thing applies.'

'Just don't blame that nice girl Goldie, Ryan. Blame me.'

'Listen, mate, I know the man I want is that git with the ringlets.'

'Dave Fowler.' Bright groaned.

'I know it's him, I feel it in my big policeman's bones. So, you screwed up, sure. My respect for your reputation is now zilch, okay? But you have not screwed up my investigation, believe me. You'd be better employed hanging out round that Dave if you feel like giving me a leg-up.'

Bright grimaced.

'Yeah, he's a mate of a mate of yours. But you're a copper, John. And he's a feckin' paedophile or something close to it. I don't like him. I want him caught.'

Bright hadn't the strength to give him an argument. 'Are

you running a check on Mark Leighton's activities in London? As you're so sure he went there.' He stood. The headache rolled like a boulder from over the left eye to over the right. He winced.

Ryan gave a cruel grin. 'I'll bring it up at morning prayers. He looked at his watch. 'Where I'm meant to be in five minutes. The IO's a stickler.'

Crossing the tarmac yard, Ryan said, 'We did check Mark Leighton's story as a matter of fact. They do have a flat in London like he said. And it did look quite tidy. Like he could have been there and cleaned it up.'

'But he wasn't seen there, right?'

Ryan shrugged. 'You know what London's like. No one sees anything. You all walk round with your eyes shut there.'

28

Going to Work

Kate sat white-faced in the kitchen. Maisie hovered, anxious. Lizzie whirlwinded round them: 'I drank too much. I never drink too much. I'm not used to it. I was awake all night. I'm going to be late.' She swallowed scalding coffee, insisted on washing up the cup.

'Just go, mum.'

'Where's my handbag?'

'Ankate? You're sitting on it.'

'Oh yes.'

'For heaven's sake, Kate, what is the matter with you?

You weren't nearly as drunk as me last night.'

'She's nervous, mum.'

'Nervous? What about?'

'It's her first day of rehearsal.'

'Oh, that. Well, you shouldn't have got yourself a hangover, should you?'

'The hangover will probably help. The more brain-dead the better.'

Lizzie pulled up short. 'Oh, God, Maisie, you'll be alone here today.'

'I'll be all right.'

'Don't go out on your own.'

'I won't. Don't worry, mum.'

'Of course I'll worry.'

'John Bright's meeting me at the theatre at lunchtime,' Kate said. 'We'll drop in here.'

'I'll make lunch for you.'

'Thanks, Maisie. If we're facing food by then.'

'Go on, mum, or you really will be late.'

'Sarah-next-door is blowing her horn.' Kate waved from the window. Sarah gestured at her wrist-watch with a frantic finger. Maisie kissed Lizzie and pushed her out of the door. 'Phew!' she said.

Kate walked down to the theatre. To get some oxygen to her brain. She wasn't hung-over. She was sick with nerves. *I can't go through this again. It's too hard on the nervous system. I can't do it any more. I've forgotten how to act on the stage. Anyway, the part's beyond me. I don't know what makes Rosalind tick. I don't know what I'm doing. That will be obvious to everyone. Colum will realise he should have cast someone else. He probably knows that already. I was probably a last resort anyway. For Christsake, you'd think you'd never done this before. Why doesn't it get easier? Why does it get worse?*

143

Maureen was still the stage door keeper. 'Comforting that some things don't change,' Kate said.

'Nice to see you back, Kate. It's great you're doing Rosalind. You must be looking forward to it.'

'Are you joking?'

'Ah, you'll be great.'

'Ha.'

She climbed the stairs to the rehearsal room. Sun beating already through the high windows. A table a mile long. Hundreds of people, it seemed. Alan Tate hugged her, saying into her ear, 'This is the reason I do movies, I've just realised. You think it's too late to pull out?'

'No. Let's go now.'

'Kate!' Colum's face was a little more lined than last year, the only sign he might be more than fourteen years old. A lanky Derry lad with a chrysanthemum of curly brown hair, he didn't look like a director. 'Oh, Kate!' Beaming, he threw open spider arms. 'I'm so glad to see you.' He whispered in her ear, 'I'm shitting bricks actually.'

Kate laughed but felt no better. This time she was going to be found out. She smiled, sickly, at ten people she didn't know huddled round the coffee table, spilling milk and sugar, scalding mouths, till the DSM called them to order.

Some sidled up to the table, eyeing those already seated. Should you sit next to the actor you'd be working most with in the play? Should you just for safety sit next to the only actor you already knew? Should you in order to seem in control of things sit confidently any old where? Should you hide down the end of the table farthest from the director, hoping not to be noticed?

And then the reading itself. What was the form? Go for it or hold back? Perform or mumble? Commit yourself or wait to see what others were doing? Or make no decision at all, just go with the flow and see how it comes out?

Lots of arranging of things: the script, the pencil, the

polystyrene cup, the cigarettes. Kate sat close to Colum for protection. A little dark girl hovered close by. Kate smiled at her. 'Hi, I'm Kate.'

'I'm Gemma. I'm playing Celia.'

'I suspected as much. Sit next to me? Since we're together in nearly every scene.'

Gemma sat, grateful to be asked. Kate hadn't dared speak to the Orlando. He was too young and beautiful by far, made her shy. Then she saw him too hovering, poor thing, not knowing what to do. She bravely smiled at him. 'Sit with us?'

He actually blushed, nodded gruffly, frowning, and sat opposite. Ian McLean, fatter than ever these days, puffed along next to him. 'A nice s-slim little thing like you,' he said, 'can surely f-fit me in?' The boy looked scared then laughed. 'After all we're f-family,' Ian said. 'Us c-city folk.'

She suddenly in a rush began to feel good. In here no young girls had been abducted, no one's father was under suspicion, no one's niece was in possible danger. This was real life. This was where the real thing lived. Between these walls between the hours of ten and six life was going to be okay.

Colum began his introductions. He started with Orlando on his left: 'Rupert Angel' – Ian murmured, 'so aptly named' – and finished with Kate on his right. Gave a little speech in his attractive flat Derry tones. 'I'm not going to say much. Just I'm really glad to see you all. It's a tremendous play. You know me, I keep things open, I haven't got a firm concept. I can feel all the big themes, I expect you all can, but I don't want to say, Oh this play is categorically about this or that, because I think we're smaller than Shakespeare and I think he'll show us the amazing connections as we go along. I don't want to set up in the audience's expectation something smaller than the play is. I think if we go for the truth we'll find out some amazing things. Sandy and I agree we should set it in the present day, just because we can signal more immediate messages that way, especially to young audiences. And, listen, I do just think this one thing: this is a *young* people's play. It's *about* young people, young people falling in love, and doing other reckless things, and how badly the grown-ups treat them, the shit place the adults have made the world. But that's not all it's about. I mean, the townees' attitude to the country. It's just awful the way they treat the country people, isn't it? Well, I won't go on. As usual, a really cogent well-thought-out speech. This is the longest one you'll hear from me. I hope. It's you doing the talking from now on. Okay?'

The reading began. Kate was blind and deaf with nerves for fifteen minutes and then she started flying. And taking in what was going on around her. Alan Tate had a real line on Jaques, not just a cynic but a man with a tragic longing not to be. She watched the faces round the table aghast at Ian McLean's stammer. She'd worked with him before, so knew that it disappeared the minute he got his performance right. Even with the stammer he got laughs, not so easy with Shakespeare's clowns. And Celia too was funny. Impossible to tell about the Orlando, Rupert. He was a mumbler, too scared to commit himself. Kate always went for it, hook, line and sinker, at the read-through. Took big risks, making mental notes. After this, pull back and explore the murky emotional depths, but fly here this once, get an idea of the speed and the trajectory of the flight.

Big laughter at coffee break, relief at having got the blocks off, tested the water. 'I feel worn out,' Alan Tate said. 'You're sparkling.'

'Oh, I love it. I forget how much. Each time I forget.'

He poured himself a coffee, murmured, 'Your sister's rather a stunner, isn't she?'

'Oh, is she? I thought you were just giving her the treatment.'

He gave his wolfish grin. 'She's a bit of a challenge, I admit.'

'She's no pushover, Alan.'

'Will she be around much?' he said in a casual tone.

'You may see her from time to time.'

'Hmm.'

Getting up from his third coffee in the front of house bar, John Bright raised an eyebrow. 'What set you on fire?'

Kate laughed. 'Relief. Listen, do you mind going up to Totterdown for lunch? Maisie's alone. Just to check. You know.'

'Sure. Anything for a sight of that little cracker. I'm seriously in love.'

'She's amazing, isn't she?'

In the car he said, 'How could that long-haired git Dave walk away from Maisie? You understand that?'

'Come on, John. Life's complicated. You know. Anyway, it was Lizzie he walked away from. Marriage. Being a family man.'

'He walked away from growing up. He's still walking.'

'Yes, well . . .'

'Maybe this business will shake him up a bit.'

'They don't still suspect him, do they?'

Bright didn't reply. She turned to look at him. Eyes on the road, he didn't glance her way.

'Do they?' she said again.

'Ryan doesn't like him. But that's not evidence. That's all I can say.'

'Are you in big trouble there?'

'Not nearly as bad as I thought. Thanks to Dave.'

'Thanks to Dave how?'

'Ryan doesn't believe the bloke I lost is the bloke he's looking for.'

'So he does think it's Dave?'

'I did not say that.' He still would not look at her.

147

They got out of the car. Kate hunted in every pocket and the depths of her bag.

Bright said, 'What is this with you and keys?'

'I have only a tenuous connection with all my belongings.'

'Tenuous, is it?' He rang the bell. 'Maisie'll let us in.'

Kate scrabbled a little more, at last found the key folded in a page of her script. Maisie had still not answered the bell. They went in.

'Maisie? We're back!' Kate walked through to the kitchen. Bright followed. 'Not here.' She looked down into the garden. No one there. 'She must be in the loo.' Kate ran up the stairs. Bright followed. They pushed open the door of each bedroom then of the bathroom.

Maisie wasn't there.

29

Desperately Seeking Maisie

Kate started to shake. She shook so that her mouth would not form words and she could not hold on to things. Bright said, 'What's Lizzie's number at work?'

Kate could only shake her head. At last she got out, 'Not Lizzie. Not yet.'

'Maisie might be *with* Lizzie.'

A gasp came out of Kate. She scrambled through her Filofax for the number, showed it to him. He asked for Lizzie. Said to Kate, 'She's gone out for lunch,' and into the phone, 'Was her daughter with her?' Pause. 'And she hasn't been there this morning? You sure? Tell Lizzie to phone home the minute she gets back. Thanks.'

'Dave,' Kate whispered.

He was already dialling. 'Dave? John Bright here. Is Maisie with you? And she hasn't been with you this morning? She's not in the house. And she's not with Lizzie. That's right. Might be a good idea.'

Kate's brain had gone into paralysis. She could only think, *Maisie promised. There was no one she would have gone with. Nowhere she would have gone. She promised. She promised not to go out.*

'Neighbours.' Bright opened the front door. 'You take this side of the street. I'll take the houses opposite.'

A mysterious person rented Lizzie's basement. He came and went. They barely knew him, even by sight. She scrambled down the stone steps and banged on the door. She looked through the window, and through the letter box. Piles of bills and junk mail on the mat. He wasn't there. Sarah-next-door was out at work with Lizzie. And Laura, the nice girl in Sarah's basement, gardened for the council. She'd be out. Kate rang anyway. No answer there either. The man at the off-licence with the beer crates outside said he hadn't seen Maisie. But he hadn't opened up till late. Eleven or so, he said.

The old couple opposite had been in their garden out back all morning. The people either side were away on holiday. Bright and Kate stood in the street. Bright got the Alison incident room on his mobile: 'It might be a false alarm but another girl is not where she should be.' He gave succinct details and rang off.

Kate's brain was back in gear. 'Alison's family live in Stevens Crescent.' They ran down the hill, turned the corner by the little mosque, crossed the road, and ran uphill again to half-way along the crescent. Stevens Crescent was more upmarket than William Street: a man was painting his house Mediterranean blue. Several families of West Indian origin lived up here.

The curtains were closed at the house. Flowers were piled against the low brick wall. Kate said, 'I've never met the mother,' as she rang the bell. A black woman opened the door, clearly Alison's mother. The same proud head, the same grace. But the woman's skin had a matt grey look, the eyes red-veined with grief. 'Yes?'

'I'm sorry to bother you. I'm Kate. Maisie's my niece. This is John Bright. We just wondered if – Is Maisie here?'

'Maisie? No. She comes most days but she's not here today. What happened?'

Kate explained. The woman put her hands up to her face. 'Oh no. Oh no. It's a curse, it's a curse.'

'What's the matter, Louie?' A deep voice. Little trace of West Indies in the accent. Alison's father came to the door. No resemblance at all, except for his height. A tall square-shouldered man with a slightly severe face. Like his wife he said, 'Oh no. Oh no. Who is doing this?'

Bright said, 'We're not sure yet that anything bad has happened. Don't let's jump to conclusions. Where do you think she could have gone?'

They looked at each other. Mrs Holt said, 'There's only the school. That's where the girls hang out. It's a place for them to be, you know?'

'The school!' Suddenly Kate had hope. If one of the girls had come by – It was possible, it was! She said to Bright, 'Will you go back to the house? Someone should be there.'

'No. I'll go down the school. Give me directions. I'll walk.'

'Down there, straight over the hill, over that way, to the railway side. You'll pass the place where—' She stopped, seeing the faces of Alison's parents in front of her.

'Where our daughter was found,' Mrs Holt said.

Mr Holt said, 'Through the barrier, and the school is right there on your left.'

Bright took off, running.

*

The house was as she had left it. Empty. Silent. She stood in the hallway desperate. Then the doorbell rang. Dave stood there, dishevelled, dismayed. 'Any news?'

Kate shook her head.

'What can we do, Kate?'

'Nothing except think. John Bright's gone down to the school. You could go down too. The girls hang out there, you know? Just a place to be.' She repeated the words of Alison's mother.

'I could search the streets.'

'Which streets?'

'I could do what the police call a house-to-house.'

'We've done the immediate neighbours.'

'I could go to meet Lizzie.'

'Lizzie.' Kate wrapped her arms round her stomach and groaned.

Dave called the pottery in Clifton. They told him Lizzie was on her way home. Kate remembered she should be back at work in a minute. She called the theatre office. It only occurred to her then that maybe Maisie had taken it into her head to go down to the theatre for lunch. So first she asked cautiously if anyone had seen this slim tall blonde girl, fragile, with a lot of frizzed-out hair, fifteen years old, very pretty. 'Your niece?' the secretary asked.

'Yes!'

'She was at the opening night of *Hedda*. She and her friend used to come to all the shows. Theatre mad. Her friend's the one who—'

'Yes.'

'Is your niece all right, Kate?'

'We don't know.' Kate started to cry.

'Don't worry. If she's been anywhere round the theatre today we'll let you know. I'll ring you as soon as I know.'

Kate managed to give her the number. 'And please tell

Colum I can't be there the rest of the day. I'm so sorry. I'm so sorry.'

Lizzie got out of the taxi and ran up the steps. The driver shouted something. Kate ran down and paid him. Lizzie stopped in her tracks at the sight of Dave.

'Lizzie—'

She ran on, all round the house, making sure for herself. She wrenched open the kitchen door and ran down the steps into the garden. She ran up again peering at the surrounding gardens. The dogs penned in the cage four gardens down howled and yelped. That would go on for hours now. She came back into the hallway. 'Where are the police?'

'John phoned them. They'll be on their way.'

'Why aren't you doing something?' She accused Dave.

'He wanted to run down to the school. John had already gone. He should be back soon.'

The phone rang. Kate grabbed it. The nice secretary from the theatre. Nobody had seen Maisie anywhere near the theatre that morning or at lunchtime. She had asked everyone. But they would continue to look. They would keep their eyes peeled. Everyone. As Kate put the phone down it rang again. 'John?'

'Yeah, me. Any sign of her?'

'No.'

'She's not at the school and hasn't been seen there. A few of the girls have been there since nine this morning keeping a vigil. They haven't seen her. I'm dropping in to Alison's house again, on my way back. See you soon.'

Kate put the phone down. She shook her head. There was no need to speak. Lizzie looked as though she might never speak again. Her eyes were wild. Even her hair, normally neat and sleek, seemed to stand out from her head as though electrified. Dave stood like a tree suddenly deprived of water, foliage withered, branches drooping dead.

He stepped towards Lizzie and she moved as though about to fall forward. He put his arms round her, not in his usual come-to-Mr-Powerful-he-will-take-care-of-you way; they came together like two crash survivors. She clung round his neck. He round her waist. Kate sat on the stairs. The fridge stopped making a noise. There was no sound in the house. None.

30

Making Connections

'Mr Holt, is there anyone at work, a colleague or an employee that you've had trouble with? Sacked maybe? Or just had cause to reprimand? Someone you've had a difficult time with? Someone—'

'Mr Bright, I've thought and thought about this, don't you think I haven't? I told the police. There's no one. Truly. Is there, Louie?'

'And you, Mrs Holt?'

'I'm a teacher, Mr Bright. There's always little things going on. With little kids there's always something. Their parents come up to the school or whatever but it's all over quick and everybody's happy again. There's never been anything serious. No.'

'You never got promoted over anyone who might have borne a grudge?'

'Mr Bright, that would be the day.'

He heard the bitterness of a life of racial discrimination and didn't pursue it. He turned to Holt. 'And you?'

'Strangely I have been promoted regularly in accordance

153

with Civil Service rules. This is not a racial thing, Mr Bright. I've said so from the start and at last that's proved at least.' He answered his wife's look: 'If Maisie has gone too, that means this is not a racial thing, Louie. Maisie is as white as the driven snow.'

She moaned and rocked back and forth. 'Don't say that, Desmond. Don't speak like that.'

'The police thought it was a racial thing,' he explained to Bright. 'But racial things are generally cruder. In my experience.'

'A-ha.'

'This killer has extreme finesse. This is not a normal person. This is a sick person. Sick.' The man got up. He walked fast up and down the room, shaking his fists in a fast rhythm and controlling his breath.

Bright waited, then said, 'Is there anyone you used to be close to and then you stopped being close with?'

Mr Holt gave him a sharp look. Bright's squint intensified so you couldn't tell where he was looking: at you, beyond you or to the side of you. If he were a dog his ears would be cocked.

'You mean at work?' Holt said.

'Wherever.'

An odd expression crossed Holt's face. He began to speak, stopped, then began again: 'There was a young man at work. He was very good. Keen. He asked my advice a lot. He was a bit too keen actually. Worked too hard. I told him to cool it. He clung to me a bit. I didn't mind but colleagues started to comment. You know, he was always there at lunch and breaktimes. I got a little bit fed up with it myself once I started to notice it. So I started to avoid him a bit. Nothing that he would notice, I hope. I didn't want to hurt his feelings. And then he got transferred to another department, so the thing was solved.'

It was clear to Bright that this person was not the one

who had first come to Mr Holt's mind. The person who had first come to his mind was someone he did not wish to discuss in front of his wife. But this could wait. Bright shot an arrow into the air: 'Was his name Mark Leighton?'

Both the Holts looked stunned, horrified. Holt nodded slowly. 'Yes. Why?'

'His name is on the suspect list. I knew he worked in the same department as you for a bit. It doesn't mean anything.'

'No.' Holt's head shook from side to side. His wife stared into his eyes. 'No. No,' he said.

Bright watched as a new light began to surround this person from the past. A person of previously blameless character. The light of suspicion.

'He couldn't.' Holt's deep confident voice had lost all resonance. 'He was a – he was a nice young man – he was – okay. I didn't – do anything bad to him. I didn't do anything he could want to – take that kind of revenge for. Kill my daughter? Kill Alison? No. Not Mark.'

Mrs Holt said, 'Why not? I can think anything of anybody now. Everyone I see, I wonder, could it be you? Life was simple before this. There's no way to know what anybody is. My neighbours. My own relations. You can't tell. I don't trust anybody now.'

Holt pulled his wits together. 'Mr Bright. Even if Mark did – even if he is the one – why Maisie? He has some quarrel with Maisie's folks too?'

'That's what I have to find out. Can you think of any connection?'

'He did his degree at Bristol University.'

'Oh, did he?'

'Maisie's father is a lecturer there.'

'A-ha. I know.'

'Does he know Mark?'

'I don't think he's been asked. Up to now.'

The Holts stared at each other. She reached out her hands. Her husband took them.

'Mam?' The door at the back of the room opened and two small faces looked in. 'Can we come in now? We can't think of no more things to play.'

'Come in, love.' Mrs Holt looked at John Bright. 'Will you find out who did it, Mr Bright?'

'Have they put you in charge?' Mr Holt assumed he was the big gun sent from Scotland Yard.

Bright didn't disabuse him. 'I've been helping out on an informal basis up to now. But that might change. Believe me, if I can find this bastard, informally or formally, I will.'

'Will they question him? Mark Leighton?'

'You bet they will.' *If they ever find him again*, Bright thought but did not say. It was possible Mark had returned and was even now in the clutches of Ryan. It was possible and as unlikely as hell.

Kate opened the door. Lizzie and Dave now sat on the stairs, hands locked together. They stood when Bright came in. He said, 'Dave, before Ryan gets here, do you remember teaching a Mark Leighton? Maybe seven years ago?'

'Mark Leighton?' Dave looked blank.

'About five foot ten, slim but strong apparently, longish hair – well, it is nowadays, curly, mid-brown. Nice neck, I'm told. I've never seen the guy, don't have a picture, this is just hearsay. Scruffy stylish clothes.'

'Mark Leighton.'

They stared at Dave as at the oracle.

'Has this man got Maisie?'

'It's a possibility.'

Dave put both hands over his face. They waited. He took his hands away and shook his head. Tears came out of his eyes. He wailed, 'I can't remember him!'

Then Ryan arrived. Came in the house like a mammoth.

156

Huge. Filled the hall space. Looked at no one but Dave. 'Shouldn't have let you go, should I, Mr Fowler? This is a warrant to search your premises. You'll come with us, please, make sure everything is done by the book.'

Hearing this, Lizzie said, 'I'm coming too.'

'Sorry, Mrs – er . . .'

'It's our daughter who is missing, Mr Ryan.'

'We'll find her, Mrs . . .'

'My name is Creech. Maisie's name is Creech. And I'm not *Mrs* anything.'

'I'm sorry. Get Mr Fowler over there quick. Now, Mrs Creech. We've already started a house-to-house in the neighbourhood. Every house in this part of Totterdown will be visited by one of my officers. We've pulled men off other cases. This is priority. Time is of the essence. It's unusual for a disappearance to be reported so quickly. Normally people wait a few days or even longer before contacting us. But we know about this right away. It will be on all the news bulletins this afternoon. Do you have a recent photo of Maisie that we can borrow now?'

Lizzie's shaking hands went through the recent snaps, fumbling them, dropping them. She handed one over, Maisie in her wispy frock, the one she had worn to the first night of *Hedda Gabler*. Standing next to Alison.

'Is this a good likeness?' Ryan asked.

They all simply looked at it.

They had him by the arms, one on either side. They almost ran him up the stairs. The place was swarming with police. Turning it over. They shook pillows out of their cases, they heaved the mattresses up and over, they pulled out drawers, shook out the contents and left the lot on the floor, turned out cupboards, mess spilling everywhere. Papers, photographs, clothes, books opened and shaken, some left open with their spines bent back. Lizzie watched dead-eyed.

They started to throw stuff off the sleeping platform. They said, 'Bring him up here.' Dave went up the ladder, a policeman in front and one behind. Lizzie followed. The platform was maybe ten foot by twelve, half of it covered with mattress. Bedding had been thrown off, pillows and cushions flung about. One mattress stood up against the wall, the other had been lifted off the floor and two policemen were holding it up. On the floor where the mattress had lain was a small polythene bag containing brown powder, and another polythene bag containing a dried greenish herbal material.

'Just to confirm that you witnessed us finding this, Mr Fowler,' Ryan said.

'I didn't.' Dave said the words but they lacked hope.

'You didn't?'

'No. I came up here and saw the stuff on the floor. I did not see anyone lift the mattress and discover it. I did not put it there and you know I didn't.'

'This is your premises and the stuff was found here.'

Dave didn't bother to reply. Lizzie couldn't.

'David Fowler, I am arresting you on suspicion of dealing in illegal substances. You do not have to say anything . . .'

They went backwards down the ladder. Two policemen took Dave out to a car. Lizzie watched from the dark doorway. Ryan said, 'Can we drop you back home, Mrs Creech?'

Lizzie said, 'He didn't do this. He didn't do any of this. You should be searching somewhere else.'

Dave didn't even look back at her as they drove him away. She walked home. She walked home by way of a million streets. Looking for Maisie. She went by waste ground searching the rough grass.

31

Excerpt from a Diary

vii

Well, it was so easy. I knocked on the door and said I had just been at Dave's. She has seen me of course a few times at Dave's. So she invited me in. She was lonely. And bored. And grieving with no relief. She said she wanted to visit Alison's parents. She has seen them every day since Alison went missing. And since the death she takes the children out. She takes them to the playground on Windmill Hill. It gives them all something to do. She loves the children. They are heartbroken and the little one can't understand that Alison is never coming back. 'I can't understand it myself, come to that,' Maisie said (she has a most attractive Bristol accent) in her light little husky voice. She takes them to the school sometimes. They go the long route over the hill, behind the school and then round. So as to avoid the site (and the sight of the site) of Alison's laying-out. The children like that, she said. And she's very worried that this morning they'll be at a loss without her. But she promised her mother she wouldn't go out.

'I'd go with you,' I said.

She looked doubtful, as well she might. But I'm used to dealing with distrust. I get over it, round it and through it several times every day in my job. I said, 'Well, let's phone Dave then. He could come over and take you.'

That convinced her I must be above board. She did not call my bluff. Though if she had it would only have put this off to another time. She was bashful too at seeming not to trust me. A respectable person such as I, youngish, not at all dangerous or villainous, must surely be okay. It's awfully insulting after all to suspect a person you know of doing the things I have done. I said, 'You could leave a note for your mother to say where you have gone.'

'No,' she said, 'it's okay. I'll be back before lunchtime and Ankate will be here then with John Bright. He's a detective inspector from London.' She spoke with pride. And a slight hint of my-dad's-a-policeman defiance. I adore her. She is ravishing. I can't wait to have her to myself. I can't wait.

So out we walked into the sun and into my car. Oh yes, of course I have another car. The grey Renault is my cover in every sense. And when in the car I suddenly said, 'Oh, Lord, I forgot my asthma inhaler, do you mind if we go via my place?' although she became a little alarmed she was too well brought up to show it. And when we got to my place, though she sensibly got out of the car so as to be able to make a run for it if I should attempt anything, when I from inside my doorway cried out, 'Ouch! Oh God!' or words to that effect, pretending to have injured myself, she called out, 'What's the matter?' and came running into my arms. Well, not literally into my arms. Just into my domain. When I locked the door behind her she was simply astonished.

The things that happen to young girls simply because they are too polite. People spend their whole lives teaching children to say yes, when the major thing they should teach them is to say no. No, no and no. To all adults. They pretend to children that adults are for the most part kind and good. This is a lie. Most adults are corrupt, cowardly, cruel, bullies who will abuse any creature weaker or smaller than themselves, and who lie and cheat. Men particularly. Because the most important thing to most men is their image. The image they have of themselves that must be upheld at all costs. People sacrifice their lives, whole nations have sacrificed themselves, to preserve one man's image of himself.

Some children of course are corrupted almost right away. They accept the adults' picture of the world and the adults' picture of themselves. Lies are wicked, say the adults, lying themselves all the time about everything. Most children accept the picture: yes lying is wrong wink wink now let's lie to our heart's content. But some children believe the adults, and have a hard time reconciling the picture they present with the reality that the child's clear eyes see. Some children never reconcile the image with the reality and they go mad. Others add it all up eventually and remain sad and disillusioned, never able to trust that they will not be betrayed. Some, like Alison, like Maisie, shine like moons in a black night, gliding above corruption. BUT THEY WILL BE BROUGHT LOW. THEIR LIGHT WILL BE EXTINGUISHED. AND THEIR CORRUPTION WILL BE THE WORSE BECAUSE THEY SHONE SO BRIGHT. I will not live or let them live to see that happen. The drugs, the sex games, the power games, the prostitution to employment and worldly power and to worldly goods. These will not be allowed to bargain for the souls of these bright children. They have the best. They have been the best. Flights of angels sing them to their rest. The rest is silence. Who can be sad at Hamlet's death? Or Ophelia's? They were pure. They were the good and the pure. They were truly not for this world. Death is not tragedy. Death is triumph. I shall convince Maisie of this.

I shall tell Maisie the truth from the start. She will know what I mean to do. I tried to deceive Alison but she guessed. She was nobody's fool. Maisie too is intelligent and perspicacious. She deserves nothing less than the truth. I shall discuss my theories with her. I have never discussed my position with another human being. I have never dared. Perhaps Maisie will raise telling arguments that will shift me from my position. Who knows? I believe that by now my position is too entrenched, too solid to admit of argument. But you never can tell.

161

Do you like my quotations from plays? Dropped in here and there for your eyes? What do you think of my theories? Do you suspect that I envy you, and that my actions are a kind of revenge on you for the gifts that you have and that I lack? Please do not think that of me. I have seen in your work a wide and profound understanding of the ways of human beings, even the human beings that horrify the general run of human beings. Your Medea, your Hedda, your Clytemnestra. These are all people who killed from a powerful belief that death was better than a corrupt life. You have depicted powerfully for the world the motives for these actions. You have brought understanding to dull minds. If only for the duration of the play they have understood and sympathised with a human being whom in life they would condemn and vilify. You are their interpreter to the world. And when you present these notes, this account for publication, you will do so again, in a different role.

I had meant to send you my diary in instalments but that was, I now realise, a rash decision made when I was in an exalted state. I have no doubt the forensic experts, infinitely more competent than the dummkopf constabulary, would trace the pages somehow back to me. But I beg you to publish this account after I am gone. I really do beg. The only desire for which I have ever begged. I need the world to understand. Its understanding is always limited. But occasionally a crack appears into which light penetrates if only for a brief flash. Out out brief candle and all that. And none of that she-should-have-died-hereafter stuff. Most people should die BEFORE they do, not after. Withered old leaves that the poor old tree of life can't shake off. Clinging on for grim life.

I know you understand. I know that, though you will feel pain, you will see that this is the best time for Maisie to die. Now while she is perfect and uncorrupted. Now before she

162

starts to decline. Into physical and moral degradation. I know you understand.

Well, enough of this polemic. Maisie is here, safe and well. For the moment she is unfortunately blindfolded and gagged and her hands are tied. I did this as gently as possible. She fought of course, that's only natural, but I am strong and have now had experience. This whole thing has been easier than it was with Alison.

I asked Maisie to sit down while I explained things to her. She did so. I taped her hands behind her before she knew what I was doing. She screamed and lifted the chair with her and thrashed about. I managed to tape her mouth. I'm sorry to say I did this cruelly. I'm afraid I slightly hurt her neck on the back of the chair. I had to. I would not have chosen to. The gag will be removed later. But not before she is introduced to her own special room, you understand: I cannot allow her to shout and scream. Also, I cannot reveal to you the location of her special room, in case my whereabouts are discovered. After the gagging, blindfolding her was relatively easy.

The idea of the special room came to me some years ago. I was in the sixth form at school. A group of us doing Media Studies were taken to London. One of our visits was to a Radio Studio at Broadcasting House. A production of *Cymbeline* was being rehearsed/recorded. You were giving one of your award-winning performances as Imogen. You will recall that, I'm sure. Just as I am sure that you will not recall meeting me. Though naturally I do remember meeting you.

One area of the radio studio was called the DEAD ROOM. I was overcome with the symbolic significance of the name, naturally. This room had padded walls and ceiling. Conical stalactites of foam rubber, covered with a greyish muslin, protruded inward and downward as though the dead all round were trying to punch their way through. No, that is fanciful. The padding was to deaden the sound. Kill the sound.

The open air (mountain, garden, forest, street), it was explained to us, reduces the resonance of the human voice, thinning it, 'deadening' it (you of course know this), so scenes set in the open air are played in the Dead Room. (You indeed were recording the Milford Haven scene, begging Pisanio to kill you – *the lamb entreats the butcher – where's thy knife?* I was greatly affected by this scene. By your playing of it. And also by your speaking of the dirge to the innocent dead: *Fear no more the heat of the sun . . .*) But enough of fond reminiscence. Thus my Dead Room is padded, not just the walls and ceiling but the floor too. The padding kills sound. So the inhabitant can make as much din as she likes. No one will ever hear.

I have spent much time myself in this room and have observed a curious phenomenon. This deadening or thinning of the voice has a strange effect. Speaking becomes a less than pleasurable experience. I discover that all of us literally enjoy the sound of our own voice. When we are robbed of that sound we become disorientated, lost, afraid. We force our voices to make more sound, but although we shout at the top of our lungs we cannot hear ourselves any better. (The aural equivalent of drowning, perhaps, or of looking into a mirror and seeing – nothing.) We are filled with a kind of despair, as though perhaps we are ceasing to exist. Whether this effect contributes to the choice of death over life I do not know. Alison in fact died in my Dead Room. And she died willingly. And so, I hope, will Maisie. She will die painlessly, peacefully, and she will be reconciled to her death. You must not worry about her. You must be glad for her. I may decide to die with her. If I decide that, through you, sufficient understanding of my motives will be reached, disseminated – *broadcast* if you like – then my work will be completed and it will be time for me to die also.

32

Changing Allegiances

Kate rang Colum to tell him what had happened. He made a harsh intake of breath like a sob. 'Oh God, Kate, what are you going to do?'

'We're helpless, Colum, helpless. We sit here. Then we go out. We roam the streets. People watch from their windows. They all know. They gaze sympathetically. They don't dare speak to Lizzie. No one can speak to her. I can't, myself.'

'Are you pulling out of the play?'

'I don't know, I don't know.'

'Don't decide yet. There's time.'

'The show must go on?'

'Well, it must actually. Yes.'

'It seems obscene to be acting make believe when this horror is happening in real life.'

'This play is more than make believe.'

'No, Colum, it's not.'

'What else would you be doing?'

'Sitting helplessly next to Lizzie staring into space waiting for news.'

'You can get news at the theatre.'

'Yes.' Kate was not convinced.

Strangely, the only person Lizzie could bear to have around was John Bright. He brought her cups of coffee and tea, placed them in her hands and made her drink them. He cooked spaghetti and made her eat, at least a forkful or two. He found some Mogadon in her bedside cabinet and made her take one so that for a few hours she might sleep.

At 2 a.m., when they had put her to bed, he and Kate sat in the living room. He said, 'This is my fault. I know who did this and I forced his hand. I blew it. Don't interrupt. If they'll have me I'm going to try to get leave to join the team.'

'Will they—?'

'I might be able to swing it if Ryan puts in a word with the IO.'

'The what?'

'Investigating Officer.'

'I thought that was Ryan.'

'No. He's just one of the two DCIs on the team. He heads one of the shifts. If the IO gives the say-so I'll be in. I'll do it voluntary, just use my leave. I'll get her out alive. I will, Kate.'

Kate looked up. Lizzie was standing in the doorway in her dressing-gown. She and John Bright stared at each other for a long time. She nodded several times. So did he. Then she turned round and went back upstairs.

Kate's mouth made a movement that resembled a smile. Bright just looked desperate. 'Some way to get your sister to tolerate me,' he said.

'Where do you begin to look for this person?' Kate whispered.

'His mother's house.'

'But he left—'

'The trail starts there. Even if all we find is a picture to circulate. His history. What the mother has to say about him. See, Ryan is fixated on Dave. The whole team is. You can see why.'

Kate made the same noise Colum had made on the phone, an inward-breathing sob, an ugly grunting sound. 'Dave didn't – Dave didn't—'

'No.' Bright's expression was grim. 'Dave didn't.'

'So . . .'

'So if I get on the team I'll get them to let me pursue this line. See, the guy has a link to this area. He's visited families round here. I can start with them. They're still doing the house-to-house. I can get them to ask.' Bright started to pace, bouncing on the balls of his feet, rattling the change in his pockets.

Kate kept still. She did not share her sister's faith. She felt the way she had felt sitting in her kitchen that day clutching her heart. When she had heard about the missing Bristol schoolgirl and known it was Maisie. She had lost Maisie now. She had lost Maisie because she had gone to the theatre to rehearse a play instead of staying with Maisie, her niece, whom she knew to be in danger. They had all done the same. Maisie's mother, and her father too. But it was no use telling herself that. She was responsible. One great love had lost her another. She felt utter despair.

'Here. You take a Moggie as well. You got to sleep.' He pulled her to her feet. 'Ah, Kate.'

'Yup.'

'What's going on?'

'How do you mean?'

'In your head?'

'Same as you. Only I can't do anything. Nothing I can do.'

'You be with Lizzie.'

'She doesn't want me. The sight of me is anathema to her. Haven't you noticed? It's terrible.'

'Is that right?'

'Yes. She only has eyes for you, dear.'

'Is that right?'

'Yup. She believes in you.'

'And you don't.'

Kate looked at him.

'A-ha,' he said.

'Not just not in you. Not in anything.'

'Go back to work then. Do the play.'

'How can I do the fucking play with this going on?'

'Here.' He handed her a Mogadon and a glass of water.

They were all awake and in the jolly kitchen at seven in the morning. Bright had the merry clown teapot in one hand and the mobile phone in the other. 'A-ha,' he said, 'a-ha.' Then, 'Ryan, listen – ' He put down the pot and went out into the hall. Kate poured tea. Lizzie drank hers in one ravenous gulp burning her mouth.

The sun shone like yesterday, like all the days, the sun gentler at this time of morning than it would be later. Kate went out on to the steps. Sarah-next-door was in her garden. She silently mouthed to Kate: Any news? Kate shook her head. Sarah wiped her eyes with her skirt hem. Kate went down the steps. Sarah whispered, 'How is she?'

Kate did not need to speak.

'Would she like me to come round?'

Lizzie appeared at the top of the steps. She saw Sarah and came down slowly. Sarah said, 'Oh Lizzie. Shall I come into yours? I can't see me going to work somehow.'

Lizzie nodded. Sarah disappeared up her own steps. Lizzie went back inside. Kate followed, after looking round at all the gardens lower down the hill. As though Maisie might suddenly appear: *Hi, I'm here, gave you all a fright, didn't I?* Then she followed Lizzie. The bell rang. Bright opened the door. Sarah came in. Lizzie walked into her arms and they stood there locked in support. Kate looked on. Bright caught her eye. His unmoving mask expressing – she could not have said how – sympathy, irony, solidarity.

Lizzie and Sarah went into the kitchen. Bright said, 'Is she going to stay with Lizzie?'

Kate nodded.

'Go to work, Kate.'

'What does Ryan say?'

'He's been on to the IO. The IO's a bit startled. It's unprecedented, apparently. But he's getting on to my guv'nor now. If my guv'nor goes for it he'll ring me. Then it'll be settled.'

'How can they spare you?'

He gave her a look. 'I've got leave due. And luckily we've just closed a case. And I'm more dispensable than you are.'

' 'Fraid not. The show will go on with or without me. There are probably thirty actresses out of work at this moment who could play Rosalind as well as me.'

'Go to work.'

She went into the kitchen. Sarah and Lizzie sat at the table. Lizzie held Sarah's hand. Sarah said, 'I'm staying, Kate.'

Kate smiled at her. 'Good. Shall I phone the pottery for you?'

'No, I'll do it.' She went to the living room to phone.

Kate said, 'What can I do, Lizzie?'

Lizzie did not look at her or reply. Bright came in shoving down the aerial on his mobile. Lizzie looked at him as a dog looks at its beloved master. 'I'm on the case,' he said.

Lizzie covered her face with her hands.

'I'll be at the station for an hour or so probably. And this is my mobile number if you need me.' He wrote it on the kitchen message board. The previous message had been written by Maisie: *Mum. We need bread and milk.*

Lizzie said, 'Thank you.'

Going out of the front door he said to Kate, 'Go to work.'

'You seem to have learned that line. You're delivering it quite well. Could you move on to the next one now?'

'I'll call you later. At the theatre.' Before he was down the steps he was on his mobile again. She heard: 'Permission to pursue this line of investigation . . .'

She sat round the house. She hoovered. She washed up. Lizzie ignored her. Sarah tried to compensate by making conversation. In the afternoon she went to the theatre.

33

Bright Goes His Own Way

'Bright, we have the stations watched, the motorways, the ferries. Feckin' Eurostar. Coach stations. The guy did a runner.'

'I need to get in the house. Question the mother.'

'It's no use questioning the mother. She doesn't speak.'

'And I'd like to take Helen Goldie with me.'

'You're supposed to be helping us, Bright.'

'A-ha.'

'Hear you're a good interviewer. Question Dave Fowler for me first.'

'Can't do that.'

'Why not?'

'Couldn't be objective, mate. Friend of the family.'

'Little gobshite.'

'Who? Me or him?'

'Take your pick.'

'I'll take Goldilocks. To see Mother Bear.'

'Get the hell out and get back here for the briefing at five.'

Bright sprinted to the incident room.

A plump woman in navy blue opened the door and let them in. 'She's sleeping just at the moment.'

'We'll wait.'

The hallway gleamed with the same civilised brilliance as yesterday. Was it yesterday? No. The day before. Seemed a year ago. The flowers were still alive, twisted stems, feathery ruffs, purple, crimson, ultramarine, scarlet, faces with hairy grasping black middles. 'Are they anenomes?' Helen asked.

The woman said, 'Enemies? Who?'

'Er – no – the flowers.'

'Anemones,' John Bright said.

'I thought you meant Mrs Leighton and her son. Enemies, I thought you said.'

'*Are* they enemies?' Bright said.

'Well, she looks frightened if you mention him.'

'Frightened of him or frightened for him?'

'Oh. I don't know. I can't tell.'

'But you thought Helen said enemies.'

But the nurse thought she had said enough. 'Wait in here, please. I'll let you know when she wakes up.'

Bright took out a hankie and slid open drawers in the sideboard: perfectly arranged canteens of cutlery, napkins, cruets. In the desk perfectly arranged wedges of writing paper, envelopes, folders of bills paid on time. The signature on the bills was not Mark's. Bright presumed it was the mother's. The initial was E. Cheque-book stubs showed only the payments of these bills, no other items. Mark's stuff must be elsewhere in the house, in his own quarters. Helen, on watch at the door, signalled the return of the nurse. Bright pocketed the hankie and stood at the window.

'She's just woken up. She's a nervous type. Don't upset her, will you?'

'Don't worry.' Helen was conciliatory. 'We'll be careful.' She let Bright go ahead into the room. She murmured to the nurse, 'What actually is the matter with her, do you know?'

The nurse made a face. 'Well, she doesn't get out of bed.

Her legs appear to be paralysed. There's the most amazing arrangements. She's got a commode and she can lever herself out on to that. She has a Teasmade thing and an electric ring and a wheelchair. So she's not confined to bed. She can get about.'

'But only on this floor?'

'That's right. Not much of a life, is it?' The nurse was settling in for a good old chin-wag. Helen smiled and slipped into the room after Bright.

The curtains did not quite meet. A stiletto of sunshine sliced between them and cut across the bed. But the room had a rosy dimness. The colours were faded and dim too, the worn Persian carpet, the soft Indian cotton quilt, the curtains themselves a rosy velvet faded in strips by the sun.

Mark Leighton's mother sat supported by pillows. She wore a pale grey fine jersey top with a silk scarf at the neck. She had a noble face, pale indoor skin. She was younger than either of them had imagined. No more than forty-five. She must have had Mark when she was very young.

She shrank back when Helen came in. 'It's okay,' Bright said. 'This is Helen. She's a friend of mine. I was just saying to Mrs Leighton – '

The woman shook her hand in a shooing motion to correct him.

'I'm sorry – Miss Leighton – she must have been only a girl when Mark was born.'

'I was a child. I was a schoolgirl. I was seduced by the father of my dearest friend while a guest in his house. I lost everything. I lost all my friends. I lost my family. I lost everything.' She recited this like a litany.

'But you gained your son,' Bright said.

A strange expression crossed the woman's face. She held the quilt with both hands, drawing it closer to her chin.

'Where is Mark now, Miss Leighton?'

172

Helen couldn't believe the way his nasal South London croak transformed itself into a catlike purr. This frightened weird woman seemed to trust him. But not that much. 'Has he gone?' she said.

'He's gone, but he hasn't told us where. Is there somewhere he goes when he goes away?'

She whispered, 'We have a little flat in London.'

'A-ha, I know. He hasn't gone there.'

'I don't know where it is he goes. Mark is very good to me. Very good.'

'A-ha. I know that, I can see that. He's a good son. When do you expect him back?'

'Back?'

'Did he tell you when he's coming home?'

'No, no. He never says. I'm all right here. You see I have everything I need.'

The room was wonderfully equipped, a small fridge, a pretty little sink and cupboard, the simple cooking arrangements.

'For a few days, yes.'

'Oh, I'm never alone for longer than a few days. I have never been.'

'I believe you have a daughter in Ireland.'

'In Ireland?'

'That's what Mark said.'

'Is she in Ireland?'

'He didn't tell you?'

'I didn't think she was so far away.'

'Doesn't she keep in touch with you?'

'She comes to see me.'

'Often?'

'Not often, no.' The woman's voice was mournful.

'Don't her and Mark get on?'

The woman looked bewildered for a moment. 'We miss her,' she said.

173

'But you've got her address?'

'No.'

'You don't have your daughter's address? You don't write to her? She doesn't write?'

Miss Leighton stared at him all this time, not responding to the questions in any way, as though trying to work out what they might mean.

'Did you quarrel with her? How many years ago? What happened?'

Miss Leighton's expression didn't change. But her eyes changed their focus so that though they seemed to rest on Bright's face as before, in fact they looked inward or far off. He was not going to get an answer, he could see that. He was stumped. He squinted at Helen fast then away with an expression that almost made her laugh aloud. He said, 'Could we have a look at Mark's room? Would that be okay by you?'

She looked away a moment towards the window. A hiatus. They waited. It was not clear whether she would bother to reply. Or even whether she had heard. Then she said, 'Yes. I think you may,' in a voice that sounded as though she had leapt a chasm.

'Where is it, Miss Leighton?'

'Nurse?'

The nurse's head came round the door, looking for trouble. 'Yes?'

'Will you show these people Mark's room?'

The nurse looked nonplussed. 'I don't know where it is.'

'It is on the floor above. Will you show them to it?'

Only the upper classes, Bright thought, could give people orders in quite that way, make their wishes clear without saying a word that could cause offence. The order was: accompany these people and keep an eye on them so they don't overstep the mark or steal the silver. The nurse was not accustomed to this mode of address. It took time for the penny to drop. 'Oh yes,' she said at last. 'Of course. All right.'

This was a narrower staircase but graceful. A long window on the half-landing gave them the whole city and the hills around and the river shining and winding here and there. The shimmer of heat over the distance. Helen said, 'Wow.'

'Not bad, is it?' Bright stood a moment near her and smelled a light perfume. She turned her face to him and he moved on up. There were three rooms up here, a bathroom at the head of the stairs and two rooms interconnecting by double doors. Fitted coir carpet. White walls. Narrow bed in the back room. White bed cover. White curtains on all windows. Ikea desk, in the front room, lap-top computer, good laser printer. Apart from the computer, with closed lid, the desk top was clear. No papers, notebooks, photos, pens. Both rooms were obsessively neat.

Bright said to the nurse, 'The son has gone missing. I'm going to have to search the drawers. She said it was okay. I just want you to make sure we don't do anything out of order. Right?'

'Oh.' She was worried and reassured in one. 'Yes. Very well then.'

'You're a witness, you see, that Miss Leighton gave us permission and that we don't overstep the mark.'

'Yes.'

'No pun intended.'

The nurse looked blank and again Helen felt a desire to laugh. For some reason Bright cheered her up. She knew he was in a state about the missing girl, but she could see that here, doing something about it, doing his job, he was in his element. She could see he had this finesse about him that wasn't like any of the other coppers she'd worked with up to now. And then, watching him, his hands had this precision and delicacy, the way they went through things —

'Come here, Helen.'

Startled, she went across to him. He held open the pine chest of drawers: one drawer socks, one vests, one underpants, one sweaters. Neatly lined with white paper. The cupboard held shirts on hangers, jeans on hangers, jackets on hangers. The upper shelf had two travel bags. Bright lifted them down. They zipped them open, felt inside. Nothing at all, not even an old plane ticket or gum wrapper. They replaced them carefully, Bright standing on a chair and feeling across the whole shelf just in case: lined also, and clean. Under the bed, not even a scrap of fluff. 'Clean guy,' Bright said to the nurse in passing. 'Unusual.'

'Most men . . .' the nurse said, and rolled her eyes.

'A-ha. Bit funny, you think?'

'Well, not for me to say. But he is a mother's boy, isn't he? You can see the way he takes care of her.'

'A-ha.' While the nurse talked he had started on the desk drawers. One side two filing cabinet drawers, the other four ordinary small drawers. 'You take that side,' he said to Helen. She opened a small drawer. 'Surprise surprise,' he groaned: neatly stacked paper, envelopes, pens, pencils, instruction manuals for the computer, the software, the printer. 'Don't miss anything though.' He was warning her.

He went through the files. No bills with Mark's signature. Nothing with his handwriting. A receipt or two, for clothes or computer stuff, all paid in cash. No credit card receipts. No cheque-book. No cheque-book stubs. He put those on one side. No address book. No diary. No photographs. A letter informing him he had got a job with the social services department. A letter saying they were transferring him to another department. This letter friendly in tone and signed by Mr Holt. Alison's father Mr Holt. No letters from the sister or from any family member or friend. Some theatre programmes. Bright stopped dead. Helen felt him stop breathing.

176

A picture of Kate. The programme for *Hedda Gabler*. Bright went through the others. Kate's Mask Play. The programme for the Bristol Old Vic Studio and also for the Donmar Warehouse where the play moved to in London. Kate. Maisie. Dave. Maisie. Mr Holt. Alison. Maisie. Alison. The guy had left his story here. The bare bones but a story. It was like he'd left it on purpose. This was the story he wanted to tell. Was that right? Was Bright being too clever, thinking this way?

The rest of the damn drawer was empty, nothing slipped out of a file, no photos. Nothing. He opened the lower drawer. White as the driven snow. Virgin. Zilch. He stood up and looked round. One bookshelf. Mostly plays: Becket, Chekhov, Pinter, Shakespeare, Shaw, and some Bright had never heard of, foreign names, in strict alphabetical order, naturally. He dutifully opened them and shook them out, one by one, not expecting results. 'Thank Christ there's only one shelf.' And there behind a book by a geezer called Grotowski, stood three photographs.

Bright picked up the photographs and looked at them. He said to the nurse, 'I'll be taking these. With his mother's permission of course. Right?'

'Oh. Yes. Well, fine.'

'Get copies. I don't know how many. A lot. Ryan'll sign the order.' He was on his way out of the incident room.

'Where are you going now?'

'Why?'

'Don't I get to come?'

He looked at her. His mask look. The unfocused squint. She suddenly knew he liked her. She hadn't been sure before. She usually was sure, to her fingertips. It was intriguing not to be sure. She took a risk: 'Would you like to have a drink tonight? Forget all this?'

'No.'

Oops. She'd got it wrong. 'Oh. Sorry.'

'It's okay. I'm off the booze, that's all.'

She knew this was not the reason. But there was no use arguing. He turned fast and went, with the file of evidence from the Leighton house in his hand.

He slapped the file on to Ryan's desk. 'This is the story, Ryan! He is connected to every area of this case.'

Ryan slowly finished filling in an interview form. Slowly pulled the file to him and opened it. Sighed heavily. Slowly turned over the items one by one. Theatre programmes from four shows featuring Kate. A snap of Kate at the microphone in a radio studio holding a script. The two letters from Desmond Holt. Three pictures. The first two portraits. The third a Polaroid: grass, and sitting on the grass Dave with two young girls. Standing, gesticulating and laughing, a young man, slim, curly brown longish hair, jeans and torn sweater.

'Mark Leighton,' Bright said. 'Helen Goldie gives a positive ID.'

'Mr Guru Man Dave Fowler?'

'Looks like they were friends, right? Dave has totally forgotten him. No recollection now.'

'Says Dave.'

'No reason for him to lie.'

'No reason that we know of.'

'Okay, Ryan. You show this colour snap to Dave. See if he remembers the guy.'

'Oh, I will, I will.'

'And Desmond Holt. Look! Look at the letter. I told you what Holt said. They used to be friends too. Then Holt virtually sacked him. Both blokes reject him. He abducts Holt's daughter. He abducts Dave's daughter. Mark Leighton is giving us the story on a plate.'

'You're the one giving us the story.'

'What's that mean?'

'Too feckin' clever by half.'

'So what? We don't have another story that holds up.'

'It's no better than my Mr Guru Man theory.'

'The boy *is* clever. That's why you've got nothing on him, can't trace him. He's cleverer than us.'

'Speak for yourself.'

'I am doing.'

'What's this with your actress friend?'

'He doesn't know her personally. He's just a theatre buff.'

'Unless *she's* forgotten him as well.' Ryan laid on the sarcasm thick.

But Bright stopped pacing a moment. 'You might have something there, Ryan.'

'Well, God forbid there could be a hole in the perfect theory now.'

'Kate's connected to Maisie, for Christ's sake. Maisie's her niece. Kate's known Dave for nearly twenty years. She could have known this lad when he was friends with Dave.'

'Oh, I see, right, there is no hole in the perfect theory after all.'

'Come on, Ryan. You should at least get a look at that house. The guy's seriously weird. No one keeps things that neat. There's nothing there except what he wanted us to find.'

'According to the perfect theory.'

'There's something wrong about the set-up. The mother. Everything!' Bright buzzed round the room.

Ryan got bigger, more stolid, more fixed, his eyes grey, cold, like frozen shards of winter sea. He sat back and looked at his watch. He stood up. 'Time for the briefing,' he said.

But at the briefing he passed out copies of the pictures, with Helen Goldie's description. A young DC asked was this the prime suspect.

'No.' Ryan looked at Bright. 'The prime suspect, David

Fowler, is still in custody. We're processing him, as you know, at the moment on possession with intention to deal, but we are accumulating evidence. This photograph, as you see, has him with two young girls considerably younger than himself.'

'They're not missing, are they, guv?' It was Helen who asked with an innocent face. Ryan's not so innocent face flushed purple. But he spoke with perfect control: 'Perhaps you'd like to look into that, constable.'

'Yes, guv. Okay.' She caught Bright's eye – which eye she couldn't say – and again had this wild desire to laugh.

Coming out of the briefing, Bright said, 'You be careful. Don't get carried away. You're a brave girl but don't push it. You've got no clout yet. Watch it, okay? I want you on the case.' He held her eye for only a moment – no squint, she could swear – then walked off. He said without turning round, 'See you tomorrow.'

34

Returns

Colum said, 'I'm pathetically grateful, though I think it'll be good for you as well as us.'

Alan Tate gave her his heavy-lidded look: 'Thank Christ you came back. We were having the horrors.'

'Who could they have got to replace you at such short notice?' Ian McLean murmured. 'Hattie Jacques?'

Rupert the Angel gave her a shy pleased brief smile.

Celia/Gemma looked wild. 'Oh God, am I glad to see you!'

She was touched by their tact and their sympathy. She was depressed and uninvolved in the proceedings.

Colum said, 'As Kate is, thank God, back with us, we'll go back to the top of the play. Let's just read it quietly to each other, scene by scene, and find out what's going on.'

At the end of the afternoon of quiet reading and quiet discussion, Kate was still uninvolved, still profoundly depressed. She felt she had contributed nothing, could contribute nothing. Wasn't really there. She said, 'Colum? I don't know if I'm doing any good here.'

'What?'

'I've no idea what's going on in Rosalind. She's like a different character in this first bit of the play. She hardly speaks.'

'That's right! That's true! I hadn't realised till this afternoon.'

'She's just – nothing. Not there. I can't do anything with it.'

'You think Shakespeare just forgot to write some lines for her or what?'

Kate was dumbstruck. An idea began to form. 'She's silent for a reason? You mean her very silence is significant?'

'Well, maybe you should think along those lines.'

'Yes.' She pondered. 'Yes . . .'

She walked back to Lizzie's, all her mind searching for Maisie. Everywhere she looked there was Maisie. Only it never was Maisie. Each time it was a girl who could have been Maisie but wasn't. She stopped outside Dave's place. His windows were dark. No use to ring the bell. But she did. No answer. Just the sound of the echoing: Dong dong dong, just like the last time, Maisie ringing it.

She stopped on the foot-bridge and looked into the water. Crowds of people on the quay outside the Ostrich Inn.

181

Summer dresses, shorts, young men with bare chests. A picture of Rupert the Angel in the wrestling scene came into her mind. *That's when Rosalind comes to life! Then! After she falls in love. Before that she's like a space in the world, empty. Empty like I am now. With loss. With hopeless unspeakable loss. Loss! That's it. She has lost everything – her father is banished. The man who banished him, his brother, her uncle, has taken her in after purloining all his money and land. That is, her father, her money, her home, her land, her prospects for any kind of life, married or otherwise. She is tolerated only because of the love of Celia. It's Celia who is the talkative funny confident one in this part of the play because she's in every sense 'at home'. If Rosalind betrays the loathing and rage and sorrow she feels, this villain her uncle will do something worse, bump her off, use her to attack her father. Whichever way she jumps she jumps into a trap. So she doesn't jump. She stays expressionless, betrays nothing. And she loathes her position. That's the reason for her silence. She is profoundly unhappy, powerless and stuck. Like me now. With loss. Like me now.*

Kate put her head in her hands. Her skull expanded, the way it always did with rehearsal inspiration. She felt gratitude to Colum from the bottom of her heart. Such directors are rare. The releasers, the enablers. Excitement flooded her, sizzling through her veins. In spite of Maisie. In spite of Maisie's abductor. In spite of her own desperation and guilt, Kate stood flooded with excitement on the little bridge. The bridge over troubled water. That's what the play might come to mean for her. The bridge from Maisie to no Maisie.

'No.' Bright's small brown eyes speared her. 'She's alive. Never forget that. Alison was alive until the night before they found her. And there was not a mark on her. She had not been harm— physically harmed, she had not been –

182

attacked, she had not been— See? And she stayed alive for three weeks. And the search for Maisie started right away, in these cases even a day can make a difference. Look.' He took them to the window where a helicopter circled low over Totterdown and disappeared behind rooftops in the direction of Bedminster. 'The heat-seeking camera. I'm not saying we've got three weeks or anything like that. But Maisie's got staying power, know what I mean? More than Alison maybe?'

Kate looked at Lizzie. For the first time she saw a little hope. Quickly doused because hope was more painful than the effort at acceptance of loss. Lizzie looked at Sarah.

'Yes,' Sarah said. 'Allie was more, like, soft.'

Lizzie cleared her throat. 'Compliant,' she said.

'The house-to-house has come up with nothing. Nobody saw her. Nobody saw anyone come here.'

'Come here?' Lizzie sat up. 'You think someone came here? But she went out. Someone grabbed her in a car.'

'That's how you see it?' he said. 'Why would she go out when she said she wouldn't?'

Lizzie shook her head.

'No one phoned,' he said. 'We checked the phone calls. Someone persuaded her to go out. They had to come here to do that. And they must have given her a good reason. No?'

Kate said, 'Yes.'

Sarah nodded, blind faith in anything he might say.

Lizzie, in a tangled collision of fear, rage, loss, hope, despair, lifted her shoulders and shook her head.

'And it was someone she knew,' Bright said.

Lizzie stood up. 'It was not Dave. Don't you tell me it was Dave.'

Bright moved his hands to calm her. 'It was not Dave.'

'They've got Dave.' Lizzie's fervid eyes. 'They won't look for the real person. It will be the cause. It will be the cause.'

'Sit down, Lizzie.' His nasal South London voice took on a hard metallic ring. 'I'm looking for the real perpetrator. And so are the investigating team. And we'll find him.'

Shocked, Lizzie sat.

'Now listen. It was someone Maisie knew. She would not have gone with a stranger. And it was someone with a convincing message. From you, or from Dave, or maybe from Kate. Someone who knows you, or Dave or Kate. See what I mean? This is the way we've got to think. There is no other way she would have gone out.' He waited. No one spoke. 'Now, what would be a convincing reason? One of you needed her?'

'I'd never send for her because I needed her.' Lizzie spoke with scorn. 'She'd know that.'

Kate said, 'She wouldn't know that, Lizzie.'

Lizzie's eyes darted her a snake's tongue of hate that took Kate's breath away. Then she went on calmly to Bright, 'She would go somewhere for Dave. Or for her' – indicating Kate with a slight move of her head – 'but not for me. Not once I'd told her not to go out.' She turned and glared again at Kate. Her eyes said, *Don't tell me what my daughter would say or do.* As if it were Kate who had taken Maisie away.

Kate saw now that Lizzie had always resented her relationship with Maisie. Their collusion, hers and Maisie's, had hurt Lizzie. And that one kind of taking away was mirrored in this physical taking away, so that, to Lizzie, Kate had become responsible for the one as for the other. And Lizzie had concealed her pain and fury until now when all her fences were down.

Bright watched this behind his expressionless mask. In the tumbling silence he put an envelope on the table. Out of it he pulled three photographs. One was a photo booth snap for a passport. One was a blurred colour print. One was a black and white portrait, amateurishly lit, shadows crossing the face like black hands. They were all of the same person. 'This,' Bright said, 'is Mark Leighton.' He passed the pictures round.

A young man. A lovely face. Dark curling hair, looking lighter in the colour snap. The colour snap taken on grass under trees with three other people. Mark has his back to the camera but his head is turned to the side. His hair is back in a short pony tail. He is in a long sweater and jeans. He is laughing. He is standing. The other people are sitting on the grass. They are looking up at him. They are, curiously, not laughing. This gives the innocent-looking snap a sinister air. One of the people sitting on the grass is Dave. The other two are young girls.

'Do you know him? Have you seen him?'

They all study the pictures closely. They look hard. They try hard. They shake their heads.

Bright said, 'Maisie probably did.'

'Is this the—?' Lizzie stopped.

'A-ha. I'm not saying it's him. But he's the one who's done a runner.'

Sarah said, 'He looks so nice.'

'I've had these printed up and handed round. Learn him off by heart, okay? He can't stay hidden. He went off with nothing, a small bag, that's all. Unless he's . . .'

They all looked at Bright, waiting. He got up and went to the kitchen window. He turned round, slow. He said, 'They've been checking trains, coaches, motorways, Eurostar, ferries, they've been going long distance. The clever little bastard knew they'd do that so maybe . . . Maybe he's round here somewhere. And if he is round here that means maybe so is Maisie.'

35

The Sins of the Fathers

Holt came to the door looking red-eyed. He'd drunk a fair amount. 'Have you found her?'

Bright shook his head. 'No. Can I come in?'

Leading the way into the living room Holt slurred, 'Wife and kids in bed. Got be quiet.'

Bright moved a miniature fire engine and sat on the couch.

'Beer?'

'Sure.' He opened the can and drank warmish carbonated stuff.

'Why you come to see me? If you haven't found her.'

'Ryan questioned you today.'

Holt shook his head. His eyes filled up. 'Again.'

'Not nice, is it?'

'Even my wife has started to think—'

'A-ha.'

The man covered his face with his hands. Then he wiped his eyes and his face. 'And you? That what you think? I killed my beautiful daughter and now I killed her best friend? You think that, Mr Bright?'

Bright looked at him. A hard stare. No squint. No doubt about where he was looking. 'You're lying though, aren't you, mate?'

'Lying?'

'Lying.'

'No. No!'

'Oh yes you are. Not about this maybe. But about something. Your wife senses it. Just like I do.'

'No!'

'Listen, it happens to all of us one time or another. We get involved. Something goes too far. Tell the truth about this. It might help. Might clear up at least your wife's mind. Even if it's something you're ashamed of.'

Holt stood there silent then said, 'I shouldn't have invited you in.'

'Yes, you should. Listen. When I was asking you about Mark Leighton—'

'I told you the truth about that. A bit of hero worship on his part. I cooled it. He got moved to another department. That was the end of it.' A moan came out of him and his hands covered his face again. 'Oh dear Lord.'

'So what really happened? Gonna tell me?'

'Give me a minute.' Holt got up. He kept his hands over his eyes. He walked round the back of his chair. He turned and put his hands on the back of his chair. His eyes down, not looking at Bright but at his own brown hands on the chair back, he said, 'My wife mustn't know this.'

'Look, mate—'

'No. You don't understand. We're members of the Pentecostal Church. We are very serious Christians. It means something. It's not like these casual Church of England people who make the rules up as they go along.'

'Okay okay. I'm not gonna run upstairs and invite your wife down to hear this, okay?'

'But no one else must know.'

Bright groaned. 'As far as I can, I'll respect this as a confidence. Whatever you like to tell me. Okay?'

'Okay.' The man's voice had nearly deserted him. 'Well . . .' He folded his arms across his chest. Took a deep breath. 'After I – cooled things off with Mark, he wrote me a few letters. They were weird, man. They were like – they were like letters from a woman, you know? Well, I felt – dirty. I mean, I've never been involved in anything like that.

187

I've never been – that way inclined. I had no idea. It never occurred to me. He was just a young man I was showing the ropes, you know?'

'A-ha. I believe you, I believe you. You still got these letters?' Bright asked this knowing what the answer would be.

'Are you joking? I shredded them in the office shredder.' He spoke with disgust as though contaminated by their very touch.

'And what then? He start pestering you at work, ringing you up, what?'

Holt shook his head slowly. 'His sister came to see me.'

'His sister?'

'She came to the office.'

'The one who lives in Ireland?'

'She was visiting, she said.'

'A-ha?'

'She told me Mark was in a bad way. She told me he had a tough life, looking after the mother, all that stuff. If I would just see him. He didn't want any more than that. Just to be my friend still. All this stuff.'

'Did you agree?'

'No, I said no. I put it as nicely as I could, but I said that for his own good it would be better if he moved on. I told her he needed help. You can get help on the National Health – I don't mean for being – you know – gay or whatever, but for being so – needy. I could give her the names of several therapists and so on.' Holt stopped.

'A-ha? Go on.'

Holt sighed. He came round the chair and sat down. He rubbed his face with both hands. He said, 'I don't know if I can tell you this.'

'Oh yes, you can. It's easy once you start.'

'You don't know.'

'You fell for her.'

'What?'

188

'Well, didn't you?'

Holt looked at him speechless.

'You fell for each other. You had long talks about it on park benches, right? Discussing what you should do? She's betraying Mark. You're betraying your wife.'

'My wife and kids, my religion. And Mark.'

'Yeah, both his beloveds in one go.'

'You talk about it cheerfully, as if it's nothing. Something that happens every day.'

'It does, mate.'

'Not to me. Not to people like us. To people on the telly, in the soaps, in the movies, yes. But to real people? No.'

'You'd be surprised.'

'And believe me, it's nothing like the soaps. They don't tell you about the real pain.'

'What's that?'

'The lying, deceiving. Pretending. Always having to think what to say when you've always been open and clear and true. It's true love I have for my wife. Good love. And for God too. I'd stand in church with all the good people not knowing how to face my God. Come home not knowing how to face my wife. I was nearly destroyed.'

'I see.'

'I doubt if you do.'

'Well, no. So what happened? Anything happen? Between you and the sister?'

'She had problems too. She'd been seduced when she was a student. By one of her lecturers. She'd never say who he was. She'd really fallen for him. She was completely inno-cent. She thought it was love for life. Marriage and children. All that. Apparently she went to bed with him. He deflowered her as she put it. And then he seemed to forget her!'

'Forget her? She was still a student of his?'

'Well, she meant forget about the – incident – as he

would have seen it. Just one among many, apparently. A man of no morals. When she confronted him he said he wasn't ready for the sort of commitment she had in mind!'

'A-ha.' Bright sounded weary.

'This may seem a common thing in your experience. But to God-fearing people it's not, believe me. It had destroyed this girl. So she was afraid to start another relationship. And knowing I was married and so on – '

'But?' Bright sounded even wearier.

'Don't belittle this.'

'Listen, mate, I can tell you the story. There's nothing new. You have all these secret meetings, lying about where you've been and who with. You can't think about anything else. You smell her everywhere you go, like she's on your skin? Even though you haven't done anything yet, you've done plenty in your mind. And eventually one night things get a little bit out of hand, in your car? Up on the Downs? Over the other side of the Gorge, Leigh Woods maybe, less close to home? Down a lane in the back of the car? Or at her place? Anyway, you do it. The big bad deed. Live up to your expectations, did it? Yeah, probably. All that guilt and fear dresses it up a bit, doesn't it? Makes it more exciting than between your God-fearing marital sheets. Okay, so you done it. What next?'

Holt stared, dumbstruck, offended but astounded beyond offence. 'Is this really so common, so ordinary? Don't tell me that. I'm ashamed enough.'

'Nah. It's different for all of us. But the story's roughly the same.'

Holt closed his eyes. 'It has never seemed a common experience to me.'

'So what happened next? She run screaming rape? She threaten to tell your wife and insist on marriage? She get pregnant?'

Holt gave a faint smile. 'I never saw her again.'

190

'What?'

'Oh? I have managed to surprise you?'

'You never saw her again? By mutual agreement or what?'

'She wrote to me. She said she couldn't break up a marriage. And she couldn't betray her brother. She had done enough damage. It had to stop now before we destroyed more lives. Not to try to get in touch with her.'

'Still got the letter? Need I ask?'

'I kept it for months. I threw it in the river in small pieces only a few weeks ago.'

'Scattering the ashes.'

'Precisely so.'

'And did you try to get in touch with her?'

'I couldn't. The only way I knew to reach her was through her brother. That was out of the question. I didn't have a number for her. I assumed she had gone back to Ireland.'

'Directory Enquiries?'

'I tried, yes.'

'A-ha.'

'I didn't know which part of Ireland. There was no trace. There were several M. Leightons. But none of them was she.'

'What's the M stand for?'

'Margaret.' A frisson of pain passed over his face when he said the name.

'A-ha.' Bright pondered a minute. 'Did she look like him?'

'Like Mark? Well . . . yes, I suppose in a way she did. But she was so unlike him in manner, in the way she thought and spoke. She had a lovely voice.'

Bright felt an inner shiver. Millie's voice. His mother: *Kate has a lovely voice. All actresses have lovely voices, ma.*

Holt said, 'He said she has a lovely face. God in his mercy lend her grace.'

'What?'

'"The Lady of Shalott". Tennyson.'

'Oh. Poetry. Yeah. A-ha.'

Holt said, 'I was punished. I went on longing for her. More than before. And now I have been truly punished. By the loss of my beloved daughter. Let's hope He has lent her grace. Oh Christ, Oh Christ.' Holt bent his head and began to sob.

Bright said, 'Have you got a picture of her? Margaret, I mean.'

Holt shook his head, blowing his nose.

Bright stood up. Looked down on the dignified man so distraught. He said, 'You'll feel freer now you've told someone. People always do.'

'He won't.'

Bright looked round. The voice had come from the doorway. Holt's wife stood there in her dressing-gown. Holt raised his wet face. He said, 'Louie.'

She said to Bright, 'I thought it was something worse. It's a relief actually.' She didn't sound relieved. Or as though she would find it easy to forgive. She sounded as hard as a woman can who has lost her daughter and thought her husband had something to do with the death.

Bright said, 'The coppers knew you were hiding something. They knew you were guilty of something. You can't hide these things if you're not a villain. If you'd told them all this, you'd have been off the hook weeks ago.'

Holt said nothing. He gazed at his wife as though an unforgiving God were about to speak through her.

Bright said, 'I'll let myself out.'

Ryan said, 'Told you he was hiding something. What do you bet it was Dave Fowler seduced the sister?'

'Give Mark a motive, wouldn't it, Ryan?'

'What, he takes revenge on two men for seducing his sister, by killing their daughters? Come off it, Bright.'

'Anyway it's more like this Margaret was taking the revenge on Holt for rejecting her brother. She seduced him if you like, then left him high and dry. The more I see of it the more I think this Margaret's a significant factor.'

'Fowler can't remember Mark. But then Mark's a bloke. Not the Guru's primary interest. Maybe he'll remember the sister better.'

36

Aides-Mémoire

'Well, Dave, remember a Margaret Leighton in your trawl through the student population of this city?'

'Margaret Leighton, like the actress?'

Ryan was nonplussed for a moment. 'I guess – yes. Though I don't imagine she shares any other characteristics with the lady. You remember a student of that name?'

Dave tried to concentrate. Miles of students like those fold-out paper dolls stretched back nearly twenty years, dancing in front of his eyes, featureless. He shook his head, despair and exasperation. His hair, normally clean and shining in waves, was lank and greasy, tied back in a knot. Ryan wanted to take the shears to it. And not just to his hair, either, the ponce. 'All one to you, are they, Fowler? Don't even remember their names?'

'I've been teaching for seventeen years. That's an awful

lot of students. I can't be expected to recall every one. Was she exceptional, this Margaret Leighton?'

'No. You seduced her. I wouldn't say that was exceptional, would you? You sick bastard.'

Dave, arms tightly crossed on his chest, stared hard at a spot on the wall. He must not allow this man to shake him. He must keep his thoughts where this man could not reach. He said, 'When is this supposed to have happened?'

'We're about to find out. We think at least six years back, if not more.'

'You asked me about another Leighton? A male student of mine. Am I supposed to have seduced him too? What is your theory exactly?'

'And you still don't remember him either.'

'I'm afraid not.'

'Here.' Ryan thrust the blurred snap under Dave's nose. 'Recognise anyone there?'

Dave took it. His fingers trembled, Ryan noted with pleasure.

He studied the picture. For a long time. Ryan crossed his big legs, wagged his big feet. But he didn't speak, let the Guru take his time.

Dave said, 'Oh God.'

'What?'

'I remember him. This guy with the pony tail, is that him?'

'What about him?'

'He was my student. He was doing English and theatre studies. He fancied himself as an actor. He had some talent, but there was something weird in his nature.'

'*You* thought *he* was weird?'

Dave closed his eyes, praying for patience. 'He couldn't form relationships. He talked *at* people. *When* he talked. He'd be silent then talk in a burst. And it was way-out rap, full of references to all sorts of esoteric stuff that the other students hadn't heard of and most of the lecturers hadn't either.'

'Showed you up, did he? You wouldn't like that, would you?'

'It was disconnected. It didn't add up. It made people uneasy. You can see here in this picture he's on one of his riffs. I can't recall what it was about. But you can see he thinks it's funny and the rest of us don't; we're disturbed by it. I don't remember this specific occasion. It was one of a number.'

Dave's long fine hand came up to his face. He brushed back his hair. Ryan almost winced watching him. He'd rarely felt such antipathy, even with the worst villains he'd had to deal with and he'd dealt with a fair few. 'Well?'

Dave said in a flattened voice, 'He might have a motive. For harming me. He might have two motives. He failed his degree. Because I gave him low marks.'

'You're kidding me.'

'I assure you I'm not, Mr Ryan.'

'And the other convenient memory return?'

Dave said, 'I rejected his sister.'

'Rejected,' Ryan said, sardonic, 'in what sense?'

'I turned down an offer of marriage from her.'

'What?' Ryan laughed in spite of himself. 'Now you are definitely having me on.'

Dave looked sad. 'No. She wasn't a student of mine. She wasn't a student at all as far as I know. She turned up at my place, brought by someone else, no idea who. Introduced herself. Apologised for her brother. Said he was a difficult character. She used to hang around after the others had left, waylay me on the way to work, that kind of thing. I realised she had a bit of a crush. It's a hazard of the job, nothing to do with one's personal qualities.'

'Really.' Even more sardonic. 'And?'

'I met her in the street one day. Got off my bike to walk

195

with her because she said she had something important to ask me. That's what it was.'

'Would you marry her?'

'Yes.' Dave didn't rise to the sceptical rudeness of Ryan's tone.

'Why? She was pregnant with triplets or what?'

Dave took some time to answer.

'Well, come on, Fowler.'

'She was pregnant, yes. The man had abandoned her. He was married. She couldn't tell her mother, who was an invalid. Or her brother, who she thought was rather disturbed.'

'And what did you do?'

'I said I couldn't marry her. I was opposed to marriage.'

'Ach Jesusmaryandjoseph—'

'But I would give her some money if she needed it, either to go away somewhere or—'

'Or what? A quick private abortion, that it?'

'I offered her money if she needed it. She looked at me as if she would like to kill me.'

'Well, it wouldn't seem much to the likes of you, would it?'

'As a matter of fact I am not in favour of abortion, on all kinds of grounds, religion not being one of them. The mental health of the mother for instance, afterwards. Certain women just can't handle it. Anyway, these problems arise all the time with students. I was not responsible for her. I assumed she had sorted it out. I was too busy to think of her. Yes, if you like, Mr Ryan, I'm an unmitigated shit. So are most men. So what.'

'Don't take that tone with me, my lad.'

Dave shook his head. He said, 'Do you think that this could have given Mark Leighton a reason to take revenge on me? It seems far-fetched. But he was disturbed. He wasn't normal. I assure you he wasn't. Where is he now?'

A heavy silence. Dave looked from Ryan to Bright. He addressed Bright for the first time: 'You met him, you know.'

'I met Mark Leighton? When?'

'At my place. You know the night you came with Kate and the girls – after the opening of *Hedda Gabler*?'

'A-ha.'

'The girls—' Dave's voice gave out. He gasped with pain. He controlled himself and said on a breath, 'The girls danced. We all stopped to watch. It was so beautiful.' Tears dropped down his face. He ignored them. 'He was – Mark was – standing next to you.'

Bright looked at Ryan and back to Dave. He remembered the young man. Enraged, ravaged at the notion of what the world could do to innocence. Their brief conversation. 'That was him?' he said.

'That was Mark.' Dave's tears had stopped. 'I hadn't seen him since his student days. He arrived with some other people. Just before you and Kate and—'

'A-ha.' Bright took the picture off the table and studied it. He shook his head. 'I can't see any resemblance.' Ryan handed him the portrait picture with the atmospheric shadows. Again Bright shook his head. 'He didn't look like this. I mean, I guess if you knew the guy you'd see it. But I damn well can't.'

Dave said, 'You met Margaret too.'

Bright and Ryan looked at him. There was a long pause.

Dave spoke to Bright: 'It was the night Lizzie came.'

'I was out of my skull.' Bright looked sick. 'I can't remember her.'

Dave said, 'I hadn't seen her for years. Not since—'

Bright thrust the pictures into Ryan's big fist. 'Ryan, I got to talk to you.'

Ryan managed to tangle his big foot with the leg of Dave's chair. The chair almost toppled and Dave with it.

Ryan walked on without looking back, slamming the door behind him.

Outside, Bright said, 'You've got enough circumstantial now. Mark Leighton is our perpetrator. We've got to find him. He's got to be brought in.'

'We'd better find the whereabouts of this Margaret.'

'Mark might have gone to her, you think?'

'No trace of him entering the Republic but you never know. Hasn't the mother got the address?'

'She says not. We couldn't get anything out of her.'

'Try again. Ireland's not that big. But it's a great place to hide.'

'Are we in touch with the Irish police?'

'They don't like to hand people over to the Garda, over there. They believe in a Higher Justice with its own rules.'

'He's motivated. He hasn't finished with these people yet. He's still got an agenda. To do with Dave. Maybe—' Bright hesitated. 'Maybe even to do with Kate Creech.'

Ryan folded his arms across his chest. It was hard for him: giving up Dave Fowler as his prime suspect. He glowered at the floor, then from under his eyebrows at Bright.

'I don't think he's left the country.' Bright waited.

Ryan said, 'The house-to-house in Totterdown gave us nothing.'

'We didn't have a picture then. We didn't know what we were looking for.'

Ryan's beefy hand rubbed over his rough hair, down over the big forehead, the boxer's nose, and covered his mouth. He growled.

Bright said, 'He knew we'd find this stuff. He's giving us the story—'

'Stop saying that.'

'Okay okay. Look. We've got the revenge angle, right? On Holt for his sister, now on Dave, also for his sister. But

'I'm telling you, this bloke is hung up on innocence. He's got this thing – You know, Ryan, that night when I talked to him? That night could have been it. You know. The time and the place when he flipped. When he decided to take Alison. Take both of them. Maybe it was just coincidence it was Alison first. It could have been Maisie first if it had worked out that way. Jesus, Ryan, I was there. And he knew I was a copper! How did he know that? He'd know that because of my connection with Kate. That case was in all the papers. All that Body in the Bath stuff. He's followed her career. Jesus, Ryan—'

'You not telling me he's going after Kate Creech next.'

'I've got to remember what he said to me that night. He didn't like the blokes looking at the little girls dancing. He was beside himself. We had this argument about innocence. He said they'd get – what was it – sucked in or something, something like that – sucked in, corrupted.' Bright stopped and met Ryan's eyes. For the first time the big man was listening. 'Christ, Ryan. He's killing little girls to stop them growing up?'

'To stop them getting corrupted like his sister.'

'Not just his sister, Ryan. Some upper class git seduced his mother when she was – ah Christ – fifteen.'

37

A Mother's Word

That afternoon posters were printed and placed in post offices, shops, bus shelters, railway stations. Mark Leighton's picture appeared on the front page of every newspaper, and on every television screen. In addition to that, a battalion of uniformed police distributed leaflets to every house in Totterdown, Windmill Hill and Bedminster.

All Mark's clients were questioned again. They hadn't seen him for a week or two. They were mostly vague about times. They liked him. They were fond of him. Most of them said he wouldn't hurt a soul. But nobody had seen him.

Bright said, 'Get the uniforms to report any house they couldn't gain entry to. Get them to explore every empty property. If they couldn't gain entry once, they go back again. Twice no entry, they gotta get in some other way.'

'And leave me to pick up the complaints?'

'You'll find a way, Ryan. Come to that, I'll find a way.'

'In the meantime I'm keeping my hands on Fowler. A suspect in the hand . . .'

'Margaret? I remember her!' Lizzie's face took on some life. 'She said she'd heard about me from Dave. She seemed like an old friend of his.'

'She didn't say anything about where she lived or – ?'

Lizzie shook her head. 'I can't remember! I mean, it was the first time I'd been to Dave's, and we were thinking about Alison and – ' She swallowed and her face settled back into grey fatigue. 'And how to get Maisie through it. I wasn't noticing much. I just thought – you know – another of his girls. Though she seemed different. Not his type. Brighter. Nicer. Dependable. Sort of good.'

'Where is your daughter, Miss Leighton?'

She held the bedcover up to her chin. Terrified.

'Miss Leighton?' Goldie's soft Bristol voice soothed the woman's terror. 'Listen, it's okay. It's nothing you've done. And nothing Margaret's done. She's not in trouble, honestly. But she might know something that can help us.'

'Help you?'

'Well, to find Mark.'

'What has Mark done?'

Goldie looked at Bright, helpless: What do we tell her?

Bright left the room, talked to the nurse on the landing. 'What sort of state is she in?'

'She's a nervous woman.'

'Yeah but how nervous? What's her medical condition? Is she gonna have a heart attack or a nervous breakdown if we give her bad news?'

'She's on tranquillising medication. Apart from that she's physically quite strong. It's just she can't walk. She seems to function fine otherwise.'

'So it's okay if I give her some bad news?'

'Is her son dead or something?'

' 'Fraid not. As far as we know.'

'Miss Leighton? You still haven't heard from Mark, right?'

'No.'

'And you don't know where he might be?'

She shook her head.

'And he hasn't done this before? Run off, left no address?'

She shook her head.

'Miss Leighton, we suspect that he is implicated in the death of Alison Holt.'

Her eyes round, she began to gasp. Goldie gave her water. She drank. She said, 'Oh oh oh oh,' on a rising scale.

Bright said, 'That's enough.'

Shocked, she stopped. Put a trembling hand to her mouth.

'Now listen. I said we suspect; we *don't know*. But he can only clear himself if he comes forward. We also suspect him of abducting another girl, Maisie Creech.'

The woman closed her eyes. Her head flopped back on the pillows. She moaned.

Bright said, 'Stop it. That won't help. We don't want this girl to die. She's fifteen years old.'

'Fifteen,' the woman whispered.

'That's right, Miss Leighton. The age you were when – '

'Yes.' A sigh like wind in grass.

'Is it possible that – '

She began to nod, hands over her mouth. 'Yes,' she said. 'Yes, yes. Oh yes.'

Goldie looked at Bright. Bright said, ' – that Mark might have – ?'

'Yes.'

'Why do you think this, Miss Leighton?'

'I can't say.'

'You know but you can't say?'

She nodded, rigid little nods like a bird.

'You know for certain he's done it?'

A sighing groan: 'No. No. But . . .'

'But what? Come on, Miss Leighton. Help us.'

Something seemed to stiffen in the woman. 'He cares too much.'

'About what happened to his sister?'

Again she gripped the bedcover and pulled it up to her chin. She didn't speak.

'Would his sister be harbouring him, Miss Leighton? That's the thing. If he went to her would she take him in?'

She blinked. This seemed to mean assent.

'Are you sure you don't know where she is? Are you sure you do not have an address for her? Are you sure?'

Minute nods of the head.

'If you are lying, Miss Leighton, you will be prosecuted. I know it's hard. I know you want to protect your child. Your children. That's natural. But another child is in imminent danger of losing her life. Her life. Not her virginity. Or her innocence as your Mark would call it. Her life. At fifteen years of age. If you know, you've got to tell us. Where is Margaret?'

'Lost,' she said. 'Gone. A long time ago.

'And no address? You're sure?'

She shook her head steadily from side to side. 'My fault. I favoured Mark. Margaret went away.'

'If either of them gets in touch with you, you will get in touch with us. Right away. And get an address before they hang up. If you can. Do you understand?'

'Yes.'

'Do you agree? Do you promise me?'

'He won't. He won't get in touch.'

'Stay with her. The IO's sending reinforcements. They'll search the house. Don't let them frighten her. You search this room yourself. Keep the nurse with you as witness. I gotta go.'

38

Excerpt from a Diary

viii

It's rather wonderful to be free of mother at last. Margaret has been free for a long time. But I have not until now. It's as though Alison was my payment to mother. Her death has freed me from my obligations. I don't like to think that Alison's life was some kind of payment to mother. But maybe in some sense it was? It is mother who has always stressed the primacy of innocence. The wanton destruction of a young girl's innocence the Great Offence. *'T'were better a millstone* and all that. And she herself the living example. Always in my sight. But now I have actually lived out my duty, I am at last autonomous. At last I can act alone. For my own ideals. For my own beliefs. Ironic, isn't it? At last, I say. And it is truly at last. I don't think I've got long.

If I were not prepared to give my own life, it would not be fair to have taken someone else's. It would not be right. The only way I could justify it would be if I were to continue my crusade. I would have to be alive, I think you would agree, to do that.

It is the suitability, the perfection almost, of these two deaths, that makes them so unutterably satisfactory. Each of their fathers had ruined the innocence of those younger and purer than themselves. Neither of these fathers deserved his daughter. I do not take the lives of the girls for this reason, naturally. But it satisfies me beyond all wonder that the preserving of these two innocent souls for eternity should punish their guilty fathers their whole livelong lives.

Their mothers? Strange how I barely think of their mothers. Well, their mothers should have taken better care of them. Lock Up Your Daughters. Lock them up. You don't deserve them otherwise.

Maisie is proving not quite such a delightful companion as I had hoped. She refuses to speak to me. I have been unfailingly pleasant to her. I have made it clear that I like her very much. Admire her. Respect her. As soon as she was ensconced in the Dead Room, I removed her gag. I expected the torrent of incoherent words I had got from Alison, begging, pleading, appealing to my better nature, appealing to my worse nature. Yes, Alison even offered herself carnally to me. But in such an innocent simple way, poor child, it only increased her innocence in my eyes. It naturally did not help her cause.

But Maisie remains silent. She looks at me with a cold gaze. She does not answer me when I speak. I do not know if this is fear disguised, or simple loathing. It looks like bitter cold hatred and could hurt me badly if I allowed it to penetrate. I smile and make it clear that I am waiting, that's all.

I feel stupid now for not understanding right away. It came to me last night. I had taken in her food. A deliciously tempting little salad: avocado, cherry tomatoes, green pepper, spring onions – my version of guacamole, very pretty. It always tempted mother. Maisie said nothing. She never took her eyes off me. 'How are you feeling, Maisie? Is there anything I can get for you to make you more comfortable? A book to read perhaps? I have some books.' I listed a few of my authors. She watched me. My voice was thin. I began to think she couldn't hear me. I explained about the Dead Room. She watched me coldly while I did so. I must say my heart began to fail me. As did my voice after a while. 'You see, Maisie,' I said, 'I can't allow you to be heard, shouting or making noise of any kind. You understand, I'm sure.'

Of course when I left the room, shutting the second door behind me, it came to me, the reason for her hostility: Alison! She knows me to be responsible for the death of her friend. Which in a sense I am. But only in a sense. Alison was brought kindly and skilfully to acquiesce in her own death. As I hope will Maisie be. But I can see Maisie is a more difficult task. A tougher character. She doesn't look it, with her butterfly-frail appearance. But she has great strength. You must be proud of her.

She ate the salad. But not till I left her alone. As I discovered this morning when I took in her breakfast. She has a hearty appetite, by the way, doesn't she? I kept her company a while. I don't always like to be alone. I sat and wrote my diary in her presence. I wanted her to ask, What are you writing? or Are you a writer? or Are you writing about me? To show some interest. But she did not. She ate

205

her breakfast, as best she could with her wrists bound together, licked the spoon, and threw it into the dish. A thin clatter it makes in this acoustic. So strange. For a moment I saw in her eyes a hint of vulnerability. The loss of sound is a strangely disorientating thing. She will eventually speak to me.

This afternoon the police came visiting. Again. I went into the Dead Room with Maisie. She had not heard the knocking of course. I must make sure from now on that no lights are to be seen at night. The nights are still light till quite late and will be for some weeks yet. I shall shut myself in here after dark. With Maisie. The police must not be allowed to interfere with the inevitable course of events. I have enough food in the freezer and in my storage jars to last for months. Perhaps from now on it would be safer if I did not go out at all. Though I would miss the newspapers. The police must surely have found the trail.

They have pictures now.

I broke off there because Maisie began to perform the most extraordinary series of physical exercises, as best she can with bound ankles and wrists: back bends and somersaults and press-ups. A rather intimidating exhibition. As perhaps it was meant to be. After a while I realised it was a good idea: if we can't go out, we can still keep fit. I joined in. Maisie stopped. I felt rather dispirited, explained that I had to sleep in there with her and switched off the light.

In the middle of the night I was woken by an odd sound, small, muffled but unmistakable: crying. I listened for some time. I wanted very much to go to her and offer comfort. But I knew this would not be welcome. I pretended to sleep until she slept again. It is slightly gratifying to discover that she is at least human, to find out at least that her hard impenetrable demeanour is a front. That inside she is frightened, lonely and distressed. I was beginning to wonder. She has remarkable will. But the carapace will crack. It won't take long.

It cracked this morning, I thought: she thanked me for her breakfast! Speech at last! I was touched. I realised immediately however that she has a strategy. She is carrying out a plan. But of course I must respond as if I don't know that. She said, 'You know my Aunt Kate, then.'

I thought for a second. 'Only from her work,' I said. 'Which I admire very much.'

'Wouldn't you like to meet her?'

Good heavens, this child is patronising me. She sees me as a freak. Some kind of pathetic anorak. To be bought off by a promised meeting with the great Kate Creech. Oh no. We can't have this. 'As an exponent of her craft,' I said, 'she interests me, as I said. As a person I have no curiosity about her at all. Those artists whose work we admire never live up to our expectations in real life.'

'Aunt Kate' (her Bristol accent makes it sound like Ankate – very sweet) 'Ankate would live up to them,' she said. 'She's really straight.'

'I should have expected no less of her,' I replied. I smiled at Maisie.

'It'll kill her if anything happens to me,' she said. 'She'll definitely think it's her fault.'

'Why should she think that?'

'She thinks everything's her fault. Her brother died when he was about my age. I think that's why.'

'Subtle psychology, Maisie, for one so young.'

'Don't patronise me,' she said. 'You sick git.'

That's what she said. I couldn't believe it. In this little tiny voice etiolated by the dead acoustic: 'You sick git.' I was amused. So much so I had to leave the room.

'*You sick git.*' Am I? Sick?

Many people would think so. Of course. I don't think so. Of course. Well, I wouldn't, would I? I think the world is sick. So sick I don't want to live in it. And I don't want perfect creatures like Alison and Maisie to live in it. I suddenly find myself moved and shaking. I will not let Maisie live in this sick world. And if she thinks that's sick, then, tough. '*You sick git.*' I did laugh.

Ruminations in the morning. Have they made the Margaret connection yet? Mother would never tell them where Margaret is. Even if she knew. And she hasn't known for years. Amazing how Margaret got free. Free of mother. Of course mother wanted Margaret to be free. I was the one she wanted to enslave. Margaret will always come to my aid. No matter how sick she thinks I am. I can always call on her. She got free of mother. But not free of me.

Sorry, this has become rather introspective. It's a stressful time. Maisie is throwing up questions Alison didn't. Please believe me: I want to do the best for everyone. For everyone who matters, that is. You. Maisie. Margaret. There isn't anyone else.

39

Exploring a Character

In rehearsal Kate was surfing the stratosphere, flying on automatic. Rehearsing full of anxiety and grief was like performing when exhausted: inspirational, all the nerve ends exposed, ready to catch any idea on the wing. She said, 'Colum, Rosalind comes alive when she falls in love. She's released.'

Colum said, 'Yes, that's the transition. How do we create a moment for it? Something the audience will immediately grasp.'

They tried this, they tried that. Nothing quite worked. Then like a sleepwalker she walked alone on to the set, marked out with tape on the rehearsal room floor. She walked around the marked-out wrestling ring, empty now, the wrestling match over and Orlando gone. She looked at the imaginary wrestling ring. A stool in the professional wrestler's corner. A stool in Orlando's corner. Orlando's towel still there on the floor, hanging over the imaginary rope. She suddenly climbed into the ring, miming the ropes. She went to Orlando's corner. She took his towel in her hands. She looked at it. Then she closed her eyes and brought the towel slowly to her face. The watching actors made a collective sound, a kind of sigh.

Colum said, 'That's it.'

She came back to herself. Rupert's gaze was fixed on her. She returned a long slow look. Then she smiled. She said, 'Yes but Orlando doesn't *know* I feel like that. That's the hard thing in this play, Colum. Remembering how much you don't know.'

At this moment she reached out her hand to Rupert's face, took his baseball cap and, pushing her hair up inside it, put it on her head. She said, 'Could Orlando leave his cap behind in the wrestling ring? That's what she does! Takes his cap! That's why she's determined to be the boy when they run away to the forest. She wants to be Orlando! It's a talisman.'

She couldn't stop talking. She couldn't stop discovering. It was terror transformed into creativity. If she hadn't been taking Lizzie's Mogadon at night she would never have slept. She was motoring on high octane fuel.

That evening Bright told her and Lizzie what he had found out. About Mark Leighton and his connection to Alison's father and to Dave. And about his sister. 'His sister?' Kate marvelled.

Lizzie said, 'She left at the same time as you.'

'Left where?'

'Dave's.'

Kate stared at Bright: 'That was her? That night? Margaret? Margaret is his sister?'

'You remember her?'

'Don't you?'

'Three of Renato's grappas. I was out of my box.'

'You talked to her. You asked her questions.'

'Did I?'

'She left with us.'

'Did she?'

Kate said, 'I walked all the way back here with her.'

'Here?'

'Well, up to the top of the steps, down at the junction of Richmond Street and . . .?'

Lizzie said, 'Pylle Hill Crescent.'

'Yes? She said she lived down there.'

'Which house?'

'I didn't ask. I wasn't interested. I didn't look where she went. I said goodnight and walked on up here. I think she went off along the crescent but she could have gone back down the steps.' Kate's eyes were wild.

Bright grabbed her by the upper arms. He kissed her on the mouth then on each cheek.

She said, 'It might not be true.'

'Why would she lie to you?'

'If she's protecting him. Giving him sanctuary. Covering for him.'

'Why would she do that?'

'I'd do that for my brother.'

210

Lizzie said, 'Typical. Disgusting. Romantic rubbish.'

Bright said, 'If he'd killed a fifteen-year-old girl? Abducted Maisie?'

Kate said, 'I'd have a problem.'

Bright looked at her in a funny way. Then he phoned Ryan and told him Kate's story. He said, 'Talk to the IO. Not tomorrow, Ryan; now! Every house. I don't care how late it is. Tomorrow it could be too damn late . . . Right.' He shut down his phone. 'I just heard what I said. About tomorrow – I only said it – '

Lizzie said, 'I agree with you. Can we go? Now?'

'Lizzie. This might not be a good idea.'

'We're four more people.'

Sarah shook her head. 'Not me. I couldn't.'

'Okay, three more.'

Kate stood up. 'Let's do it, John. Otherwise we just sit here and wait. It's intolerable. And we know what she looks like. The police don't.'

House after house in Pylle Hill Crescent. Nobody knew Margaret. They held a discussion at the top of the steps. Lizzie said, 'If you go down the steps a bit the next crescent down is St Luke's.' Irate residents, disturbed watching the telly, became sympathetic on hearing what it was about. They tried every front door in St Luke's Crescent, every basement entrance. Not every house had a basement, because of the extraordinary slope of the street. Kate knocked at a blue front door, no basement. There was no reply. She knocked louder, though the windows were dark. She caught a glimpse at the window blind of the slightest of movements. She knocked again. She was what she called white-tired, wiped out, the ground rocking under her feet. She waited. At last the door opened. Margaret stood there.

It was a strange flat. Not what Kate would have expected.

Slightly bare. A stripped wood floor. Grey walls. Mattress-ticking curtains and a black sofa. All monochrome. Like existing inside a black and white photograph. It was just one room, knocked through, with the kitchen at the back and the bathroom next to it. They were cramped, all squeezed in there. Bright had been on the mobile. Now he said, 'Where do you sleep?'

Margaret pointed at the black sofa. 'It's a sofa bed.'

'A-ha.' He looked at the garden. Rather good expensive paving that looked like York stone, wall to wall. A few big pots with yukkas and other spiky exotic plants. No flowers. In the dark, the light from the kitchen window rendered the garden monochrome too. Like a photographic negative. 'Low maintenance,' Bright said.

'I'm away a lot.'

'Ireland, right?'

She nodded.

'Write your address there, would you?' He handed her a small notebook. She wrote and handed it back. 'Beara?' he said, not sure of the pronunciation.

'It's a remote place. Not everyone in Ireland knows it. Here it's hardly known at all.'

'Is that where your brother is?'

'I haven't been there myself for a year. I sold up and came back here.'

'Why?'

'It wasn't working out. The person who helped me. Well – she left. So I became too tied to the place. I couldn't leave it to come and see my brother any more.'

'Your mother said she hadn't seen you for years.'

'A year at least.'

'You came back here but you didn't see your mother.'

'I do not get on with my mother, we are not compatible. She has always tried to annihilate me.'

'That's heavy stuff.'

212

'Yes.'

Lizzie said, 'Haven't you seen him? Your brother. Don't you know where he is?'

Margaret looked at her. She shook her head. Her frank straightforward face expressed compassion. 'You're Maisie's mother,' she said. 'I saw the posters today. And the local paper.' She indicated the *Bristol Evening Post* folded at Mark's picture.

'Did you know before that it was him?'

'I don't think even now that it is him.'

'Dave Fowler told us you thought Mark was disturbed.'

'Then. Yes. Because he was doing badly on his literature course. But I believe he's better now. He loves his job. He's good at it. He helps the helpless, you know.'

'So do you,' Kate said.

Margaret looked taken aback. 'How?'

'The donkey sanctuary.'

'Oh that. Yes. But animals are easy. To help people is harder, don't you think?'

Bright said, 'Mark has done a runner. He is lying low. Has he ever done that before?'

Margaret seriously thought. 'No. He has never done that before. He has always been there to look after mother. Who is doing that now, by the way?'

'A social services nurse. Will you do it, now you know?'

Margaret shook her head. 'No. She would find some way to blame me. My presence does not improve her quality of life.'

'Will Mark get in touch with you?'

'I hope not.'

'You hope not?'

'Because then this will become my responsibility. I can't face giving him up. Not yet. I wish I could.'

'So if he does contact you, we can't depend on you to let us know.'

213

'I don't know.'

Kate thought Lizzie was going to leap on the girl and shake the life out of her. 'John? I think we should go.'

Bright nodded. Kate steered Lizzie out. As they passed her, Margaret said to Kate, 'I'm ashamed to be the cause of such distress. But I love my brother as she loves – well . . .'

As Kate steered Lizzie down the path a girl leaped out of a car and ran towards them. She was blonde and young and a little plump. She stopped in their path. They all moved left then right then left. 'I'm sorry. I'm looking for DI John Bright?'

Kate indicated the front door. 'In there.'

The girl ran past them.

'Who's she?' Lizzie still spoke through clenched teeth.

'A policeman, I think.'

'This is my colleague, WPC Goldie. Helen, this is Margaret. She's Mark Leighton's sister.'

'You're his sister? Oh.' She asked no questions. Great restraint. Just one amazed glance at Bright, then her eyes wandered over Margaret and around the strangely colourless flat.

'Ms Leighton is going to let us look round. That's right. isn't it, Margaret?'

'Oh yes. Please. Whatever. Of course.'

Bright opened the kitchen cupboards one by one. Margaret sat, tucking her cotton skirt under her knees, and watched.

He went into the bathroom and tapped the panel that boxed in the bath. Opposite the bathroom door a pair of light louvre doors. Bright opened the louvre doors. The corridor of the flat had been partitioned off. It now formed a deep walk-in closet back here to hang clothes, store suitcases, vacuum cleaner, ironing board, the usual domestic junk, neatly stowed. He came back in and stood in front of Margaret. 'Come with me,' he said. She obediently stood. He led her into the little lobby between kitchen and bathroom. They stood looking into the long narrow cupboard. 'Good idea,' he said, 'doing that with the corridor. Will you empty it out for us, please, Margaret?'

Margaret looked dismayed.

'Sorry, but I can't get any sense of the size, what with the hanging rail and everything. Just want to get a proper look. You don't mind, do you?'

'Will you help me?'

'Sure. So will Helen. Won't you, Helen?'

The three of them toiled. Margaret discovered a tennis racket she had forgotten. And a box of audio cassettes. And a box of clothes belonging to her brother. 'We'll take this, if you don't mind. Helen will get you to sign a chit. All right?'

'They're just his old clothes. I was going to give them to Oxfam.'

'Well, we can do that for you. After we've finished with them.'

'Why do you want them?'

'Heard of DNA?'

'Oh. I see.'

'Up to now, see, we've only had circumstantial evidence to connect him to Alison. If these clothes had traces of her—'

'Oh, they couldn't. I took them to Ireland with me by mistake. Years ago. And again when I came back they just got packed up with the rest of my stuff. I meant to throw them away. It really isn't worth your while taking them.'

'Just sign there, okay?'

'Sorry. Of course. You have to do your job.' Margaret took the chit. Bright handed her a pen. She finished signing and said, 'You still think I might be harbouring him?'

'What do you think?'

'I have never been involved in a police investigation of any kind. I don't know how you work.' Her voice, which was deep and melodious, quavered a little.

'Well, I don't know either, Ms Leighton. We'll probably discover the answer to that as we go along. But now that I've found you I'm reluctant to let you go, know what I mean?'

Helen watched him half amused, half really scared. There was something slightly manic about him. Under his dead calm exterior, she felt he wanted to tear the place apart with his bare hands.

'Okay then.' He spoke to Margaret very pleasantly. 'We're off. Sorry to leave you with this mess.'

'I expect the police often leave messes behind for civilians to clean up.' Margaret gave a sad smile which took the edge off this remark.

Outside by Helen's car Bright said, 'What did you think?'

'There was nothing in that walk-in cupboard,' she said. 'There was nothing anywhere.'

'How did that flat make you feel?'

'A bit weird, wasn't it? Sort of – colourless like?'

'A-ha. Nothing else?'

'Sort of – empty. No heart.'

'A-ha?'

She tried hard. Knew he wanted something to inspire him, something that would rip a hole in the curtain that hid Mark Leighton from him. But she couldn't think of anything. 'That Margaret seems . . . Well, I dunno. Well, she's quite like him in a way. But, like, he's all clever and sort of showing off and, I dunno – gleeful? But she's sort of – like, good, isn't she? Sincere.'

'You don't think she's lying then?'

'Well . . . no.'

'Okay. Good girl. Get off home. See you in the morning.'

She was going to suggest a drink, but he patted her arm, shut her car door on her, and went off up the street. Not even a backward glance.

Lizzie was in the armchair, head back, snoring. It was the first time she had slept since Maisie had gone. Impressed, Bright whispered, 'What did you do?'

Kate silently shut the door and led him to the kitchen. She held up an empty scotch bottle: 'Two large ones. She'll be awake in three hours I should think. I'll be up, keeping her company while she hates me in spades.'

'What did you think back there?'

'Curious person, isn't she, that Margaret?'

'How?'

'So calm. So nice. And what Lizzie said: somehow good. Only – '

'A-ha? Only what?'

'Well, I think the psychiatrists would call it loss of affect.'

'What's that when it's at home?'

'Are you playing ignorant copper?'

'It's Yank-speak. Don't know if I know what it means.'

'Well – lack of – reaction, emotion, the ability to be affected by things, I suppose. Too calm. Too cool. Like you could stick a pin in her and though she might feel it she wouldn't cry out.'

'And what does that mean?'

'I don't know.'

'Fat lot of help you are.'

'Thanks.'

They were lodged between the kitchen table and the stove. He crashed his body at her like a missile. They clung together. Their mouths roamed searching: eyes, ears, neck, cheeks, then mouth to mouth, mutual resuscitation. They tore at clothes fumbling, trembling. They began standing,

Kate back to the kitchen table, Bright back to the cooker, and ended on the scarlet linoleum floor. A grim ecstatic coupling, silent in case Lizzie should hear and be scandalised. They stared afterwards with horror and friendship into each other's eyes. He said, 'I thought it would never happen.' She said, 'So did I.' He closed his eyes and placed his hot brow on hers. She said, 'We can't go on lying here under Lizzie's kitchen table.' He said, 'Why not?' Kate kissed him and sat up. 'She hates me enough already.' When Lizzie did open the kitchen door they were making decaf as though nothing had occurred.

40

Excerpt from a Diary

ix

Well, it happened. They came here and they did not discover the Dead Room. I am amazed and know not what to say. Isn't it incredible? Even that little cross-eyed London policeman. His eyes are like screwdrivers. I remember thinking that night at Mr Wonderful's place, his eyes could screw secrets out of the sphinx. He's the first real test this place has had. It passed with flying colours. Good old Margaret. Her open candid face, her calmness and goodness. They work every time. I owe everything to her. It was meant to be the other way around. I was meant to be the one who fought the battles, stood up for the so-called weaker sex. Well, over the years, I guess we have complemented each other. Sometimes she has defended me. Sometimes I have defended her.

I debated whether to tell Maisie they had been here – her mother, her 'Ankate', her friend the policeman. I decided to keep it for a future occasion when she has really annoyed me. I don't like to think of her in this antagonistic way, but she really is recalcitrant. I would like to shake her sometimes. I do not, I have to admit, like her thinking me 'sick'. It causes me a curious shaking anger in the pit of my stomach. I have several times had to leave the room, afraid of what I might do.

This seems crazy, I know, when my whole aim is that Maisie should die. But I do not want my motives to be mixed. I want this to be a perfect act: a pure end to a pure life. I must summon all my resources of patience and logic to bring her to an understanding and appreciation of my motives. My aims.

This resolve was good, it appears. She asked me at lunchtime if she could have pen and paper. 'With what in mind?' I asked.

'Writing actually,' she replied. Then she smiled, for the first time since I brought her here. She has a wonderful childlike smile. This took the edge off her sarcasm and pleased me. 'Writing what?' I said patiently.

'My experiences here. My thoughts.'

'I am here. You can speak your thoughts.'

'You're going to kill me. I want to leave a record. I got the idea from you. Writing in your diary every day. We can compare notes if you like.'

'How do you know I'm going to kill you?'

'You killed Alison.'

'Alison died voluntarily.'

'I don't believe you.'

'I can't prove it. But there wasn't a mark on her, was there?'

'Alison never would. She wanted to have six kids. She loved her mum and dad. She loved her little brothers. She never would.'

'You don't have to believe me.' I shrugged.

'It must've been because you sapped her will. It must've. You must've made her believe – You must have given her drugs or something – ' She stopped herself saying more. She changed her tone. She said, 'Okay then. You explain it to me.'

She was humouring me, the sweet child. I decided to indulge her. 'You see, Maisie, you and Alison possess something precious, the most precious thing there is. Do you know what it is? No, you don't. It is innocence.' I waited. Maisie screwed up her eyes and looked at me as though from a great distance. She didn't reply. 'Yes,' I said, 'it is a rare quality these days, rarer and rarer. The world, you see, is corrupt. Most of the people in it have become degraded, compromised, before they are even old enough to know what has happened to them. Somehow you and Alison managed to escape that. But you were both on the brink, on the cusp. You were both ripe for the—' I heard myself and stopped. I was in danger myself of corrupting the mind of the child. What was I thinking of?

'On the cusp of what? Not being virgins any more? Is that what you mean?' Maisie waited and watched me to see how I would take this.

I was shocked, I admit. But quickly apprehended what she was trying to do. I smiled. 'You are trying to shock me, Maisie.'

'I'm not. That's what you mean, isn't it? How would the human race go on if people didn't lose their virginity? Are you a virgin? Is that your problem? You can't lose yours so you don't want anyone else to lose theirs, that what it is? I tell you what. I'd rather lose my virginity than lose my life, if that's the choice I've got. And Alison would say the same. I know.'

This child came out with this stuff. Her innocent sweet mouth spat forth this worldly claptrap. The hackneyed

220

nature of her thoughts only served to reveal her true innocence. 'You know not of what you speak,' I said. 'You have
not experienced such a choice.'

'You don't have to experience everything to know about
it,' she averred.

'Oh yes,' I corrected her, 'you do.'

'You don't!' she said. 'My Ankate – '

Ah, she is going to quote her other guru. I waited with
bored expression and bated breath.

'My Ankate says that we have all experienced everything
by the age of five. You can't learn anything more, you can
only remember. And imagine.' She saw my bored expression and her voice faltered a little: 'Well, that's what she
says. I wouldn't know, myself. Not yet.'

'In this field,' I replied, 'you can only speak for yourself.'

'You're not giving me any choice,' she says, changing
tack. 'Do you think that's right?'

'But I am! That's what you're going to understand. I am
going to convince you that it is better to lose your life than
lose your precious innocence. You see, I am not talking just
about physical integrity but moral integrity. Moral simplic-
ity. Innocence of mind. I talk in this way because I think
you are able to understand.'

At this point Maisie gave me a look. You know those
looks. She knew I was talking up to her in order to talk
down to her. She is unusually subtle, isn't she? A worthy
opponent.

By this time I had talked so much I had strained my
voice. The effect of the Dead Room. When you can't hear
your voice you start to think you are not there. You can't
hear yourself breathing either. The sense of one's own presence is literally vital. You know this. I know this. Before, I
have seen its effect. This time I was experiencing it for
myself. I admit to a sense of panic.

The Dead Room acoustic, or lack of acoustic rather,

221

contributed greatly to Alison's desire for death. I know she became disorientated. She became terrified. And when I explained that she could choose either to stay with me for ever in there, or to die, she did not hesitate long.

Maisie has raised a doubt in me. I have to admit. I get out of the Dead Room, I come and go as I please. But to be in there continuously day and night is the worst kind of sensory deprivation. Not to hear your own breath, is to experience a kind of death. With Alison this did not seem unfair. My sense of mission, my knowledge of the path awaiting her, were stronger than – Oh, I see what is happening here: Maisie is seducing me. She is bringing me round to her point of view, I am seeing through her eyes. Clever child. She is also aware of the effect of talking in the Dead Room. She is talking little to make me talk too much. I see! It won't work. She may have to be dispatched more quickly than Alison and possibly even without her consent. I must be on my guard.

You have a wonderful niece. When she is gone you will appreciate her more, not less. She will remain as you know her now. Perfect. Unsullied. Pure. That's better than seeing her grow up, grow away from you, turn into the usual ambitious tart, making the right career moves, being taken by this man, then that, then possibly having children, growing older and plainer and sadder while her man goes off plying other young girls with his attentions and she sinks into grey middle age. Is that what you want for her? Well, that's what you'll get if she lives. That's life. And that's why I am intervening in her life's inevitable course. And nobody will talk me out of that.

I must stop for tonight. It has been a nerve-racking day. Resolution: I must not talk so much. Confine my thoughts to these pages, don't waste my energy on Maisie. Let things take their course.

*

Next Day.

I took off the night-gag and Maisie screamed. Her mouth opened, she screwed up her eyes, but I heard no sound. She closed her mouth, looked at me cheekily and started to eat her breakfast.

When I recovered from the shock I saw she was playing a joke on me. A bitter joke about the effect of the Dead Room. She was also letting me know she was not going to waste her breath on me. Her voice on me. I smiled at her. She smiled back, like a little cat. She licked her spoon and put it in the cereal bowl. She sat back and stared at me. I looked away first. I pretended I found her defiance tedious, beneath my consideration. She knew that was not the case.

When I came out into the outer room I was shaken. I know the difference here. Alison did not take me seriously. She did not believe I would actually take her life, or keep her for ever. To convince her, I told her about her father. What he had done to Mark. And to Margaret. I allowed my hatred of her father to show. To interfere with my pure motives. I told her I had kidnapped her to blackmail her father. I told her he had refused to pay the ransom. I now believe this was the reason Alison cooperated in her own death. She despaired. At the time I felt this was another sin on the head of her father. But no. I refused to admit it at the time, but it was my fault for not telling her the truth. I will not make this mistake with Maisie.

But Maisie knows that Alison died. She knows from the start it's serious. She is ready for me. She is a match for me. I have met my match. These everyday expressions. Match can mean opponent, or mate. A perfect match. A match made in heaven.

41

Going Behind their Backs

'You got me out in the middle of my dinner to toil up and down that feckin' hill. For what? The sister's place is clean. And she's a nice young woman. She said she wouldn't give him up, but believe me, after I talked to her she saw that there was no other way. That it's for his own good. If he gets in touch with her now she'll let us know all right. Believe me, she will.'

Bright stood silent. Ryan looked at him: 'What's up with you?'

'Meaning what?'

'You're not arguing with me.'

'Oh. Right. Yeah. No. A-ha. That's right.'

'Are you quite well?'

'I'm not sure, Ryan. Ask me when I've got my hands on Mark Leighton. Ask me when I've got Maisie back unharmed. I'll tell you then.'

But Rosalind's joy filled Kate like helium. So much joy, so much delight, so much fear, so much excitement, and so much incomparable language to express it: O *wonderful, wonderful, and yet more wonderful, and after that, out of all whooping!*

After one of the mock-love-mock-quarrel scenes Kate took off the baseball cap and threw it in the air, terrifying Celia. Her mass of hair fell loose and she felt freedom, experienced her womanhood, longed to be able to show herself to Orlando as she really was. Then rehearsals stopped for lunch.

Rupert sat with her. He was getting braver, like a bird she

224

was taming. She felt the tenderness for him that she would feel for such a creature. He asked her how things were. She told him about the visit to Margaret. He said, 'You must go to see her again.'

'You think?'

'It's the only way to find out anything. What else have you got?'

She looked at him with narrowed eyes. She'd thought him too beautiful and too young to be this sharp, this direct in his thinking. Blinded by his extreme beauty and his youth she hadn't expected a mind at all.

Sandy came in at teatime to discuss costume. Today Rupert was wearing long loose shorts, a loose sweat shirt and Birkenstock sandals. Kate said, 'I want your clothes. I want all your clothes.'

Rupert looked horrified. 'You want me to strip off now?'

She went on without even a smile. 'Jeans is no good because men and women both wear jeans and it's always quite clear which gender is which.'

Rupert nodded, serious. 'It's the bum that gives it away.'

Kate flicked him a look.

Sandy said, 'Trouble is now males and females dress so much alike.'

'In Shakespeare's day, put a bloke in a farthingale, or a girl in doublet and hose, and *voilà*!' Colum clicked his fingers. 'They'd changed gender!'

'That's an idea,' Sandy groaned. 'Let's do it in Elizabethan dress!'

'Now now, Sandy, you can do it, don't despair.'

Kate hovered light as a feather midway up the steep stone steps. The evening light laid gold over the park far below and long shadows over the streets. She could go up and see Lizzie, not a cheerful thought, or trot down St Luke's Crescent and try Margaret Leighton's door.

225

No one answered her knock. She waited. She was curiously tired, empty, weightless, separated from herself by events. Unable to think a coherent thought but open to impressions, the slightest pressure on mind or body would leave a bruise, a tender place. The copper-coloured sun clasped her in heat, blinded her. She sat on the low wall and closed her eyes. When she opened them, turned away from the sun, Margaret was climbing the slope of the crescent with a plastic carrier.

Kate stayed where she was. She thought Margaret hesitated a second, seeing her, but then she shaded her eyes with her *Bristol Evening Post* and walked up faster, smiling. 'I thought you might be what they call a police presence.'

'No. Just me.'

'You seem tired.'

'Yes.' The young woman's sympathy might dislodge Kate's fragile control. 'Cup of tea might help. Just couldn't face the rest of the steps just yet.'

'You walked from the theatre?'

'Yes. A breath of air after the day. And before hearing there's no news. And walking, there's more chance of seeing – Well, you feel there is.'

Margaret nodded, sympathy not overdone. She got out her key and Kate followed her inside. The room was cool, airy from an open window on to the terrace at the back. 'Nice to have that,' Kate said.

'Yes, except it faces north-east. Hopeless for growing things, or sitting in the sun.'

'Some of the houses down here have basements and some don't,' Kate said.

'That's right. They all have cellars though.'

'Oh?'

'Yes. And because the ground slopes up so steeply at the back, some of the back yards are very deep down. Those ones have buildings in the yard behind the house.'

226

'But you don't.'

'No.' Margaret shuddered. 'Those buildings are very gloomy and sinister, like air raid shelters or something. Mostly full of rotting rubbish, and, I suspect, rats. No. This was just dusty earth. I paved it for easy maintenance. I'm no gardener. How do you take your tea?'

The front room was held in a shaft of copper light. Margaret cleared some papers off a chair. 'My pathetic efforts.'

'How are you getting on?'

'Well, I may be getting somewhere. Who knows?' She studied Kate as she sat. 'No news then. Of Maisie.'

Kate shook her head. 'Margaret. I've come here to plead with you really. I don't know what else to do. Or where else to turn. If you have any idea where your brother is. Where he might have gone. Where he might have taken – I know you don't think he did. But I know you thought he was unbalanced once, and maybe he has become unbalanced again. It can happen—'

Margaret stopped her, a cool hand on her wrist. 'If I knew, I hope I would tell you.'

'Margaret, that's not enough. I had a brother. He died young. I'd have done anything for him. So I know it's not easy. I know the struggle between loyalty to someone you love and doing the right thing for – well – society, I suppose, I know that's the toughest choice there is, probably.' Kate found herself in tears. 'I only loved two people that much. Liam and Maisie. I'm sorry—'

Margaret handed her a box of tissues and watched her as she mopped up. Her gaze was more detached than sympathetic now. Kate felt she'd blown it. 'I didn't mean to do this. I came here to plead with you but not to use emotional blackmail.'

Margaret said, 'It's not that. I have a plan, you see.'

'A plan?'

227

'I know that Mark will get in touch with me. When he does – assuming it is not too late to save Maisie's life – I will try to persuade him to give her up. To give her back. I will probably be able to persuade him. I have always been able to in the past.'

'But this time he has gone where you can't find him. Perhaps because he knows that and is determined that you won't persuade him.'

'Well, if that is the case, I can't help, can I?'

'No.'

'Persuading him myself will be easier than handing him over.'

'You'd let him get away to do this again?'

Margaret turned her head away. Kate waited. Margaret stood up. She came towards Kate. She spoke quietly, keeping her voice under control. 'He won't live after doing this.'

Kate could barely speak: 'What do you mean?'

'I know him. These acts. Alison's death and now abducting Maisie. These are extreme acts. The acts of a person *in extremis*. Aren't they? I know Mark. If they are his acts. If he is responsible. If he has done these things, he won't want to live afterwards. He is a good person. I know it seems strange to say that. But he does not have a sanguine view of the world.'

'We love Maisie. Lizzie, and Dave. And I. We love her. She has a life to live. It's nobody's right to take that life.'

'I feel like that about my brother.'

'Nobody is threatening his life. Except himself, if you're right.'

'They would lock him up and he would never know freedom again.'

'He must know he is taking that risk.'

They were sparring now. Kate had not intended this; only to appeal to Margaret's better nature, and also to the True

228

Fan in her, calling in a debt. The True Fan seemed curiously to have died in the fight for her brother.

'You all talk as though you're sure it's Mark. But you can't be. It could just as easily be Dave Fowler. Mr Wonderful, as Mark calls him. Or any of the people who hang out with Dave.'

'Yes.' Kate decided to agree with her, not get her back up any further. 'I seem to have blown this. Thanks for the tea.' She got up.

'No. You haven't blown it. You have shown me something. Something I hadn't imagined. Our imaginations are weak when it comes to other people's – feelings, point of view. I've been so concerned for my brother – I was even shocked last night to see Maisie's mother, to see face to face how she is feeling.'

'If only your brother could see it.'

'I don't believe my brother would avoidably cause an innocent person to suffer.'

'I'm so sorry if I've offended you.'

'No.' Margaret covered her face for a moment. When she took her hand away she had calmed down. 'Actually I'm honoured to have you here. In other circumstances I'd be over the moon.'

Kate gave a wan smile.

'How is the play going?'

'Wonderful, I think.'

'How do you manage to act with this on your mind?'

'It's the one thing that stops me going round the bend. When you're doing it, when you're rehearsing, there's only that. Nothing else exists. When it stops, the real world comes back. At the moment the real world is so unreal the unreal world seems real-er.'

Margaret gave her extraordinary smile. 'I envy you.'

'So you should. So should everyone. It's the greatest thing. To be able to turn sorrow into joy. To be able to

229

make *use* of the bad things to create something else.'

'Yes,' Margaret said. 'That's the true alchemy.'

'But you're a writer. You do that too.'

'Your voice takes on a hollow ring when you say that.'

Kate accepted this challenge; no point denying it. 'That's because I haven't seen your work. I don't know how good it is.'

Margaret looked at the sheaf of papers: 'You won't see it yet. No one will. I'm going to finish something before I show a word.'

'Well, if you change your mind and want an opinion – and it would only be one opinion, I don't set myself up as a judge – I'd be glad. I feel you're good.'

'Good?'

'Original.'

'Why?'

'I think you have an original mind. Cool. With a dispassionate over-view.'

Margaret's eyes filled with tears. Kate was astonished. The girl had seemed to her strangely emotionless. Now she got herself back under control quickly with no fuss. 'Oh. What a surprise. Sorry. Never do that. But nobody before has appreciated those qualities in me. They are precisely the qualities I've always hoped – that I've striven for. Nobody has touched that – ambition – suspected it even – before. And that it should be you. I'm grateful.'

Kate trudged up the steps, as tired as if she'd been physically wrestling with a powerful opponent. And she didn't know the result. No referee. Was it a draw? Or had she been overthrown, as Rosalind says to Orlando? *Sir, you have wrestled well, and overthrown more than your enemies.*

On her left a row of cottages with country-ish front gardens, beyond them, far below on the other side of the

230

railway cutting, the city of Bristol. Brunel's lovely railway station quite clear and small. And on her right the end house of St Luke's Crescent. She saw what Margaret had meant by the steep slope at the back. The side wall of the end house rose as steeply as the steps.

Half-way up the final flight of steps at a cobbled resting place, she stopped to get her breath. Here, at right angles to the steps, there was a narrow opening between the backs of the St Luke's Crescent houses and the houses of Pylle Hill Crescent, above. This alleyway did not look inviting. She could not see where it ended: it curved with the crescents. But down it she went.

The back yards of the St Luke's Crescent houses were on her right. The walls were too high for her to see over. But twenty yards along the alley, a wall was broken down. She looked over the jagged bricks. She could see clearly now what Margaret meant. Some of the yards were incredibly deep and dark. Some, less deep – the houses without basements, she guessed – had earth banks that sloped steeply up from the house to the end wall. In most of the deeper yards a flat-roofed building filled the entire space, its roof level with the ground floor.

The backs of these houses were not only sinister but also confusing. It was impossible to tell what level of the houses you were looking at. At the front, some of the houses appeared to have basements, some not. But at the back some had double basements, one over the other. Or did they? Her tired brain could not work it out.

She counted down to the house where Margaret lived. But she could not see into that yard. The alley came to a dead end, a gruesome dark corner, piled with black garbage bags, chewed, spilling out unrecognisable gunk, old push chairs, a car seat, tyres, a burst football. The picture of her despair.

She made her way back to the steps, climbed to the top,

and carried on up Richmond Street, high, airy, the houses backing on to the railway cutting painted pretty colours, with restored stonework, original windows and doors.

Bright greeted her in the hallway. She didn't know how they'd look at each other today. She'd had no time, and no room in her mind, to consider what had happened between them. They stood in Lizzie's hallway in a momentary hiatus, then pressed body to body from forehead to knees, holding tight like there was nothing else in the world to hold on to, which was the truth. 'All right?' he said.

She nodded: 'How's Lizzie?' All this in whispers.

He made a face – not good.

Lizzie sat wrecked in a chair, uncombed, in her dressing-gown. Sarah sat with her, distraught.

'Do you want to go home for a bit, Sarah? I can be here,' Kate offered. But Lizzie grabbed Sarah's arm and Sarah shrugged: 'No, Kate, thanks, I'm fine.'

In the kitchen Bright was cooking an omelette. His deft movements, his hands cracking the yellow eggs into the white bowl, his hands and the swift motions of the fork, made a calm centre in Kate's universe, just for now.

'I checked out donkey sanctuaries.' He swirled a nut of butter in the pan.

'Margaret?'

'A-ha. No donkey sanctuary in miles of here has heard of her.'

'What?'

'Except one. Near Minehead. She worked there for a month ten years ago in her school vacation.'

'Why should she lie?'

'Want to ask her?' He poured the eggs into the pan. She watched the edges become opaque, then set and curl, the middle a swirl of golden liquid. He sprinkled little stars of parsley over the yellow and, a moment before the whole thing set solid, with the spatula, folded one side over the other, enclosing the perfect slightly liquid centre under its frilly edge. She took two hot plates from the oven and he expertly chopped the omelette into two and slid them on to the white porcelain. He placed a slice of good brown bread on each plate and a spoon of salad, picked them up with a tea towel and carried them through. Then he came back to the kitchen.

'Will she eat?' Kate said.

'If she can't eat that she can't eat anything.' He poured them each a glass of wine. He sat at the table and held on to Kate's hand. 'Margaret lied because whatever she was doing all those years, and especially what she's been doing recently, she doesn't want us to know.'

'Brilliant deduction.'

'Yeah, clever clogs. Now why doesn't she want us to know? Is it something to do with her brother? Or some secret nothing to do with all this? We're checking out the Ireland story. So far no one's heard of her over there.'

'I've just been to see her.'

'On your own?' Bright was shocked.

'What do you think she would do to me? Hit me over the head with a meat cleaver because I want her to betray her brother?'

'You shouldn't do that. You've got to tell me first.'

'Anyway she's a True Fan, I thought I might have some influence because of that.'

'And have you?'

'I fear not.'

'Nah.' He rubbed his eyes.

'But there's an alleyway between the backs of her houses and the street above. The houses have a weird construction. Some of them, the whole yard is filled with a building. You come out of the back door deep deep down, and across a narrow yard, no more than three feet from the house, is this

233

flat-roofed building. The roofs are just big concrete blocks. It's the most sinister unpleasant backs of houses I've ever seen. Have those buildings in the yards been searched?'

He got up from the table and took out the mobile. 'Helen? A-ha, it's me. No, don't put me through to Ryan, I don't want to get up his nose. Listen, find out something for me?' He explained then covered the receiver and spoke to Kate: 'Is there one of these buildings at the back of Margaret's place?'

'The alley doesn't go all the way. I couldn't get far enough to see.'

'From inside it looked like a paved garden, simple.'

'I know. But the kitchen units go all along the back window. You can't see straight down the back of the house without clambering on to the kitchen sink. It looks like the paving comes right up to the back wall of the house but – '

Bright was back on the phone. 'Find out if those buildings in the back yards have been searched. Ask around. Call me back.'

The sun had gone now, an orange glow low in the sky over the hill. They climbed up and over Richmond Street, Pylle Hill Crescent off to the left at the end. Down the first section of steps, to the alley. More uninviting in the gloaming. Bright took out a small torch. They peered over the broken wall. 'I see what you mean. Villains' paradise. From the inside you wouldn't suspect. I mean, even here it's hard to tell what level you're on. Completely different levels front and back. Never seen anything like it.'

Something scurried over Kate's foot. She gasped and lifted both feet. She couldn't see in the dark of the litter at the wall's base what the animal had been. She hoped cat and doubted it. Bright's warm dry hand held hers. 'Margaret's place is a bit further along, right? Two houses? Three?'

They counted their way back along the alley then continued down the steps to St Luke's Crescent. They counted the houses along to Margaret's. 'Four,' Bright said, 'from the end of the alley.' They walked on past. There was a light in the window. Margaret sat at her small desk, her head bent over her papers, writing in longhand. She looked concentrated and easy. Happy even. Bright and Kate walked on down the crescent. His phone rang. 'Yeah?'

He listened, said 'A-ha,' once or twice, then, 'Thanks, Helen. Talk to the DCI on the next shift, not Ryan, the nice guy who knows about the drug scene. Get him to institute a raid or something. The pretext doesn't matter. He's got to see the inside of every one of those buildings, okay?'

Shutting off the phone he said, 'This is dealers' paradise, apparently. The basement flats are in big demand in certain circles.' They were passing a house with metal shutters over the windows. It appeared to have no basement but there was a ventilator grille in the front bay. 'They were doing a bit of refining and packaging in the building out the back. Mixing brick dust with the browns.'

'What?'

'Heroin. They call it the browns. It's brownish powder, looks like brick dust, so they use brick dust to bulk it out a bit. Ten quid a go.'

'No.'

'That's what these kids are squirting into their veins. Cheers you up, doesn't it?'

As they reached the bottom of the street three squad cars came round the corner. No blue lights, no sirens, quiet and sweet. Helen Goldie got out of the first car, with a man in a brown sweater and casual trousers. A nice bank manager on holiday, he looked. Bright whispered, 'That's Pollock. He's a good bloke. Hasn't got solid ivory between the ears.' Two uniformed police in each car. They spread out up the hill, four or five houses each, up the steps to front doors or down to basements. Bright bounced on the balls of his feet, rattled the change in his pockets. Kate said, 'I wish you wouldn't do that.'

She saw his teeth in the dark. 'Finding fault with me already?' He took his hands out of his pockets and put an arm round her. 'About last night –'

'We'll think about it later,' she said. 'Some other time. How about that?'

Doors opened, closed, oblongs of light coming and going, shadowy figures appearing on steps, disappearing. 'That's Margaret's place.' Kate moved up the hill a little. Saw Helen Goldie and Inspector Pollock go inside. Bright was bouncing again, his change rattling like mad. Kate walked down then up then in a circle, then got off the pavement to let some people pass.

'What's this then?' A mulish Bristolian voice.

Bright shrugged. 'Dunno, mate. Looks like a raid.'

'Which house they gone to then?'

'Seem to be trying them all.'

'Christ. C'm'on, less go.' The two men backed off down to Windsor Terrace then ran down to the main road. Kate could see Bright's instinct to give chase. Instead he got on his mobile and gave a description: 'Short, stocky. Blondish. Round heads, short haircuts, satin baseball jackets.' Shutting the phone down he said, 'Yeah, fits ninety per cent of the blokes round here.'

'Mulish manner,' Kate said. 'You didn't mention that.'

Bright gripped her arm. Pollock and Helen were coming out of Margaret's place. They came down the hill towards Pollock's car. Bright and Kate shrank back a bit. Before Helen got into the car she shook her head, a minimal movement easy to miss. She could have been shaking her hair back if it hadn't been back already in its neat arrangement. Bright's shoulders drooped. Pollock and Helen drove off.

42

Excerpt from a Diary

x

Well well, my sister is good, no point denying it. Such cool, such sang-froid. 'Oh, of course,' she says. 'Yes, do look. I do have a basement now I come to think of it, well, it's more a cellar. I never go down there because it's rather spooky, but by all means look.' So she goes into the broom cupboard that used to be the corridor, and she shifts a few things.

'You didn't tell us about this before,' says the little policewoman, very quiet so that the man can't hear.

'Well,' says Margaret, 'I just ignore its existence, as far as possible.' She gets out the last box and she uses the edge of a shovel to lift up the trap door. She tries not to look at the little policewoman. She doesn't want to make her feel any more foolish. 'The trap door is very hard to see,' she says. 'It used to have a handle but I took it off.'

The man says, 'Well, it would get in the way of storing things, wouldn't it.' He's humouring Margaret, of course.

Margaret pretends she doesn't know this. 'Hold on,' she says, 'I think there's a light somewhere.' She feels around and finds the switch, and turns it on. The feeble bulb swings on that dangerous-looking wire thick with cobweb fluff, over the rickety open-tread stairs. 'More a ladder really,' Margaret says apologetically.

The man goes down first. The girl looks at Margaret closely. 'I met your brother,' she says.

'Did you?' says Margaret.

'I liked him, actually,' says the girl.

Margaret looks really touched.

'Up close, you're quite alike,' says the little policewoman – sorry – woman police officer, actually – her little Bristol voice, her charming plump soft skin. 'Aren't you?' she says.

'I've always hoped so,' Margaret says.

The little policewoman sees Margaret's too moved to say anything else. So she goes off down the cellar steps after the chap.

Margaret follows them down. They have torches and they poke about, at the brick walls thick with black rime, the slimy damp red pantiles of the floor. They turn over a pile of sacks in a corner. 'Coal,' the man says. 'These were the coal cellars in the old days. You'd have to come down here with a coal scuttle three times a day, carry it all the way up the house.' They move some boxes stacked in a corner, look inside them, look behind them. Nothing there!

'I hope there's no – well – animals,' says the little policewoman. 'I'm not scared of much, but rats I just go spare.' Now there's a thought. I'd like to see her go spare, I have to admit.

She's a fine little actress, plays it so sweet with this inspector, butter wouldn't melt. She doesn't want him to know she's been here before with the little cockney one, and failed to discover the cellar. And she knows that Margaret doesn't want that known either. She really plays men on the end of her line. Though he seems oblivious. Just getting on with the job. She's wasting her time there.

They go through to the back. Margaret follows them. He shines his torch all along the back wall and finds the bricked-up doorway. Touches it. 'Yes,' – Margaret's so cool – 'I don't know when that was bricked up. A long time ago, I expect.'

The inspector says, 'What would be outside there? What level are we on here?'

'Oh, on THE level, I assure you,' says Margaret. 'Always

on the level.' No she doesn't. (Oh, I wish!) She says, 'Yes, it is difficult to work out. Some of the houses have deep yards depending on the slope of the hill. Their basements open out on to the yard. Others like this are just earth at the back, I think. Mine was when I came here.'

'You had it paved.'

'Yes, it was unsightly and I'm no gardener.'

'You've made it nice,' the little policewoman simpers.

Margaret gives her a small smile. 'Thanks.'

The officer is still feeling along the wall. He pats it all over with the flat of his hand listening for differences in sound. But the sound is flat and dead and solid everywhere, there's no difference at all. He shines his torch closely at the brick. He shakes his head. 'Why did it have an opening in the first place?'

Margaret says, 'I thought it might have been one of those storage areas that you sometimes find under the pavement in the front area of a house. Only in this case it's the back?'

The officer shakes his head. He is exasperated. Flummoxed. In other circumstances I'd have liked to help him out: the backs of these house *are*, quite objectively, interesting. 'Let's go,' he says. 'Thanks for being so co-operative, Miss Leighton. This thing is pretty hard on you, I suppose?'

Margaret gives a deprecatory shrug, too full of feeling to speak. 'Sorry to bother you,' says the nice policeman, and up they go, up the rickety steps, up through the trap and into the nice warm dry flat. Out through the front door.

Margaret watched them. Down the short path to the pavement. They opened the bin cupboard and shone the torch. Nothing there except bins.

You need lateral thinking for police work, a type of inspiration most simple bobbies are not capable of. I can't help but despise their limited imaginations.

239

43

Shifts

Bright came back with Kate to her digs. The family were in the kitchen eating. The warm glow at the end of the corridor and Thomas laughing helplessly at some story Luke was telling him. Normal life. Everyone safe. A rush of emotion to Kate's throat. Bright put a hand on her back. They went upstairs quietly, so as not to disturb that secure life.

Now he cooked an omelette for Kate and himself. They drank more red wine. Helen Goldie called. She gave him a full report. He looked fit to be tied as he shut off the phone.

He told Kate about the cellar. 'Why didn't she show us before if there's nothing to hide? There's got to be something there! Why that street?' he said to Kate. 'I've been up and down those streets, round and round that little hill. That street is weird. Why does Margaret live there? She could live in a nice street. She's not short of a bob or two, and anyway, nowhere up that bit of Totterdown is expensive. Why there?'

'I'll ask her.' Kate reached for his phone.

Bright put his hand over hers and a plate in front of her. 'Eat.'

She realised she was trembling with hunger, light in the head. 'Okay.'

They didn't bother opening the sofa bed out. They lay on the rug in front of the coal effect gas fire. 'Are we always going to make love on the floor?' she said.

He covered her up with the duvet and clung close to her. His legs circled her legs, his arms circled her back. His body was warm, dry, he smelt like autumn grass. They didn't talk. No future. No past. Just now. Just them. Before she slept Maisie's face looked right at her out of the dark. She opened her eyes and he was watching her. 'It's okay,' he said. 'It's going to be okay.'

She decided to suspend disbelief, and sleep.

She never left the rehearsal room except for lunch or the loo. She watched avidly the production come together. She watched with unusual attention the process whereby an actor makes himself a conduit through which the character can be expressed, a vessel the character can inhabit, a medium for the message. She found the process unusually moving. Particularly as the actor is largely unaware of the metamorphosis, the chrysalis stage a frustrating head-banging time, the actor thinking he's getting nowhere, while in fact the character is entering him imperceptibly, infiltrating him bone, sinew and skin.

Today she watched Rupert. There couldn't be a more perfect Orlando, so young, a fledgling. All the wildness, truth and passion of a fledgling. Because he was so serious, he was heartbreakingly funny. She was too old for him surely? Wouldn't it show?

Before lunch, Ian sidled up to Colum. 'C-Colum, I have an idea f-for the interval. May I show you after lunch?'

At lunch Kate said to Rupert, 'I'm too old for you.'

He looked appalled. 'Of course you're not!' He blushed and laughed. 'You're not.'

She shrugged, unconvinced, but glad at least he hadn't immediately agreed. A silence and some unspoken thought elapsed between them. He overcame his shyness to ask, 'Did you visit the sister?'

Kate told him the story. 'Hopeless, I think. If she knows where he is she'll never say.'

'You have to keep in touch with her.'

'I know. I don't like her, I realise. She's a True Fan, a bit embarrassing. Earnest. Not great on humour. She Wants to Write. The only time I got through to her was when I flattered her about being a writer. She seemed really touched.'

'Get her to show you her stuff.'

'Maybe I will.' She looked at him. You could drown in those puppy-like honest intelligent eyes. What was she thinking of? She found herself blushing too.

After lunch Ian made his entrance. Sandy sidled in in his wake to watch. He'd dressed his pear-shaped body in perfect Boy Scout uniform from the Mounties' hat to the big khaki shorts and knee-socks. He carried an enormous rucksack. He had found the perfect metaphor · for the dyed-in-the-wool townee off on a jaunt to the country. He was an ineffably comic sight.

While they laughed he seriously unshouldered his backpack, knelt and opened it up. Out came a series of creature comforts, alarm clock, radio, magazines, a torch, food, food, and more food. Then out came a bundle of cloth. He unravelled this to reveal it as a small tent. He proceeded to erect this tent, giving members of the cast ropes to hold. The tent up, he at last disappeared inside. The tent bulged and heaved while he settled himself to sleep. The cast applauded. Ian poked his head out with an enquiring expression. 'Brilliant.' Colum got up. 'You've decided me where to have the interval. Now look.' Colum and Ian went into deep confabulation. Ian clenched a fist and grinned. 'Right, let's try it.'

'Rupert, Ian will stay in his tent right through the interval. We'll start the second half with the sonnets on trees scene. Want to try it now?' Colum had a few quiet words with Rupert, who nodded, dead earnest, then he sat down near Kate, to watch.

Ian squeezed back into his tent while Rupert rehearsed his sweetly crazy love scene, pinning poems addressed to

242

Rosalind on tree after tree. Running off at the end of the scene, Rupert tripped on a tent rope. The tent collapsed and Ian was revealed reading *Playboy* by torchlight. In a state of wounded dignity he gathered up his collapsed belongings and removed himself, a heap of wobbling flesh. 'I th-thought I'd get a member of the audience to h-help with the tent.'

Kate cried with laughter and knew this was the whole point of the exercise, of their job: to fly people out of their troubles however bad, just for a minute, just for an hour. You didn't suspend just disbelief, you suspended your life, you put your problems on hold. She thought how Maisie would laugh, how she and Alison would be crazy about Rupert, how she and Alison –

Gemma scraped her up off the floor of the loo. Kate wept in her arms. And even while she did so she thought, This is how Celia would have comforted Rosalind. At the start of the play, this is how it would be. Her sister Lizzie had no such release. No use she could make of her sorrow, her horror. Nothing she could do. And nothing Kate could do for her, her real sister, in their real life.

After rehearsal Alan Tate sidled up in the long striped scarf he had decided to wear for Jaques. 'How's your sister bearing up?'

'Badly. Well. I don't know. She doesn't speak to me.'

'No?'

'She thinks it's all my fault.'

He blinked. 'Why?'

She sighed. 'How far back do you want to go?'

'I see. Family history.'

'Habit. Anyway, it *is* my fault.'

'Oh dear dear, no.'

'Want to come up and see her?'

Nothing so revealing as a blush had invaded his perfect

poise for years, but a kind of frisson passed over his face. 'Oh, she wouldn't want – erm . . .'

'I'm going now.'

He seemed too tall and stately for the little house. But Lizzie for the first time actually looked somewhere other than within. She was unembarrassed by her dishevelled appearance, because she was unaware of it, though he was shocked.

Sarah looked grateful to take a break. In the kitchen she said, 'Oh Kate, I feel dreadful sorry for her, but I'll have to get away for a bit or I'll go crazy.'

'That's okay, Sarah. I'll stay here.' Kate made tea in the mocking clown's-head teapot.

'Your policeman comes round regular. She's pleased to see him even when he's got no news.'

'He had no news today then?'

'Said he'd be round about seven. I need an evening off. I feel awful saying that.'

'You've been amazing.'

'Well, she's got Sir with her now.'

Kate smiled. 'Alan would like that. He does have the air of a Knight of the The-at-ah.'

'I'd just like a night in my own bed.'

Kate for a moment thought she'd said knight. They collapsed in hysterical mirth, crying tears of laughter, then crying tears of fear and grief. For the second time Kate found herself clinging to another human being, unusual for her, so undemonstrative, so contained, so independent. For a moment she felt strapped to a raft in a sea so stormy that survival was not a possibility.

She gave Sarah a tea towel to wipe her eyes. Sarah said, 'Kate? What will you do if – ?'

Kate said, 'I can't imagine wanting to go on. I can't imagine Lizzie wanting to go on.'

'Doesn't make any sense, does it?'

Bright was standing in the doorway. 'I see His Nibs has come to visit. That'll do her good. Go home, Sarah. Have a drink. Have a lie-down. Go to the pictures. Get away from this. We'll be here.'

Sarah said, 'D'you know, I never thought I could get to like a policeman?'

They stood with their arms round each other at the kitchen window.

'Anything new today?'

'Pollock, the DCI on the late shift? He's persuaded the IO to put twenty-four-hour surveillance on Margaret's flat.'

'Is she hiding him there? Her brother?'

'Don't look hopeful, Kate. It doesn't look likely, does it? We've searched twice. But if he goes anywhere near, they won't miss him. And if she goes anywhere near him, we won't miss that either.'

'She's being followed?'

'Under observation, as we say.'

Kate shivered.

'Apart from that, they smoked out a little heroin factory further down the street. Doesn't help us much but Pollock's pleased. That's his speciality. Small-time drugs and thieving. He's not used to good-quality crime.'

'Good-quality crime?'

'A-ha. Murder. High-class burglary. Fraud.'

'That's what you call it?'

'A-ha. Doesn't come better quality than this.'

When Kate went into the front room with food, Alan Tate was perched imposingly on an armchair. Though physically uneasy he seemed oddly at home. And Lizzie, miracle of miracles, was talking. She shut up when Kate arrived, naturally. But outside the door Kate heard her start up again, the occasional murmur from Alan prompting her on.

Bright was off to keep a rendezvous with Helen Goldie. He crept by the front room: the murmur of Lizzie's voice, Lizzie crying, Tate's resonant comforting tones. He raised his eyebrows at Kate. 'Didn't figure him as the sympathetic type.'

'I'm amazed,' Kate said.

'See you later?'

'Here's the keys to my digs. But I expect to be here tonight.'

'We really looked everywhere. There wasn't any way there could be a place below, or a place at the back. There was nothing there, John!' It was the first time she'd called him John. It had slipped out of her secret mind. She blushed.

'Then there's got to be another place in that street. Otherwise why is Margaret there?'

'I don't think she knows where he is. That's just her place, that's all.'

'Nah. Maybe you're right. Any news from Ireland?'

'No. But Pollock's going to start using Anna Kappa on Margaret. I got him interested. He's started going back in months, not minutes. Where was Margaret before she turned up here?'

'He got anywhere?'

'He's starting with his shift tonight.'

Bright nodded, staccato small movements of his head. 'I want to talk to the mother again.'

'She's so – '

'I know she's a bit barmy, but there's method in it somewhere. Do you believe she never knew where her daughter was all that time?'

'Well, if they don't get on very well – '

'If you fell out with your folks would you just not let them know where you were?'

246

'Lots of people do it. You know that.'

'Get back in to see her. Try and get me in.'

'John – '

'I know it's hard, I'm really grateful. I am. Sorry. It's knocking me to hell, all this. Should never get involved with friends' cases, but what can I do? We've got to get to Maisie before – '

'It's okay.'

'If there is a before. If it isn't already after.'

He left her outside her door and drove up to Kingsdown Parade. Caroline greeted him in the hall with Thomas in her arms. 'I just can't get him to sleep. He's always restless when Luke's out. He must pick up some vibes from me.'

Bright sat in her kitchen with them, drinking tea till midnight. Kate didn't come in. He slept wrapped in the duvet on her floor. Her perfume surrounded him. It wasn't Millie's perfume, it was just Kate's.

Kate went out at midnight. She found herself walking the streets of Totterdown. Round and round the hill and over and over the hill. She went down the steps and along the alley behind St Luke's Terrace, shivering with fear and a kind of sickness. Margaret's place was in darkness, so far as she could see. She stood there in the dark, hoping there would be no rustling in the garbage at her feet. She pulled herself up on to the wall hoping for a better view. No good. One or two windows in other houses dimly glowed. But it was hard to tell if she was even looking at the right house at this distance.

Alan Tate was closing the door gently behind him when Kate arrived back. He whispered, 'She's sleeping.'

'Alan! I don't think she's slept for over a week.'

'Ah, darling, all you need is one performance from me – send anyone to sleep.'

Kate kissed him. 'Thanks.'

But Kate didn't sleep. She lay on Maisie's bed holding the teddy bear she'd bought for Maisie's first Christmas. She thought about Liam, her lost brother, Dave alienated from his family, Margaret Leighton alienated from her mother, then all the dysfunctional families in *As You Like It*, all the brothers alienated, missing, exiled, plotted against. Celia takes the name Aliena when she goes to the forest. She is alienated from her father. The love of Rosalind and Orlando rises from a dunghill of hate and revenge. Her work her saviour. She floated into harried searching dreams way after dawn.

Bright caught her at the stage door before she went into work and gave her Helen's update.

'What's Anna Kappa?' She looked as bleary as he felt.

'It's this island. I forget where. South Seas or somewhere. Weather conditions. Lots of mist swirling around. It appears and disappears. Well, it's a methodology by time.'

'I'm mystified.'

'Well, you take the point of the crime.'

'The crime?'

'In this case, because of Alison, they're taking the point of disappearance, near as they can. Maisie's disappearance. They make a line backwards and forwards from that, and along that line they place events.'

'Like Mark Leighton disappearing?'

'A-ha. And Pollock's placing Margaret in the frame. Just to see. See if her movements add up in terms of Mark's, or Maisie's. It's an outside chance but you never know.'

'How did you persuade Pollock?'

'He's a good bloke. Didn't like the Margaret set-up. He'll have a hard job persuading Ryan, though. Gonna bring it up at morning prayers.'

Kate was bewildered. 'Prayers?'

248

'The morning conference. The two DCIs off each shift, and the Investigating Officer, decide on the actions to be taken, allocate personnel to the actions. The IO's more sympathetic to Ryan than Pollock.' Bright looked troubled. His shoulders sagged.

'What? Something new?'

'No, nothing new, that's the thing. Kate – '

'What?'

'They got no leads, it's not going anywhere. It's a question of resources, manpower. There's other crimes. And Maisie's disappearance isn't even a definite crime yet. It's getting on for a week. If there's no leads in forty-eight hours the heat goes out of it. It goes cold. That's the problem.'

'Oh Christ.' Kate covered her face with her hands.

'Helen and me are gonna try and get to see Mark's mother again. We'll do it on our own time, after our shift.'

'It's a risk for her?'

'A-ha. Pollock's sympathetic but she could get in trouble.'

'So could you.'

'Ach.' He dismissed this.

'Well, please thank her from us.'

They were at the stage door. Kate was going to be late. They clung together in a fierce quick embrace. 'I missed you last night,' he said.

'Yup.'

That day Alan rehearsed his Seven Ages of Man speech. The rich modulated despairing voice had the power of the Last Post played on a single bugle over fields of the dead. Astonishingly towards the end Jaques the arch cynic cried. There was no hint of crying in his voice but tears ran down his cheeks. An extraordinary silence hovered over the rehearsal room, astonished, shocked, illuminated. No one had ever done it like this before.

The sense of awe stretched even over the coffee break.

Alan gave Kate a sidelong look. Embarrassment, she thought. He said in a rich-toned mumble, 'I didn't intend that.'

'It's wonderful.'

'Oh no. You think?'

Colum approached and put a hand on Alan's shoulder. 'Is it likely to occur again?'

'Oh, you guessed it wasn't meant.'

'It was astonishing. I've never known you take the emotional route.'

'Do you think I should take it again?'

'I think it would be wonderful but don't try for it.'

'Ah yes, we all know the pitfalls of trying to repeat an effect.'

Later Kate and Rupert worked on the play's greatest, longest, disguised-love scene, Rosalind like mercury, like fireworks, like an electric storm, like a cooing dove. For Kate the piercing joy of Rosalind's love was fuelled by the piercing despair of Maisie's absence, both passions equally intense, equally acute. At the end of the day Colum looked at her with concern. 'Be careful, Kate. Don't get there too soon. Can you hold back a bit? I think you're frightening Rupert.'

'Am I frightening you, Rupert?'

'I feel a clodhopping mutt.'

Colum's eyes lit up. 'Maybe that's how Orlando feels? And he's confused too, because he's having these sexy tender feelings for a boy. We have to define those moments of confusion, make them work for us.'

Rupert groaned.

Kate took him for a drink in the theatre bar. He gazed at her with eyes full of love. He seemed almost about to make a declaration. Oh no, Kate thought, not this. I don't have time or room for this, it's the wrong time and the wrong place, *it's a lovely face but it's the wrong face* ... With Rupert, a woman in her position would have to make the first move, and such a thing was beyond Kate, so far out of character as to be impossible. If she could ever do it she'd make a hash of it. *Of course, Rosalind has precisely that problem and finds a way around it* ... She was off again. Work as displacement activity. Work as anaesthetic.

Alan Tate stopped by their table. 'I'm going to cook your sister my incomparable spaghetti this evening. No need to rush back.' He sailed on, a proud ship, through the bar.

Helen stepped down to the stone floor of the Coronation Tap. Bright sat looking at the *Bristol Evening Post*, not reading it. He looked up. Seeing her, his dead brown eyes took on their metallic points of light. 'What'll you have?'

'Scrumpy.'

'You sure?'

'It's nice here, the cider. Out of the barrel.'

'Any news?'

'They've let Dave Fowler go.'

'Christ.'

'The superintendent said it was getting embarrassing. Fowler's lawyer's been getting really tough. Pollock had this big argument with Ryan, apparently. Well, that's the story going round.'

'So now they haven't got anyone in the frame.'

'Well, Pollock's got them to definitely put Mark in it. And now we've started concentrating on his sister.'

'Thank Christ for that. Cheers.'

'I rang the nurse and asked if I could visit the mother. She said it would be okay. You'll be late for Ryan's shift.'

'Yup. I'll spin him a tale. Keep you out of it.' She looked at her watch on the smooth plump wrist. Bright found himself with a sudden urgent desire to touch that smooth baby flesh. What was happening here? Cured by Kate of a three-year paralysing obsession, turned on by Kate not just to her but to all women? Helen was young enough to be his— He buried his nose in his pint. 'We've got ten minutes,' Helen said.

'A-ha. Good. Right.'

The house did not have the shine, the gleam, it had had when Mark was there. The smell was different. Sadder. A slight cabbagey odour drifted up from the kitchen. The nurse wiped her hands on her apron.

'Sorry to bother you. I can see you're busy.' Bright's most tomcat-like purr.

The nurse tucked a lock of grey hair behind her ear. 'I'm cooking her supper.'

'That's all right, love. We know the way.' He started up the stairs after Helen.

The nurse looked harassed. 'Mind if I get on?'

'You go ahead. I'll ask you a few things later, okay? Nothing heavy. You take your time.' Her footsteps could be heard clomping off to the kitchen as they reached the first landing. Bright looked out at the back yard. Not the only time in this hilly city a basement had had him fooled. Just the first. He started to follow this thought. Had the basement here given Mark the idea? Had he got Margaret to take the flat in St Luke's Crescent because of its deceptive levels? No, that was no good. Margaret's basement had been searched now. Nothing there. He wished he could have searched it himself. He might do that— Helen was knocking on the door of Miss Leighton's room. There was no reply. Bright gave Helen the nod and followed her in.

'Hello, Miss Leighton?' Helen's voice soothed with its softest Bristolian inflection. She was learning from Bright. 'We've come to see you again. Are you awake?'

Mark's mother had not moved since their entrance. She

was no more than a hump in the bed in the dusky room. Helen went to the window and pulled back the curtain. A shaft of evening sun cut across the bed. The woman was asleep, it seemed, head back almost off the pillow. Then Bright saw her eyes were open. He'd been in rooms before where death had got there ahead of him. Helen turned from the window. Her face stiffened with shock, comic, almost. She recovered to say, 'Is she dead?'

Bright knelt by the bed. A small chenille cushion had landed on the rug there. Knocked off in a struggle? Or simply used and then carelessly thrown down? He had a quick look at the woman's fingernails. There had been no struggle.

Though it was obvious there wouldn't be one, Helen felt for a pulse. Then she called for the nurse. The nurse sang up cheerfully, 'I'm coming. Won't be a mo!'

Bright said, 'She's a witness I was here. No point making a run for it. Sorry, Helen.'

'Oh, well.' She made her report into the mobile phone. Bright circled the room like a cat, sniffing in detail, minute observations: closed curtains middle of the day, someone might have noticed that. Someone had been here. When? How did they get in?

The smell of cabbage ascended with the nurse. She carried a bowl of overcooked-vegetable soup on a tray. Helen raised a hand to stop her in the doorway. It was strange to Bright to do nothing in this situation, to have no place, no clout. Helen shut down her phone. 'Put down the tray, please.'

The nurse looked taken aback, no more. Puzzled, anxious, she put the tray on a washstand in the hall. 'What is it? Has she been taken ill?'

'When were you last up here?'

'Oh . . . Oh dear, I didn't come up at lunchtime. Her daughter came. She brought the lunch up instead of me.'

'Her daughter? You're sure?'

'Yes. Well, she said she was her daughter. She *was* her daughter. She came once before and Miss Leighton recognised her all right. She didn't seem to like her much.'

'She brought the lunch up and you – '

'I stayed downstairs to eat my own lunch in peace. Then I went out for a few things, just to the village. The daughter – Margaret, is she called? – yes. Margaret said it would be okay, she'd be here till I came back.'

'And was she?'

'Yes.'

'Yes?' Helen looked at Bright. He raised an eyebrow.

'I'd been back about ten minutes, must have been four o'clock or so. She called out from the hall, Don't worry, I'll let myself out. Mother's fine, she's asleep, don't disturb her. Don't bother taking her tea. That's what she said.' The nurse's face went quite blank for a moment. 'Oh my God,' she said. 'She's died, hasn't she? Oh my God.'

Bright stopped her from going into the room. He didn't want her to touch anything in there, though her prints must already be over everything. She sat on a stair with her head between her knees. 'It's your nightmare,' she said to Bright. 'If you're a nurse. It's your nightmare they'll die on you. I haven't neglected her, I really haven't.'

'No, no. No one thinks you have.'

'Oh.'

'You're sure it was the daughter who came?'

'Margaret. Yes.'

'Not the son?'

'Mark? No! What are you—? Is there something fishy about it, then? Is that why you're asking – ?'

'Well, we won't know till they've done the PM. But, well, it looks like it.'

'Oh no.' It was almost a whimper and her hands started to tremble.

'Listen, love, it wasn't your fault, right? Keep cool 'cause you're going be needed round here. You're the only one so far who saw the daughter here.'

'It couldn't have been her who did it. She's so nice. She's so calm.'

'But Miss Leighton here didn't like her, right?'

'No. That's right. She always looked a bit alarmed when I mentioned her. The son now, that's a different matter. She seemed to be keener on him. Why has he stayed away so long? she kept asking me. That police guard on the house, that was watching out for him, wasn't it?'

Bright didn't answer this. When Mark first did a runner there had been surveillance. It had been transferred to Margaret's place. There's only ever so much manpower to go around. But surely someone must have followed Margaret up here, at least. The ruthlessness of this killing. The smooth way it had been done. Margaret was involved, in some way. He felt it. He knew it. And he knew it would not be possible to prove.

He led the nurse down to the basement. The back door was open. He said, 'Did you leave this open?'

She had both hands pressed flat to her chest. She shook her head, swallowing. She whispered, 'I never open it. Last time I saw it it was bolted shut.'

'When was the last time you saw it?'

'I keep the vegetables down here, it's such a small fridge in the kitchen. I came down to get onions and carrots for the soup. That was this morning about ten o'clock.'

'And it was bolted then?'

She nodded her head, then shook it, then said, 'I never noticed if it was bolted. I didn't look. But it wasn't open, I can tell you that.' She had started to rally. Outrage, the sense of invasion, of being tricked, got the blood moving in her veins again. 'He was hiding somewhere then? All the time. He could have been watching me even.' She suddenly spat out, 'The little shit.'

'You're sure Margaret left by the front door?'

'Yes.'

'You saw her go? Or she just called out, or what?'

'Oh. Oh God. Hang on. She called out to me. I was busy in the kitchen. I poked my head round the door. She said goodbye. She opened the front door. I came back down here. I heard the door close.'

'You didn't see her actually go out?'

'Oh God. Margaret? You're not saying Margaret – Are you saying Margaret let him in?'

'I'm not saying anything, love. Just repeat to the officer who comes what you said to me. Great observation. Good as a copper.'

'It's the training. We're taught to look for signs.'

The noise of arrival broke out upstairs. Ryan would be spitting blood to know he was here. Bright held the door open with a tea towel, threw the towel to the nurse and went out. Into the yard. Into the mews. Deserted. The garage men had long gone home. Out into the wide street. Great long shadows everywhere, stretching over everything, like fingers.

44

Blood out of Stone

He found himself with no breath, like he'd been running up the hills, not driving. He ran now past three parked cars and down the path to her door. She opened the door and gave her shy composed smile.

'Can I come in? Thanks.' He said this like one word and

slid inside in one movement, fast on his feet, smooth as an alley-cat. She had no chance to stop him. Not that she seemed to want to. She looked a little taken aback but nothing more. Not guilty, not scared, not even alarmed. He said, 'You went to see your mother this afternoon?'

'How did you know?'

'I've just been visiting too.'

'Why?'

'To ask a few more questions about Mark.'

'And about me, I suppose.'

'How was your mother?'

'She's weak. She's gone to pieces since Mark went. She misses him. Well, he did everything for her. I felt almost guilty. I even wondered should I move back in? But that wouldn't work. It never did. And the nurse seems good. Conscientious anyway.'

Was the girl talking more than usual? Her nice modulated voice laved calm over everything, but she was talking a lot, wasn't she? 'She was okay, though? Your mother?'

Margaret's brow creased slightly. 'Yes. I mean, as well as – Why are you asking this?'

I ask the questions, Bright thought, but did not say. *Mustn't alienate the girl. Not yet. Bird in the hand. Don't scare it off.* 'Did you see Mark when you were there?'

'Mark?'

'Your missing brother Mark, a-ha.'

'You're saying Mark was there?'

'You didn't see him? You didn't arrange to meet him there? You didn't open the door to let him in, let him out?'

'Mark was there?' She put her long hands up to her face. 'How do you know? Have you seen him? Have they – have they arrested him? Oh no.'

This was all spoken in this tranquil unhurried voice, the way she said everything. He couldn't work out whether this gave an air of utter falsehood or utter truth. He was having a job working out anything. His brain seemed to have come off its tracks. He said, 'Look, love, sit down a minute, all right?' He sat himself opposite her. That felt better. He must not break the news of the mother's death, much as he wanted to; he had to wait for the local force. Pollock or Ryan would come in person for this. They should get her reaction fresh.

'Tell me what happened,' he said. 'From the moment you got there. Hang on. Why did you go? You don't like your mother. Did you get a call from Mark?'

She looked at him level, enquiring. 'I went because Mark isn't around, not because he is. If Mark were there, I wouldn't need to go. But it appears to be my duty just to look in. It's not the first time I've been.'

'No?'

'I went about a week ago, just after – '

'A-ha.'

'She's never pleased to see me. She makes me feel bad. Really bad. You know? A bad person, I mean. She doesn't mean to, but that's how it is. I stayed a while. To give the nurse a break.'

'What did you talk about?'

She tried to avoid his eye but something in that concentrated squint – was it focused on her? was it not? – forced words out of her. At last she said, 'All right. I went there to see if she knew where Mark was, okay? That's the reason I went both times. Not to see my mother. I can't believe he wouldn't have been in touch with her. But she said she knew nothing. She's heard nothing. He hasn't even phoned.' Her voice disappeared a second. She cleared her throat, and her emotion with it.

'Was she worried about him?'

'She was worried he might not come back to look after her. Her. Her. That's all she worries about. All she ever has worried about. I'm sorry to sound so bitter. But if Mark has by any chance done the dreadful things you suspect him of, it will be my mother's fault, not his. And I want to go on record now as saying that.'

You'll be on record soon enough, Bright thought. He suddenly found himself saying, 'We found your mother dead.'

Margaret stood. She backed away. She pressed her whole body back against the wall, even the palms of her hands. Her eyes were shut. Then she bent forwards, her hair ends touched her feet, her hands hung. She went down on her hands and knees. Then she sat back on her heels. It was an astonishing series of movements, carried out in utter silence. She breathed out long breaths like she was doing yoga.

Bright said, 'I'm asking you again: did you let Mark in?'

She shook her head from side to side.

'Did you let Mark out?'

Again she shook her head: no.

'Did you see Mark?'

'No.'

'Did you know he was there?'

'No.'

'Then I think you're going to be arrested for your mother's murder.'

'In that case I wish I had killed her. It would make it all worth while.'

45

Excerpt from a Diary

xi

When Margaret decided to go up to the house I was disturbed. She said she was worried about mother, but Margaret stopped worrying about mother years ago. I never like it when Margaret lies or starts to get clever. It's not like her. It churns me up. I do not like her taking action on her own. I refused to go with her.

I am really not sure what happened. She must have done things coolly, slowly, she was there for hours. And mother did not struggle. I believe she gave mother some of her sleeping pills and just waited, watching her.

Margaret has never taken action like this alone before. I could always call on her when I needed her, but apart from that she kept away. I needed her to abduct Maisie. Because of what had happened to Alison, Maisie would never have left her house alone that day with a man. So I had to send Margaret to get her and bring her here. And since then, to give me time, I have had to use her to talk to the police etc. She has had to have a high profile. It's I who have had to disappear. This way she has got back into my life. She has got too close to me. Things are getting confused between us. Blurred. I don't like this.

Margaret walked back in here, so cool. She wanted to go in to look at Maisie. I would not let her. I know that for Margaret mother's death is a liberation. A triumph. A necessity. I suppose she had always known this and that is why she went away. And if she had not been hounded and chased into this corner she would not have taken such a

260

revenge. I don't believe she meant to do this when she went up there. I believe she was overcome, taken by surprise.

I do not want that to happen to me. I waited a good while before going in to Maisie myself.

Maisie knew at once that something big had happened. She said, 'What's going on?' and I realised I had taken her no food or drink for some time and that she was scared I was going to leave her here to starve. She was more scared than she has been before and I was sorry to see that. I told her I would not let her die like that. I would not let her die till she agreed. 'I'm hungry,' she said. I brought her food. She said, 'Aren't you eating?' I shook my head and I told her what had happened. It was only then it became real to me. I realised I had lost my mother and now there is nothing in my life to cling to. Nobody who needs me. Margaret doesn't need me any more. She has freed herself from both of us. It doesn't matter, I told myself, because I'm going to die when Maisie does, but just the same I did feel utterly desolate.

I knew once again I had talked too much in the Dead Room and that this had added to my despair. Maisie strangely enough looked compassionately upon me. When I stopped crying she said, 'Now you know how I feel about my mother. Why don't you let me go to her, and just stop all this?' She said it as though she did not expect me to reply. And I didn't. She thinks it would be hard for me to send her back because of Alison. But that's not the reason.

I am writing my diary in the Dead Room with her tonight because I am afraid to be alone. I'm afraid of Margaret.

46

Going Solo

Bright thought Ryan might burst a blood vessel finding him at Margaret's. He slipped out, leaving him to pull in Margaret on his own, but the damage was done. The interview later in his office was short. Bright knew he'd overstepped the mark. Ryan threatened to make a report to Bright's superintendent at Kentish Town. The superintendent was new, he didn't know Bright yet. It could mean disaster. 'Don't do that, Ryan. I'll go quietly, okay?'

On his way out he had a word with Pollock. Pollock said he'd do what he could. 'Sorry you're off the team.'

'Thanks. Not as sorry as I am.'

He managed a short meet with Helen late that night. Not at the police station bar; it wouldn't do Helen's prospects much good to be seen with him. They were in the Coronation Tap again. Bright liked the feel of the place, it had become his home from home. 'They took Margaret's fingerprints,' Helen said. 'They're all round the mother's room, and on the front door, the banister rail, all over the house. But they would be, wouldn't they?'

'Why would they?'

'Well – '

'She hasn't spent time there for years, she says.'

'No, but she'd have gone all over the place, wouldn't she? Her first visit home and that? You explore, don't you?'

'What about the back door downstairs?'

'Only Margaret's prints and the nurse's.'

'No others?'

'Well, a few smudgy ones. But we never got Mark's to compare, did we? 'Cause Ryan – well – Mark wasn't a suspect, was he, till he did a runner?'

Bright groaned. 'They got the nurse in the frame?'

'They're not ruling her out.'

'She's helping them with their enquiries.'

'Yes.'

'Waste of time. She's got nothing to do with it.' Bright gulped a mouthful of scotch, a double, neat, one cube of ice. 'I've pissed off Ryan all right.'

'Why did you stay at Margaret's till he came?'

'I couldn't scarper once I'd told her about her mother, could I? She could have done a runner too. Could've told her brother. If he's killed his mother, it means he's gone right off the rails. It doesn't look good for Maisie. It doesn't look good.'

'We've let her go.'

'The nurse? Sure.'

'Margaret.'

He put down his scotch. 'Let Margaret go?'

'I *thought* you'd be surprised.'

'Why?'

'The mother was alive when she left. Forensic confirm it. She died at least an hour later.'

'Cause of death?'

'Barbiturates, then suffocation.'

'Same as Alison.'

Bright slowly sipped the scotch. He swirled the ice around. He stared at it, swirling. He said, 'She gave the mother the sleeping pills. She opened the back door for Mark. She left. He did the suffocation. They're working together. Can you get anyone to see that?' He looked at her. A raw recruit. Eager to get into CID. Imaginative. Ambitious. But just a kid. He was too low tonight even to

263

fancy her. He swallowed the ice cube and drained the glass. 'I shouldn't be here. I'm doing nobody any good.'

Lizzie's had a different atmosphere. He felt it outside the front door. He heard the mighty rumble of the voice of Alan Tate. But when he got inside he saw Dave. Dave looked bad. In custody he'd grown a beard. He looked like Rip Van Winkle. He'd come out of the mountain into a different world. He shook Bright's hand.

'How're you feeling?' Bright said.

'I somehow thought they'd let me out when they found Maisie. Only they haven't found Maisie. Why did they let me go? Nobody would say.'

'Mark Leighton's mother was found dead early this evening.'

Dave looked blank. 'And? She was an invalid, wasn't she?'

'She'd been helped on her way.'

'Are we talking euthanasia here?'

'Doesn't look like it, no.'

A succession of thoughts slowly crossed Dave's face. 'So now Mark Leighton's their prime suspect?'

'Been mine all along.'

'Thanks.'

'You're welcome. I'm no closer to catching him. The sister's in cahoots with him, I'm sure she is, but she comes across pure as the driven snow, and she'll never give him up. They've let her go. All I can do is keep a close watch on her.'

'Can I help?'

'More help here, aren't you?'

Dave's gaunt face expressed a rueful sense of loss. He opened the door to the front room. Silence fell. Lizzie was dressed and had combed her hair. Her face was dead tired, white, its severe expression wiped out by anxiety and grief.

264

She nodded at Bright and Dave. Alan Tate stood up. 'Well, I must be on my way, as they say.' He crossed to Lizzie. 'Don't get up, Lizzie. I'll drop in tomorrow, if I may?'

Lizzie nodded. He lightly touched her hair, and left. Bright went into the kitchen to see Kate. She looked wild, her hair, her eyes, like something bad was chasing her. He sat close to her. 'There's something I'm not getting. Something dead simple. I know that girl Margaret is aiding and abetting him, covering for him. She knows where he is. She knows where Maisie is.'

Kate said, 'I'm going to see her again.'

'I'll go with you when you go.'

'You're in trouble enough,' she said.

'I'll keep out of sight. But I'll be around.'

'You think I'm in danger from her?'

'I think she helped him to kill his mother.'

'*Her* mother too.'

'She told me she wished she'd killed her.'

'John.'

'A-ha.'

A shiver ran through Kate. All the tiredness she'd been holding at bay fell suddenly on her like an avalanche.

Bright said, 'Don't go and see her tonight. Go home and go to bed. Take a sleeping pill. I'll be keeping an eye on Margaret's place, just in case. I might take Dave with me to watch the back. Keep him occupied.'

But strolling up St Luke's Crescent, Bright recognised one of the uniforms from Broadbury Road police station, slumped in an unmarked car in plain clothes just across from Margaret's place. He climbed the steps at the end of the street to the back yard wall level, the mouth of the alleyway. Two young blokes lounged there, smoking. He knew them too, from the police station bar. He nodded and went on up the steps.

Dave and Lizzie were asleep on the couch in each other's arms, babes in the wood. He covered them with a duvet from upstairs. They didn't stir. He left the house. He walked the streets.

Helen told him next day what he already knew – that a constant watch was being kept on Margaret. He said, 'What's the matter with them? They could have pulled her in yesterday.'

'What for?'

'A crime was committed, she was there, her fingerprints were found at the scene, come on! *What for?*'

'But then she couldn't lead them to Mark.'

'No, but at least they could search her place without a warrant. PACE section eighteen: searches.'

'But Inspector Pollock already searched. I was with him.'

'Mark's there, Helen. I know he's there. He's living in that flat in St Luke's Crescent with that mad sister.'

'You think she's mad?'

'A-ha. And you think I am.'

Helen blushed. 'We really did search. Honestly there was nothing there.'

'A-ha.'

She was irritated that she couldn't convince him. He was wild, couldn't sit still, got out of the car. Paced up and down. Up here on the edge of the Downs, that amazing bridge, the river below, the lovely Georgian houses, all air and grace, and there was Maisie somewhere, in some prison, kept by a maniac capable of killing not just a young girl on the brink of life, Alison, but his own mother whom he'd looked after for twenty years. He felt like he was in one of those dreams where everything's calm on the surface and underneath something boils and ticks and you can't get hold of it.

*

266

He went to see Kate at lunchtime. He felt weird round the theatre, no business there, spare prick at the wedding. She said, 'That's how *I* feel when I'm not working. You only feel okay here when you've got a job to do.'

His small brown eyes had this desperate burn to them today. She knew he knew time was running out. The mother's death was a sign the guy had flipped. She took him to the Arnolfini. They got a sandwich and sat at a table on the grey cobbles by the water. The smart young things of Bristol milled around, eating and drinking and flirting and laughing. The sun shone. And there were they, enclosed by darkness in the sun. He said, 'He's cleverer than we are.'

'I don't believe he's cleverer than you.'

That made him more desperate, he felt like grinding his teeth. He groaned. He couldn't eat. Fed his posh sandwich to the gulls. Kate said, 'Look, we've got the theatre just for this afternoon. We're having a stagger-through. Why don't you come?' Normally she'd die rather than let someone in before she was ready. But this time there were more important things than the performance. He looked appalled. She said, 'What else are you going to do?'

'I can't do a blind thing. They got Margaret pinned down. She can't take a piss without they'll know. That's what *they* think. She's got a phone, hasn't she?'

'Won't they be tracing her calls?'

'She'll have a way. She's abetting him. I know she is.'

A juddering roar above. They looked up. A helicopter circled low over the warehouses opposite, not yet turned into fashionable loft apartments, over where Dave lived. 'The heat-seeking camera,' he said.

Kate too threw her sandwich to the gulls. 'I'm praying, non-stop, all the time, to something I don't believe in.'

He looked at her. He'd been talking to her as if she was a colleague on the case. But she loved Maisie. She gazed at him, pleading. She said, 'Come and see the run-through.'

He looked at the helicopter twinkling away over Bedminster way, then at her poor face, white like Lizzie's face, with feverish eyes. He nodded. 'Okay.'

'Provided the others agree.'

They took a vote to let him stay. Colum said, 'Sit by me and tell me what's wrong with it.' But Bright declined. Sat towards the back, scrunched down in his seat, in case the actors could see him. He dreaded catching anyone's eye. He was nervous. He was going to be shown up. He wasn't going to understand a word.

First surprise: he understands everything. That poor kid Orlando. His brother's doing him out of his inheritance, but he's a good-hearted lad, looking after this old servant bloke. Then Rosalind and Celia come on, Rosalind's dead depressed. He thinks at first, *It's Kate, she's in such a state about Maisie she can't lift herself out of it*, but then she wasn't Kate, she was changed, not outwardly but from within somehow. So it's Rosalind who's depressed about her dad who's been given the push by her uncle. Here's another wicked brother doing dirty deeds. Then they do this wrestling match. Good as the real thing. The lad throws this big tough guy. And Rosalind falls in love and this joy invades Kate, she lights up. She dresses up like the lad and they go off to the forest.

Suddenly he remembers it from school. It hadn't seemed like this then. He actually finds himself laughing when Touchstone, this little fat guy, comes on in full Scout regalia. And then the lad pinning these poems on the trees. The whole thing had been about evil and sadness and loss and now suddenly it's about love. Everyone's falling in love and it's a bit mad, because they're all out of their depth in this forest, and all that evil stuff is still there in the background. But they forget it, and so do you, except when that old misery Jaques wanders in reminding everyone. The lad gallops off to pin up his next poem and down comes Touchstone's tent and there he is reading *Playboy* by the light of a torch. He gathers everything up, mortified. Bright's laughing. He wouldn't have thought it possible an hour ago.

And then come these amazing love scenes. The girl's flying. Only she's a boy and the real boy is getting confused because he's got these feelings for this Ganymede and how can he be getting the hots for this kid when he's in love with Rosalind? And she's enjoying herself so much she's almost crazy. That nice little Celia is getting really upset. Who can blame her? It's wicked. She says to Rosalind, 'We must have your doublet and hose plucked over your head and show the world what the bird hath done to her own nest!' and Rosalind takes off her cap and throws it in the air and all her hair comes tumbling out so she's a girl again and she says, 'That thou didst know how many fathom deep I am in love!' And Bright knew.

He knew why only Margaret's fingerprints were at the scene. He knew why Maisie had gone in the first place. He knew where Maisie was. He knew who was holding her. He didn't know why. But he knew who. He stood up. Colum turned, shocked: *the show was that bad?* Nearly out of the back doors Bright stopped. He pulled out his notebook and wrote a note for Kate, not getting her hopes up, but saying he had to go.

47

Excerpt from a Diary

xii

Margaret behaved with total cool at the police station. She was incredible but I know when she gets like that, the stress is building up. Margaret is beginning to frighten me.

Maisie can see I'm frightened. Maisie whispers to me in the Dead Room. Whispering is horrible in there. But not as worrying as hearing one's own voice so thin and distant. I whispered to Maisie about our lives, Margaret's and mine. How Margaret had struggled to be herself all her life. How I had given in and become what mother wanted. 'Don't be a girl,' mother said. 'Look at *me*: this is what happens to girls.' She did not want a girl. She wanted an invulnerable, strong, male person. Sometimes she would say, '*You'll* make sure Margaret comes to no harm. You'll keep her safe. You will protect her.' She dressed Margaret in my clothes. She called Margaret Mark. She sent Margaret to school as Mark. It was fine when we were small. It seemed a joke. It made mother happy, it made us laugh. It was when Margaret started to become a woman that things went wrong. She came in one day dressed much as she dresses now, in a simple cotton frock, with just a faint tasteful trace of makeup, and mother behaved as though she had committed a heinous crime. 'Take that off. Take that off. Get out of here. Get out.'

I'm losing it. I have to try to keep control. I don't want Margaret to take over. I don't want her to win. I know in a sense Margaret and mother are the same. Both of them ruthless and cruel, and they've manipulated me between them. I've been there for them and yet because of me Margaret could never be herself, never have lovers or children or a decent life. No. Not because of me. Because of mother. But I have never been able to blame mother. I can only blame the man who did what he did to her when she was fifteen and innocent. Margaret blamed mother for passing that hurt on. When I told Maisie this, she said, 'That's what you're doing too. Just like your mother. You're passing it on. That's why you're killing young girls, you're doing the same thing the man did to your mother and your mother did to Margaret.' She said, 'Why don't you stop?' She became a little bit agitated and she had the sense to stop talking. Her small hands were trembling a little today. And I took my decision.

She's weak, from fear at being left alone so much, from revulsion at her chemical toilet which had not been emptied while Margaret was in custody. And from hunger of course. She's very hungry. I did not want it to be quite like this. But sometimes we don't have a choice. While her stomach is empty is a good time. I prepared her cocktail.

When I said to her, Here, have a drink, it will cheer you up, she said, 'Is this it then? This what you gave Alison?'

'Alison accepted it,' I said. 'She understood.'

'*I* understand,' Maisie said. 'I understand you're not going to let me out of here whatever happens. But I'm not going to take your drugs.'

I tried to persuade her. Then I gave up. I said, 'Oh all right then,' and gave her some food. It was one of my delicious curries. A mixed vegetable dish called Niramish. The barbiturates were in that. Maisie was so hungry she never suspected. And in some strange way she trusts me. I really love her. I'd like to die with her, but unfortunately I have to make sure she is really gone first. I don't have to leave her on the hillside. That cockney policeman, the one

271

with the screwdriver voice, the icicle sharp eyes, he'll find us. I knew as soon as he came here that our time was short.

You will publicise this diary, won't you? You will try to make people understand. You will understand, yourself? That I have done everything from the purest of motives, even when pushed to my limits. And I do admit limits, at last. Don't miss Maisie. Remember her as she was. Perfect. Unsullied. Her own self. She and Alison.

They shall not see corruption.

48

They Who Have Eyes to See

He phoned the incident room on the way. He was lucky, it was Pollock's shift. He told Pollock what he knew. Pollock said, 'You're barking mad.' Bright said, 'Think about it. Think through what you've got and why you haven't got more. And then speak to the IO and then get your arse down there and pull Leighton in. On any pretext, doesn't matter, just do it. You know I'm right, Pollock.'

He was just driving under the railway bridge. Even if Pollock went along, the IO would think it was a mad idea. Bright had to get there himself, and fast, and bugger the consequences. He shot along by the side of the green hill where Alison's beautiful body had been laid out by this freak, he zoomed round the corner into steep Windsor Terrace, shot left into steeper St Luke's Crescent, squealed to a stop outside Margaret's place, jumped out and hurtled up the path. He rang the bell, not too hard, not too long.

He waited. Rang again and knocked. Nothing. He broke a pane of glass and opened the door.

The place was silent. Empty. Now one of the uniforms from the surveillance car was on his back: 'What you think you're doing?' Then the lad recognised him and didn't know what to do.

'It's okay, mate. DCI Pollock'll be down here any minute. I was in the vicinity. Maisie Creech is in here. She's somewhere in this building.'

The second uniform ran upstairs. Bright moved, light on his feet, through to the kitchen at the back, looking, listening, sniffing the air, feeling his way, a tracker dog with its tail up. 'DCI Pollock says the way down to the cellar is through the big cupboard.' Swift, silent, they moved away the brooms and stuff, and there was the trap door. Bright knew that was no good. He knew it for certain in his bones. Margaret had taken them down there. She wouldn't do that if—

'Sir?' The uniform who'd gone upstairs panted in. 'Sir, I just noticed something. You can't see it from down here. Come and look.' The lad climbed on to the sink unit. Bright followed. 'Look, sir.' The lad pointed down. From here, pressed up against the window, looking straight down, you could see: the Yorkstone paving of Margaret's smart garden did not come right up to the house as it had seemed to. It stopped about two feet away and the space between the house and the paving was roofed over. There was a ventilator fan in this strip of roof.

Bright silently got off the sink unit, followed by the lad. 'What's your name?'

'Peters, sir.'

'They should make you sergeant tomorrow. Now how would you get down there?'

'Through the cellar.'

'Too obvious for this freak. And it's been searched. So

273

has this damn kitchen. I searched these cupboards myself. But then I was looking for Mark Leighton, not for a way down to a prison.' Bright opened the cupboards under the sink and the work surface. The lad cottoned on, pulled out all the stuff. They felt round the edges of the cupboard floors. Nothing. Bright opened the tall narrow cupboard in the corner. Took out a mop and bucket. Pulled at the floor. It came up, hinged at one side. A ladder led down the side wall, metal rungs down into light. A nice little kitchen area. Mark Leighton's clothes on a hanging rail, so instantly recognisable it might have been him hanging there. Margaret's cotton dress too. And a door.

Bright pulled the big metal handle. The door didn't budge. He put more effort and with a deep-throated *pfluck,* the thing threw him back on his heels. Immediately inside was a second door. He pulled. No good. He pushed. The door opened.

Leighton knelt over Maisie. Only, without the scruffy long sweater, it was suddenly clear that this was a woman's body, not a man's. Maisie's head was inside a plastic bag. Leighton turned. The face was made up, a little tasteful lipstick and eye shadow, nothing too much.

It took both uniforms to restrain her. She was screaming. 'You don't understand. Let me finish. I've got to finish what I've begun!'

Bright got the bag off Maisie's head. He began to pump at her lungs. She was far gone and fading. He could hear the uniforms calling for back-up. It might not get here in time. He knew he shouldn't move her but he had to get her some air. He picked her up and put her in a fireman's lift over his shoulder while he climbed the ladder. As he flung her over his shoulder he felt her start to heave. By the time he got her outside she had certainly thrown up, all down his back. The squad car was going off down the crescent, Leighton's face pressed to the window, he/she/it still screaming, silenced by glass.

Bright laid Maisie down. Her delicate limbs. She was so light. A crowd was forming, and no back-up yet. A woman gave him a blanket. He wrapped Maisie in it. Though she'd thrown up, her breathing was fragile. She was in big trouble, he could feel her slipping away. He pumped at her back. He turned her over. He wiped her mouth and held her nose and brought his mouth to hers, he'd give his life for her, to her, his breath for hers.

The ambulance howled up the hill as Lizzie and Dave ran along from the steps at the other end of the street. Bright watched them get in the back, together. The family united.

The murmuring crowd stayed in the street. Pollock arrived. Bright was finding it hard to speak. He showed the poor DCI what he'd missed. Now they looked at this weird padded room. It was the worst thing Bright had ever seen. Worse than the discovery under the shed floor of that pervert on the estate in Kentish Town. This was elaborate, prepared. This was expensive. This padded cave. He noticed that talking in there thinned your voice like talking on a mountain in a high wind. It made you feel lost. He and Pollock got out of there fast. Outside, Pollock shivered. 'Bloody hell,' he said.

Up in the flat, going through the desk, Pollock found this thick wodge of A4 paper in a white folder. On the front it said, DIARY. Pollock opened it. The top page was blank except for the words: *Dear Kate Creech. From one who admires dedication and excellence, a fellow perfectionist. This is for you. You will understand.*

Pollock turned to page one. Over his shoulder Bright read: *2 a.m. A moonless night. I crouched in the car listening . . .*

Maisie was on oxygen and a drip. They'd pumped her out. But the barbiturates were in her bloodstream. She was way gone. Out of it. Not out of danger, but taking a rest from life. They told Lizzie and Dave she'd live. Looking at her, nothing but a junction box for all the lines going into her and out of her, this was hard to believe.

The casualty department was non-stop. This was the middle of the night. Kate's shaking hands turned the pages. 'How did you – ?'

'Helen smuggled me a copy.'

Something about the way he said Helen told her something. She'd think about it later. She didn't care. She didn't care about anything in the world, just having Maisie back again.

REVENGE

Maureen O'Brien

Jude Craig is having an affair. What had begun as just another gardening job, has blossomed into the sort of emotions that had long been missing with her husband Dan. But when Jude leaves the young, handsome Lee Han asleep in bed, whispering 'See you next week', little does she know what is about to happen next.

Lee's flat is torched. His burns are so bad his body is unrecognisable

When Detective Inspector John Bright arrives to question Jude, she realises with a shudder that she was the last person to see him alive. Whoever started the fire had been watching the house, and had been waiting for her to leave. If that isn't traumatic enough, John Bright's questions are forcing her into a corner – how can she remove herself from the list of prime suspects without revealing her affair with Lee? How can she tell the truth without Dan finding out? Or maybe the truth is that Dan already knows . . .

Praise for Maureen O'Brien

'O'Brien is a real talent' Donna Leon

'Lots of surprises, with a stunning denouement.'
The Scotsman

Time Warner Paperbacks
0 7515 3226 6

UNAUTHORISED DEPARTURE

Maureen O'Brien

When DI John Bright puts a vicious London gangland boss behind bars, it's not long before the death threats start coming. With his DCI suggesting he lies low for a while, his girlfriend Jude insists they need a holiday, Bright, against his better judgment, agrees.

His instincts are to prove horrifically right. Passing through the French town of Neufchâtel, Bright and Jude stay overnight at the pleasant, if strange, Hotel Sanglier – an establishment dominated by the tense atmosphere between the owner Louis and his wild, voluptuous fiancée Mariela.

Then Mariela is discovered dead, and Bright is unable to account for his whereabouts. Suddenly, he finds himself in the unfamiliar position of suspect. Faced with a police force whose language, rules and customs he doesn't understand, frustrated by his virtual prisoner status, he realizes the best way to clear his name is to help them find the killer . . .

Time Warner Paperbacks
ISBN 0 7515 3248 7

You can now order superb titles directly from Time Warner Paperbacks

☐ Mask of Betrayal	Maureen O'Brien	£6.99
☐ Revenge	Maureen O'Brien	£6.99
☐ Unauthorised Departure	Maureen O'Brien	£6.99